The Good
Doctor Guillotin

The Good
Doctor Guillotin

AN ANATOMY OF FIVE

Marc Estrin

UNBRIDLED BOOKS

Unbridled Books

Library of Congress Cataloging-in-Publication Data

Estrin, Marc.
The good Doctor Guillotin : an anatomy of five / Marc Estrin.
p. cm.
Includes bibliographical references.
ISBN 978-1-932961-85-0
1. Guillotine—Fiction.   2. Guillotin, Joseph Ignace, 1738-1814.—Fiction.
3. France—History—18th century—Fiction.   I. Title.
PS3605.S77G66 2009
813'.6—dc22
2009018518

ISBN: 978-1-932961-85-0

1 3 5 7 9 10 8 6 4 2

Book Design by SH ∘ CV

First Printing

The image on page 3 appears courtesy of
Special Collections, University of Vermont

Contents

I . Prelude

II . Ça Ira

III . Allons, Enfants de la Patrie

HISTORY, WORDS, AND VIOLENCE

IV. Le Jour de Gloire Est Arrivé

When asked in the 1960s about the historical effect of the French Revolution, Chinese Primier Zhou En-lai replied, "Too soon to tell."

I. Prelude

FIVE PATHS

Five paths converging at a place, and that place is the scaffold. Five roads to this engorging center, and five ways of the five men upon them.

For the Pythagoreans, five was the number of MAN—with his five fingers, five toes, and five senses, the creature who could be placed inside a pentagram, with its center at his groin.

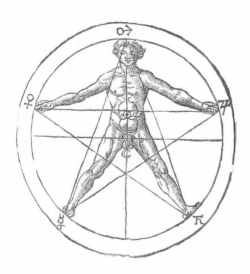

While his groin may have been near the center of the scaffold on April 25, 1792, the center of attention was his neck—the neck of Nicolas Jacques Pelletier, age thirty-six, profession "brigand," the first of many to mate with the new machine.

Five were the number of the wounds of Christ, a truth held dear by another at the scaffold, the *curé* Pierre-René Grenier, spiritual adviser and companion of Pelletier's last days.

There, too, was the builder of the machine, the "painless device"—which for a while would be known as the *"louison"* after Antoine Louis, the doctor who had perfected its design—one Tobias Schmidt, a German piano-maker living and working in Paris.

The machine's attendant was also there, of course: Charles-Henri Sanson, the executioner of Paris, who nine months later would strap a king onto the plank, hold his fallen head up by the hair, and show it to the crowd. Nine pregnant months into the birth of a new world, and the death of an old one.

A fifth person was there, too, completing the pentagram, its head, perhaps, but cut off from the event, mind tortured and heart afraid—Dr. Joseph-Ignace Guillotin, professor at the Faculté de Medicine, Parisian delegate to the National Assembly, a man charged with helping to write a constitution for an un-imagined world.

He was secretary to that Assembly, the good Doctor Guillotin, that singular man, a respectable clinician much in demand, a man doomed by laughing fate to immortal scorn. He wanted an egalitarian justice system, a more humane method of execution. In return he was haunted by repulsion and sniggering, by dirty pointing fingers and hands going chop-chop at the neck. His name became attached to a monster daughter, fathered by his Enlightenment hope for improving the lot of humankind. And contempt has followed him to the present day. On April 25, 1792, he could not bring himself to witness the event: He turned his back to the scaffold.

In a funeral oration for Guillotin on March, 23, 1814, a Dr. Bourru remarked, "It is difficult to benefit mankind without some unpleasantness resulting for oneself." Alas, too true.

Five paths to that scaffold, a pentagram of powerlessness and power. For the Freemasons, of which Guillotin was one, the pentagram inscribed in the pentagon symbolized the hermetic mystery of Solomon's Seal, the Quintessence, a fifth essence beyond fire, water, earth, and air, the burning star of the Spirit. Walking the halls of our own Pentagon, we find still the same array: would-be altruists, victims dreaming of victims, builders of efficient machines, those who use them, and those who bless them.

I.

PELLETIER

The first path:

In 1759, when Nicolas Jacques Pelletier was three, his mama first told him the story of Le Petit Chaperon Rouge. This was how it went:

Once upon a time a little girl was told by her mother to take some bread and milk to her grandmother. As she was walking on the forest path she met a wolf, who asked where she was going.

"To Grandmother's house," she said.

"Which path are you taking, the path of the pins or the path of the needles?"

"The path of the needles."

So the wolf took the path of the pins and got to the house first. He killed the grandmother, poured her blood into a bottle, and sliced her flesh onto a platter. Then he got into her nightclothes and waited in bed.

Knock, knock.

"Come in, my dear."

"Hello, Grandmother. I've brought you some bread and milk."

"Have something yourself, my dear. There is meat and wine in the pantry."

So the little girl ate what was offered, and as she did, Grandma's little cat said, "You slut! To eat your grandmother's flesh and drink your grandmother's blood! Unforgivable!"

"Undress," the wolf said, "and get into bed with me."

"Where shall I put my apron?"

"Throw it on the fire. You won't need it anymore."

When the girl got into bed, she said, "Oh, Grandmother! How hairy you are!"

"The better to keep me warm, my dear."

"Oh, Grandmother, what big shoulders you have!"

Here the boy Nicholas wiggled his shoulders around, feeling a brotherhood.

"The better for carrying firewood, my dear."

"Oh, Grandmother, what long nails you have!"

"The better to scratch myself, my dear."

"Oh, Grandmother, what big teeth you have!"

"The better to eat you with, my dear."

And he ate her.

Then Nicholas's mama made biting and slurping sounds, which he loved. Sometimes when she told the story she added chomping when Little Red Riding Hood was eating her grandmother and gurgling when she was drinking the old woman's blood. Nicolas would laugh and laugh.

Sometimes he would even discuss the story with

her, and the discussion itself became ritualized as part of the tale.

"Why does the wolf eat Little Red Riding Hood? Does she do something wrong?"

"No, Nico," his mother would say. "That's just the way the world is. You need a quick wit to stay alive."

But a quick wit was not one of Nico's attributes. Slow he was, not torturously slow, just a thick son of a thick family, a big child with huge shoulders merging directly into his head. There was a neck in there somewhere, buried in the muscle. "Little Ox," his family called him, as did his friends. And then "Big Ox," and then just "Ox," his lasting nickname and beloved totem. *"Le boeuf, c'est moi!"*

Nicolas Jacques Pelletier grew up on the outskirts of Les Herbiers, a small farming town in the eastern Vendée, that fateful region of western France. As children he and his brothers loved to climb Lark Hill to play among the seven great windmills and view the vast panorama of their land. Unlike his smaller brothers, who rejoiced only in the view and the wind, Nico felt brother to the windmills—those vast, tapered stone cylinders with their peaked, shingled roofs and great white sails. He would hold up his thick arms in the shape of a V and slowly twirl till he grew dizzy, dissolved into the rolling hills below, and sometimes fell while the younger brothers laughed.

"It's so close," he once told them, sitting dizzily on the ground.

"What? What's so close?" they asked.

"The world."

When they were cold or wet, the children would go inside to watch the milling. Unnerved by the great booming growl, Nico felt smaller than a little ox should ever feel. He wondered what it would be to be a grain of wheat or rye fed to the huge stone, to be crushed and powdered. His trek down then was always a little sad, so that after a while he refused to go inside with his brothers to watch such carnage.

Being the oldest, he was the first of them to lose free time to new responsibility, and though he would miss the view and the twirling, that was fine with him. For he was now a farm worker like his father, tending the animals, bulling it among the cows, plowing, planting, weeding, hoeing, harvesting. He found the torture of small animals instructive.

On Sundays the family would walk two miles to the Church of St. Pierre, where the child, big as a building, sensed his brotherhood with the brown stones and the huge, thick Roman bell tower. He enjoyed hearing ever again the stories of Saint Peter and Saint Paul, who greeted the family from either side of the great red portal. There was nothing as juicy as eating a grandmother in those saints' tales, but he thought of the little girl drinking blood when the priest took communion, and when he drank the blood-red wine. He liked, too, the part about Christ rising from the dead.

From Nico's early teens on, the Pelletier farm began to fail. Alternating droughts and floods, increased taxes and levies, his mother's sickness, and the ever-increasing food needs of five growing children quickly made to destroy the equilibrium of income and expense. When he was fourteen the family discussed his going to town, perhaps to earn more money and send it home. But they wondered whether the family could handle the workload without him and whether his absence would cost them more than they might gain.

Nicolas was far from ambitious; he liked his Herbiers life; he was good at it. Above all he wanted to be—and was—helpful. And secretly he was wary of what might come to pass out there, in the beyond, *au-delà*. But when three of the six cows died of bloat, the die was cast. There was less tending, less milking, to be done and a greater need for income: The family decided he would go off to Redon, four days' walk, to make his fortune and add some to their own.

2.

GUILLOTIN

The second path, a different route entirely:

In 1773, when Nicolas Pelletier went off to the big city, Joseph-Ignace was thirty-five and a doctor of medicine in Paris, three years past his thesis, "On Preventing the Effects of Rabies." At medical school, first at Reims, then at Paris, his hard work, his acute spirit of observation, and above all his devotion to the needs of the poor had won him a prize and some heightened respect as a prizewinner. He became the foremost disciple of the celebrated Antoine Petit and was thrust early on into the great public health controversies of the eighteenth century.

Paris. A smallpox epidemic in the winter of 1762–1763 forced the medical community to the forefront of the inoculation debate: With a one-in-two-hundred risk of death from smallpox vaccination, should a national policy make vaccination mandatory?

The faculties of medicine grappled with questions of individual risk and tried to balance a patient's individual interest against the general good of the state. In spite of statistics from Asia, Turkey, and England, where vaccination was long-established practice, the French were fearful, or at best ambivalent. While they would blame as a "murderer" any physician who lost a patient after a vaccination, they would also accuse those who refused to inoculate of complicity in thousands of deaths. And the doctors themselves were uncomfortable with a shift in roles—from that of healers to that of purveyors of disease.

Petit and his students, with Guillotin now among them, took a cautious but statist stand: Clearly inoculation was in the national interest. In spite of the deaths that might occur, statistically, universal mandatory inoculation would be best for France, good for economic growth, a check against depopulation. Nevertheless, good liberals all, they argued for individual and family choice. They would join the *philosophes* in opting to educate the public, hoping for informed patient consent. But it was an uphill battle, and widespread acceptance of inoculation by the French came only after the Revolution with Jenner's safer use of cowpox, instead of smallpox, for vaccination.

Post-Revolution, Joseph-Ignace Guillotin was one of the first French doctors to promote Jenner's work and in 1805 would be made president of the Committee for Vaccination in Paris. As his legacy, he hoped to substitute a role in life preservation for his previous role in its destruction. He was unsuccessful.

A moderate man, of moderate height, with strong black hair and weak green eyes, Guillotin, too, had once been a child, innocent of all these complications. He, too, had a mother, and of her he was born in the town of Saintes in the glorious month of May 1738—though he might have been born less prematurely in June. The poor woman, they say, was terrified by the cries of a man being tortured in the public square. While members of the upper class might buy their way to a quick beheading, common criminals were, depending on their crimes, either broken on the wheel or hanged. In earshot of one such breaking, Mme. Guillotin dropped her ninth child of twelve three weeks before she and he were due. Perhaps she was just good at it by then, but Guillotin *père* always joked that Joseph's midwife was the executioner, a pleasantry that finally rang most peculiar. There is no worse joke than a true one.

As in Nico's family, Joseph's mother told her son bedtime stories, too, for instance that of Le Petit Chaperon Rouge. Hers was the classic Perrault version, the one you know, read from an illustrated book. It was different from Nico's peasant tale:

Unlike Nico's, Joseph's little red-cloaked girl was frankly pretty and adored; her cape was a labor of love and loved on her by all. *Her* grandma got cakes and butter, not bread and milk. And this little girl gave the wolf specific directions, abetting her endangerment, a warning to middle-class youngsters to guard their privacy. There were woodcutters in this forest, and the spirit of Walt Disney, too, as the little girl chased butterflies, gathered nuts and flowers, and tarried in the bourgeois woodland beauty. And the wolf had not eaten in three days, a motivating detail the enlightened of the time—perhaps even Mme. Guillotin—saw as social commentary.

Joseph's little girl did not undress, not even to snuggle with Grammy. She certainly did not eat her grammy's flesh and drink her blood. And although she was eaten all the same, in performance there were no eating sounds, for spittle would have soiled the lovely book.

Joseph would always get upset, and the woodcutters, though unbidden by Perrault, would ever come to the rescue. Whatever Mme. Guillotin might think, as a mother she could not leave Little Red Riding Hood in all her loveliness simply walking into the jaws of death, devoured by inscrutable calamity. She could not scotch the notion that virtue would be rewarded, or that mistrust was to be mistrusted. So in her version, the woodcutters would cut the wolf open, release Little Red Riding Hood—and sometimes her grandmother, too, if Joseph asked—and all would end happily ever after.

Often there would follow family discussions, with eight older siblings, ages five to sixteen, offering appropriate observations, and Father Guillotin suggesting that life was hard and it might be better not to have any illusions about selflessness in one's fellow men, or that the world can be savage and even people like themselves were sometimes set upon by rogues.

In this gentle dialectic Joseph took his mother's side. He grew up an affectionate and tenderhearted child, full of compassion for *les misérables*. When some of his peers robbed birds' nests, Joseph always fought to replace the nestlings with their mother, who, to his dismay, might no longer want to care for them. For his interventions he was punched and kicked by his friends and often wound up having to dropper-feed the abandoned one. At seven, rather than roughing it up with roughneck chums, he was frequently seen walking the street alone, catechism in hand, pondering, memorizing. His family found itself sharing meals and offering beds to wanderers he might bring home with him. This bookish child was often in tears over suffering. An antivivisectionist in medical school, as an adult Dr. Guillotin was a vegetarian.

3.

SANSON

The path direct:

Let me assure you that Charles-Henri Sanson comes from noble blood. Our coat of arms—the silenced bell, *sans son*—dates from the Crusades, when Sanson de Longval was the seneschal of Robert the Magnificent, the father of William the Conqueror. You think we are mere death-stained workmen? For six generations we have been the acquaintances of kings and queens, friends of princes of the Church and of the Realm. We have known every important politician and writer of our time; I and my family have supped with bankers. I have drunk with the new revolutionaries— and with mistresses of the king.

You think these are rope-hardened fingers, filthy with the offal of the condemned? These hands play the glorious violoncello suites of Bach! Can you say the same?

And yet, I and my forebears are shunned. When I

wore blue to do my work—blue, the color of my noble blood—I was called to court and upbraided. So I put on green—and now, *voilà*, it has become the latest fashion. The Marquis de Letorière began wearing green, and now all of Versailles is dressing "à la Sanson." I am the fashion leader of high society, a respectable neighbor, charitable and kind to the poor, and damned for my brave service to the Nation!

Here's a good one—look what I have to put up with: I was hunting several years ago, out in the Compiègne. It was getting dark, so I called it a day and stopped at an inn on my way back to the city. It's fair to say, I think, that I cut a striking figure, and so I was not surprised to be asked by a guest, a noblewoman, to dine with her. I'll not mention her name. When asked, I told her my name was "Charles-Henri, Chevalier de Longeval"—which it is—and that I was an officer of the court—which I am. A little wine, some languid looks, you know how it goes, and she invited me to her room with clear intentions. As I had to be back early to prepare for an execution the next morning, I made my excuses and left. Perfectly innocent—in deed, if not in mind.

I imagine she asked the host about the chevalier she craved and found out I was the executioner of Paris. Well! She actually called me into court for the offense of having dined with her. And so that no other noblewomen should suffer the same awful fate, she petitioned the court to have all executioners wear some distinctive mark on their clothing, an ax crossed with a gallows perhaps.

Would you believe it?—I could get no lawyer to defend me. Not one in the entire city. So I defended myself: I am an officer of the law, I told the judges. I kill men in the same way and for the same reason that soldiers do—to protect France and its king and its citizens. Ask any soldier what his job is. He will tell you it is to kill men to protect France and its king and its citizens. He is not anathema for that. No one flees the company of a soldier. Whom does he kill? Innocent people, soldiers who are serving their country exactly as he is serving his.

I also serve my country, but unlike a soldier, I respect innocence. I kill only the guilty. So? Why should I be shunned? Why should it be a crime to have dinner with a beautiful lady? My job is as respectable and honorable as any other, more than many, in fact.

What happened? Her case was dismissed. And for the benefit of future generations of my profession I am proud to say that no law was made afflicting us with a dress code.

Bedtime stories? No fairy tales for *me*; only family stories from family experience. Everything I learned I learned from family experience because no other kids would play with me. "Your papa is the executioner!" "Executioner's son!" "Executioner," that was enough for shunning. Even our church pew was set apart from others'. I play Bach's violoncello suites because I almost always have to play alone. And because I am a serious sort of man.

Why don't I quit, you may ask? Why don't I get out of this job which makes me so isolated? Only a bourgeois, with a bourgeois idea of personal freedom, could ask that question. An executioner can no more abdicate than can a king, or for that matter a horse thief or a peasant. We have had two centuries of executioners in our family, and we have to marry among ourselves, for who else (except my own dear Marie-Anne) would marry us? We are members of a dynasty of executioners whose sons and grandsons and great-grandsons have followed in their fathers' footsteps, whose brothers and uncles have wielded the rope and the ax. In every major city we have hanged, burned, branded, and mutilated—in the service of France. We have broken criminals on the wheel when they have tried to break the world. And yet, we are human beings. As the great Shakespeare has written, *"Si vous nous piquez, ne saignons-nous pas? si vous nous chatouillez, ne rions-nous pas? si vous nous empoisonnez, ne mourons-nous pas? et si vous nous outragez, ne nous vengerons-nous pas?"*

I in fact am sick and tired of being treated—by the public, not by many nobles—as some kind of sin-

ister figure with thick fingers and blood-rimmed fingernails. When people deliver a message to me, they
most often place it on the ground between us.

Look at these hands, look at them. Why should
they be objects of scorn, detested, reviled, feared, as if
they were slaves to some venomous heart? My employ-
ment is not a necessary evil but a necessary *good* that is
difficult to do. My family stories are of men who loved
and hated, men with feelings and weaknesses and
doubts and fears just like everyone else. The public
thinks our race is one of proud, vain, ambitious villains, off on some self-serving career, when we can
barely keep body and soul together.

Why must we make our children pariahs? By order of the city, when my cousin Aline turned sixteen,
Uncle Rémy had to put a poster on his front door letting everyone know there was a marriageable girl in the
house—not as a kind of advertisement but to protect
the young men of Marseilles from an encounter or any
kind of involvement with a tainted bloodline. That's
right, by order of the city. So she had to marry Cousin
Claude, the executioner from Lyons, though she didn't
love him.

Enough complaining. Life is hard for everyone,
even the nobility. There is one point I want to make,
though. I mentioned it before: It is very difficult for a
public servant such as myself to make ends meet.

I applaud our revolution. I think a constitutional

monarchy is a sound and workable idea. America has gone too far, but England shows it can be done. We have a good, reasonable, adaptable king. "L'Oui" the people call him—the King Who Says Yes.

But the King Who Says Yes doesn't seem to understand my problems any more than the King Who Used to Be the Almighty. Here on the Rue St. Jean— with the shortages, with all our money gone to help America be free—my relatives have come to rely on me. Some have moved in. Two of my brothers have come to live with me, and old Uncle Gabriel, the retired executioner of Reims, who helps me with my duties. And my sick sister, Renée-Claire. I've got seventeen mouths to feed: myself, my wife, my two sons, my two brothers, my uncle and his wife, my sister, a cook, four assistants, and three cart-drivers and stablemen. What happened to the *droit de havage*? Can my assistants and I fill our hands at the market? Can we keep any of our clients' clothing and jewelry after they are dispatched? No. Gone. Replaced by a salary. But does the salary make ends meet? No.

For my two brothers I need 600 livres each, so on days when there are separate executions in different places, they can do them. I have four servants at 300, three carters at 300, a cook at 200. For four horses, 2,000. I had to build three carriages and a dung-cart. That was 300. The harnesses cost 150 and the blacksmith 200. I have to pay my mother her court-ordered pension of 1,200. Then sixteen people besides me have to eat, and that takes up about 9,600 livres. I have to support my wife and children in decent style—linen, washing, furniture, all that: 4,000. Then there's the rent for a house and equipment sheds located near my place of work. Another 4,800. Add in the taxes per capita for another 2,048, and you come up with almost 28,000 livres. Every year!

That's a lot, you say? I haven't mentioned the contingent expenses: colleagues to help when I need it—which happens all too often because of the bad character of the servants I am forced to hire, who hold me up for money because they know I need help so badly. People don't like to work in this fabled household. Then there is constant tipping if I want to hold on to everyone whom I occasionally need. And the replacement of horses when they die, or veterinary expenses when they don't. The servants get sick, and I have to keep them because I can't find anyone to replace them. All the gifts I have to give, all the miscellaneous expenses on the day of execution. And speaking of execution, all the tools must be constantly renewed or replaced to avoid mishap. There are a thousand other incidental expenses, impossible to itemize—all of which add up to the sum of another 5,000 livres.

A few further observations for when I am required to take part in torturing, or in any carpentry work: For executing torture, I need an additional assistant. For any part of the carpentry: three carriages; three horses; three harnesses; the services of a black-smith; two carters; two assistant carpenters to nail the wood together and construct the scaffold; lodging for the men, horses, carriages, and tools; wood to rebuild; upkeep; extra expenses incurred when I am required to go out of Paris; replacement of horses . . . another 18,000.

Should you add up these figures, you will arrive at a figure just short of 53,000 livres. How much do I earn? 16,000 livres. And my salary, such as it is, has not been paid for three months. You may draw your own conclusions. As the great M. Shakespeare has said, *"Tout est bien, s'il y a apport d'argent."*

Now that M. Robespierre, the deputy from Ar-ras, has given his speech to the Assembly calling for the abolition of the death penalty, I sense there will be ever more pressure against my office and ever more reluc-tance to meet my needs. I trust the king will make sure that capital punishment may continue.

Robespierre wants "the bloody laws that sanc-tion official murder" effaced from our penal code. He calls them "repugnant to the Frenchman's new way of life, and to their new constitution." He sets out to prove that the death penalty is unjust and that, far from discouraging violent crimes, it only increases them.

The calm, unflappable M. Robespierre, the "In-corruptible," is, as everyone knows, a persuasive orator.

Execution is not society's natural self-defense, he argues, but a ganging up on the defenseless, like a man slitting the throat of a child. He sees my work as cowardly murder, a solemn crime committed according to legal procedures, which deadens the sensibility of our citizens. He feels human judgments—listen to this, I'll read it to you—"are never sure enough for society to be able to put to death a man who has been condemned by fellow men who share his fallibility. To deny a man the possibility to expiate his crime by repentance or virtuous deeds, pitilessly to shut him off from any return to virtue and self-esteem, to hasten to force him into his tomb while he is freshly stained by his crime; all this is to my mind the most horrible refinement of cruelty."

M. Virtue, and by the looks of his wardrobe, M. Self-Esteem. Is he afraid that he might one day be deprived of such blessings? Debase public morality and make murder more likely, do I? "The idea of murder," according to the Incorruptible, "inspires far less terror when the law itself sets the example of it for all to see. Horror of crime diminishes when its only punishment is by another crime. We must beware of confusing the efficacy of punishment with its excessive severity: The one is fundamentally opposed to the other. Moderate laws win the support of all; savage laws provoke a general conspiracy." He wants to repeal the death penalty!

The king, I would hope, is wise enough to understand—certainly the queen is—that crowds flock to the

Place de Grève to see the pillory, to see my hangings and breakings. They come in awe of a great public act of state power which bears witness to the power of the throne. Royal authority needs those crowds to parade its majesty. Surely the court will understand that and insist that my office remain intact and well provided.

If at the moment we need to save money on torture, then fine—there are less expensive ways to extract information. I could get confessions in my kitchen just by putting hot boiled eggs in the criminal's armpits and holding down his arms. Or by hanging him from the kitchen beam by his wrists, tied behind him. Torture can be cheap. And remember, these are judged and proven criminals—their lives set against us, and against the state.

M. Robespierre, I can tell you that I sleep well enough, and my conscience is untroubled by what I do. I would, however, like to be paid for it.

4.

THE PIANO-MAKER

The fourth path:

Tobias Schmidt—the piano-maker who built the machine—was the oldest of the five men in our pentangle. Born in Leipzig to a musical family, he was nourished and inspired by his weekly, sometimes daily, visits to the Thomaskirche, to pray on Sundays with his parents and receive communion, yes, but more important for him, to listen to the fantastic choral compositions and organ improvisations of Kantor Bach. Each week would bring another masterpiece, newly written, copied out, and rehearsed, an unending flow of inspired and inspiring sound.

Would that he could join the old man's choir, but his voice, even when he was a child, was croaking and uncertain and would remain so to the end of the century. He wanted to study keyboard or organ with that genius, but Bach had little time to spare for extra students. So Tobias studied the keyboard with his mother and the violin with his father and thought and thought about building a better instrument that he would dedicate to his great spiritual mentor for Bach's enjoyment and to serve his compositions.

In Tobias's teenaged opinion, the *clavecin* was too soft to contain the master's huge emotions and the organ too huge to fit the human frame. The harpsichord had little dynamic variation and its plucked strings no sustaining power. What the master needed, Tobias felt, was another type of instrument altogether—one that would further his expressiveness while bringing his great works into the home. What to do? What could *he* do? Where were the technical lines of attack?

Little Toby had had his Red Riding Hood, too. But his was the folktale that the Grimms would turn into their classic Rotkäppchen. In that tale, that German tale, each of the characters works things through, suiting their actions to rigorous Teutonic logic. The little girl wanders off to pick flowers because "if I bring Grandmother a fresh bunch of flowers, it'll make her happy." (Instrumental.) After finding out where the sick grandmother lives, the wolf thinks, "That young, tender thing is a plump, dainty morsel and will taste even better than the old woman. I must be canny about it and arrange things to catch them both." (Systematic.) When Rotkäppchen enters her grandmother's house, she thinks, "My, I feel so uneasy today, and yet I usually so like being at Grandmother's." (Intuitive.)

When a hunter hears the wolf snoring after his big double meal, he investigates: "So here's where I find you, you old sinner!" (Judgmental.) He cuts the wolf open with a scissors (tool-appropriate), and out jump Rotkäppchen *and* her grandmother (salvationary).

Rotkäppchen quickly fetched some big stones and filled the wolf's belly with them. (Grotesquely inventive.) *When it woke up, it wanted to skip off* (stubborn innocence), *but the stones were so heavy that it at once sank to the ground and died.* (New method of execution.)

Then all three were happy. The hunter skinned the wolf and went home with the pelt, the grandmother ate the cake and drank the wine and recovered, and Rotkäppchen thought, "Never again will I stray off the road and run into the forest when my mother has told me not to." (At last obedient.)

These virtues, conveyed over and over in a hundred folktale variations, do have a lasting effect on the German soul. Tobias Schmidt was, among other things, instrumental in his approach to life, thorough and systematic, intuitively led and yet obedient, addicted to fine judgments, always tool- and action-appropriate, ever inventive of original methods and solutions, especially concerning the salvation of things and situations in need of such. Even as a child, he was a natural-born tinkerer.

And so he put his mind, pencil, and elementary shop skills to "Bach's" problem: how to design a hammer that would hit a string quickly and repeatedly, without dampening the sound, and with varying force so as to produce softer and louder notes. He realized that with the tools at hand, he could not solve it.

In 1748, when Tobias was thirteen, the organ-builder Gottfried Silbermann rolled into town, carting the pieces of a new keyboard instrument to demonstrate to Bach and other Leipzig musicians. The old man did not like it, complaining that the higher notes were too soft to allow a full dynamic range. The boy Tobias, straining to see at the back of the crowd, understood intuitively that the strings were too thin to produce enough sound and that thicker strings under more tension had to be used. More tension would mean a heavier tuning bar, perhaps even one of iron.

But Silbermann, Tobias thought, had invented an amazing thing, a device by which the player could lift all the dampers off the strings, permitting them to vibrate freely, either when struck or sympathetically when other notes were played. It was controlled by a hand stop, which required the player to cease playing on the keys for a moment in order to change the damper configuration. Thus, it was a device for imparting an unusual tonal color to whole passages. The young Tobias thought it might be controlled by a pedal, thus leaving the hands free for continuous playing, for more effective nuanced expression.

From seeing Silbermann's instrument, Tobias realized two things: one, that people besides himself were also interested in solving Bach's problem; and two, that if he were really interested in a solution, he would need to study with craftsmen who had better tools and more resources than wire, scrap wood, pencil, and paper. He would need to work with real instrument-makers who were already engaged with the problem.

When Tobias came of age he was living with his family in Salzburg, working at his father's relocated lumber, carpentry, and cabinetmaking concern, building intricate experimental mechanisms for keyboard hammers and wooing the lovely and talented Anna Maria Wohlfeil, daughter of Salzburg's chief magistrate. His method? Accompanying her violin playing on an improved Silbermann piano, now all the rage in musical circles and now "completely approved" *("mit völliger Gutheißung")* by Bach. And there, in Salzburg, when Tobias was twenty-one, another Anna Maria, not his own, gave birth to a child and named him Wolfgang Amadeus.

There are those who still insist that Mozart was a Venusian, come to earth as an interplanetary spore of higher intelligence. How else, they ask, to explain the many Mozart stories: the phenomenal childhood feats of musical memory and composition or, in adulthood, his writing three of his greatest symphonies in six weeks? His "premature and almost supernatural talents" seemed to his astonished elders "such an extraordinary phenomenon that one is hard put to it to believe what one sees with one's eyes and hears with one's ears." As the Benedictine priest, Placidus Scharl, observed:

> *Even in the sixth year of his age he would play the most difficult pieces for the pianoforte, of his own invention. He skimmed the octave which his short little fingers could not span, at fascinating speed and with wonderful accuracy. One had only to give him the first subject which came to mind for a fugue or an invention: he would develop it with strange variations and constantly changing passages as long as one wished; he would improvise fugally on a subject for hours, and this fantasia-playing was his greatest passion.*

What Tobias did not personally see and hear of his tiny neighbor, he heard about through the musical rumor mill.

He proposed to Anna Maria after taking her to a concert by the seven-year-old. Mozart had played two sonatas of his own and several preludes and fugues of Bach and had closed with a concerto by the Court composer Georg Christoph Wagenseil, with the composer turning the pages. Anna Maria was so moved by the evening, and by a vision of making music with her own children, that she accepted Tobias's hand. She died of cholera in early pregnancy.

Now, cholera is a particularly distressing disease to observe and tend. Tobias watched his beautiful wife, his child's mother-to-be, vomit and vomit again till there was nothing left but dryness to throw up. He changed her beshitten sheets, flooded in brown and tinged with blood and mucus. All her limbs contracted with painful cramps, and then her entire trunk in spasm after spasm of agonized rigidity. God was not kind: Her mind stayed clear and aware of her frightening trajectory. The doctors had no hope. And suddenly, on the third day, she lapsed into a short coma and died. *They* died. His beloved and his child. And in spite of all he could do, they—or certainly she—had not died painlessly.

Tobias had to get away. He had to hide. He left that afternoon and walked, exhausted, through the night, vaguely aware of heading west, toward the land of the setting sun. Days followed weary days. He hitched rides, slept where he could, did odd jobs, and walked and trudged and walked along one of our five paths toward destiny. München, Augsburg, Stuttgart . . . Pforzheim and a short Rhein journey south. And all the while, running through his heart and head, the monumental C-sharp minor fugue of Bach from *"Das*

Wohltemperierte Clavier" which the child had played for him and Anna. As he walked, two steps to each slow, half-note pulse, there arose in his heart a faint scaffold of hope, a vision—though encumbered by memories of shit and screams—the notion that—in honor of Anna—that great fugue might someday be played on *his* instrument, the one he had talked about with her, not a clavier, not a harpsichord, but his very own sound device, imagined for the master.

Accompanying his vision were words from Philo's *Quod Deus immutabilis sit*, the text he had read for comfort in the gloomy moments when his patient slept: "A knowledge of moral opposites" was its theme; "Such a soul is the most perfect instrument fashioned by Nature" was its verse. "And if it be well-tempered, it will produce a symphony the most beautiful in the world, which has its consummation not in sound, but in the consistencies of life's actions." Banish discord, banish pain. To Bach's melody, with this text, toward this vision he traveled—and came at last to Strasbourg.

Strasbourg, the city through which the rich musical culture of Germany flowed into France, a city with both French and German cathedral choirs, French and German opera houses, and the finest orchestras outside Paris and Versailles.

In Strasbourg, in 1784, the celebrated Austrian composer Ignaz Pleyel would become assistant *Kapellmeister* of the great cathedral. Eleven years later he would open a piano factory in Paris which would grow to become one of the largest in Europe, perhaps in part because of prompting and goading from Pleyel's new, then old, "apprentice," Tobias Schmidt.

The twenty-six-year-old Pleyel moved to Strasbourg in 1783, when his apprentice-to-be was almost fifty. Being the twenty-fourth child of thirty-eight of a necessarily impoverished schoolteacher meant that young Pleyel was used to chaos and that his decisions were a long time in the making and effecting. Being an only child, old Tobias Schmidt was used to getting his way, if only by staying on message and never letting up. But the only child and the twenty-fourth one seemed to embody some necessary complement, taking to each other like Diderot and d'Alembert, needling, mutually stimulating, sowing seeds. Their teasing converged on the developing and manufacturing of pianos: "So why aren't you doing it?" Schmidt would ask. "So why aren't *you?*" Pleyel would respond.

Though both wound up in Paris, Pleyel's piano manufactory balloon eventually landed and took root, while Schmidt's detoured to another world entirely.

5·

THE COUNTRY PRIEST

The fifth path:

The final member of our quintet was the young-est, and the last to enter the story. He had no fairy tales told him as a child, or at least nothing thought to be a fairy tale. His bedtime book, read to him at first and then perused by him, was a well-thumbed *Vie des Saints*, which had been handed down for four generations in his family. As we might expect, the story that fascinated him most was that of his own saint's-day saint, whose feast, along with Pierrot's own birthday, was celebrated on July 27. Pierre-René Grenier was born in Paris in 1763. His name-day saint, Pantaleon, had been born in Nico-midea almost fifteen hundred years earlier, one of the Fourteen Holy Helpers of the Church, a martyr, and patron saint of physicians. Father Pierre-René Grenier would be patron saint to only one.

This was the story he heard as a child, the life and death of the saint he loved:

Pantaleon was the son of a rich pagan but had been instructed in Christianity by his Christian mother. But after her death he fell away from the Christian church, and he studied medicine with a renowned physician and became physician to the Emperor Maximian. He was won back to Christianity by Saint Hermolaus, who convinced him that Christ was the better physician, signaling the significance of the exemplum of Pantaleon that faith is to be trusted over medical advice.

By miraculously healing a blind man, Pantaleon converted his father, upon whose death he came into possession of a large fortune. He freed his father's slaves and, distributing his wealth among the poor, developed a great reputation in Nicomedia. During the Diocletian persecution, envious colleagues denounced him to the emperor. The emperor wished to save him and sought to persuade him to give up his religious beliefs. Pantaleon, however, openly confessed his faith, and as proof that Christ is the true God, he healed a paralytic. For thus defying the emperor, who denounced the miracle as an exhibition of magic, Pantaleon was condemned to death.

His flesh was first burned with torches, whereupon Christ appeared to all in the form of Saint Hermolaus to strengthen and heal him. The torches were miraculously extinguished. Then a bath of molten lead was prepared; when the apparition of Christ stepped into the cauldron with him, the fire went out and the lead became cold. Pantaleon was now loaded with a great stone and thrown into the sea, but he floated nevertheless. He was thrown to wild beasts, but these groveled before him and could not be forced away until he had blessed them. He was bound on the wheel, but the ropes snapped, and the wheel broke. An attempt was made to behead him, but the *sword bent, and the executioners were converted to Christianity. Pantaleon implored heaven to forgive them, for which reason he also received the name of Panteleimon ("mercy for all"). It was not until he himself requested it that it was possible to behead him.*

At Vierzehnheiligen bei Staffelstein, in Franconia, Saint Pantaleon is venerated with his hands nailed to his head, reflecting another legend about his death.

Read it again, Mama.

G rowing up, Pierre-René said his beads, healed sick animals, counseled sick friends, and prayed for all and everyone. They called the child *"Le bon petit docteur."* What his family could afford, however, was not a medical school but the Jesuit training college in the Augustinian abbey of Toussaints in his town of Châlons-sur-Marne, the seat of the Catholic diocese, the first of his unnumbered stations of the cross.

His patron saint, Pantaleon, was beheaded, or had his hands nailed to his head, or both, at age twenty-nine. Often, with the body of Christ on his tongue, Pierre-René wondered what his own twenty-ninth year would bring.

II. Ça Ira

HOPE AND UTOPIA

In Paris, in May 1968, the following notions were
graffitied on the walls of the Sorbonne:

BREAK THE POWER OF FACTS OVER THE WORLD.

and

ANY VIEW OF THINGS WHICH ISN'T STRANGE IS FALSE.

and

BE REALISTIC—DEMAND THE IMPOSSIBLE!

and

IMAGINATION IS REVOLUTION.

Concerning which President de Gaulle commented.
"Reform, yes; shitting in your own bed, no."

The human being, Ernst Bloch asserts, is "the
animal that hopes," and for Bloch, that funda-
mental act of hoping provides the deepest insight into
both human consciousness and world history.

Human hope springs from an intuition of in-
completeness in the world and a refusal to accept the
status quo as what must forever be. At times it mani-

fests as a gnawing restlessness or psychic hunger, at other times as a sustained cry more serious than a hemorrhage.

Hope traffics in daydreams, sharing in but transcending world realities. A man daydreams of what he does not have, of a world he would like to see. Marx called it "need." Daydreams are the front between the real and the possible, and sometimes even, as in the graffiti, *beyond* the possible, a yearning for as-yet-unimagined possibilities, mutations of the given, with the not-yet given space to form. TAKE YOUR DESIRES AS REALITY, read another slogan, MONOLITHICALLY STUPID, GAULLISM IS THE INVERSION OF LIFE. The students were *Möglichkeitmenschen*—like my Gregor Samsa—throwing themselves headlong on the side of possibility.

Unlike night dreams, daydreams are vaguely anticipatory, not surreally retrospective. While "we cannot know the future," still the future must in some dim way be sensed in the here and now, shedding light upon the present, or all willed human activity would be random thrashing against meaningless chaos. It is our sense of the possible future that shapes our daydreams and present world activity.

Each of our five characters has his daydreams, his imaginative play with what it might mean to be fully human in a potentially hostile world.

Perhaps Pelletier once dreamt of a normal life with a woman who might actually love him, even

though he is an ox. Now he will dream only of strate-
gies to survive, and of his relationship to a world clos-
ing in on him.

Dr. Guillotin dreams of bringing health and
more kindness to various unhealthy and sometimes
cruel populations. He will be, to his great regret, a
crucial player in the Theater of Cruelty itself.

Sanson daydreams of claiming nobility for himself and bringing it to his persecuted profession. He is
only doing his job, and he dreams of doing it well.

Schmidt dreams of Bach and Mozart, of the cruelties lurking in the depths, and of how those cruelties
create the possibility of grace.

Grenier, too, will dream of grace, of bringing it
as he can to the most graceless of others. His day-
dream is of serving; his night dream is, alas, of death.

All five, consciously or not, grew their lives in
"the Age of Enlightenment," that time when Hope
first consciously imagined liberating humankind from
fear and ignorance. Guillotin dreamt of ridding the
world of pain and disease. He may even have imagined
medicine as ridding it of death.

We, on the other hand, are sworn to this world as
it is, and largely block all consciousness of alterity. As
Margaret Thatcher declaimed, "There is no alternative."
In the eighteenth century, and especially in the France of
Rousseau and the Encyclopedists, the thinkers still
thought that humankind could be free from want and

fear if there no longer existed anything unknown. Science would triumph, rational economics, the clever reasoning of labor-saving machinery and agriculture, the perfect order of perfect government. It was a radical notion.

But, as Herbert Marcuse has observed, our "fully enlightened earth" is a world of "disaster triumphant." The dissolution of myth and the triumph of knowledge have destroyed more than fancy. The world is disenchanted, and powerful "enlightened" men use nature and one another for domination, not for freedom. Enlightenment, for all its analysis and reflection, is as totalitarian as the system of kings and nobles it sought to undermine. This we are clear on now, since Alamogordo and its consequences. Back then, not so.

But we are infinitely clever about hoping. If the body is defeated, hope is good tactical progress. In hope we are never lost. We can always learn from our mistakes. The dichotomy between that which is and that which should be presents to us a task, some kind of model, a trial for which there are no previously registered blueprints.

For the human home seems to be, alarmingly, in utopia, in the good place, the place that is not there. In spite of today's scorn for the word "utopian," there lurks within us, as within the five men in our story, some secret, non-Aristotelian principle of identity: A = not-yet-A. And this is not strange, given our pervasive myths of the Golden Age, with its analog of Eden. Our Old Testament hope for the Promised Land. Jesus' promise for the coming kingdom of God. Marx's search for the kingdom of liberty. Somewhere in there is the Enlightenment. As Oscar Wilde wrote, "A map of the world that does not include Utopia is not even worth glancing at."

Nineteen sixty-eight was a time in which a great many people felt a white-hot, even inquisitorial, hatred for some men and some things and, at the same time, an angelic ardor for others. There was always a religious dimension in the student movement—religious yearning, religious purity, religious corruption and intolerance. Holiness rioted on all sides.

And why? Because as Bertolt Brecht so insightfully put it, "Something is lacking," *etwas fehlt.* In his Paradise City of Mahagonny:

> *Wonderful—is the coming of evening,*
> *And lovely is the talk of men among themselves,*
> Aber etwas fehlt.
> *Beautiful are Calmness and Peace,*
> *and Harmony makes one happy,*
> Aber etwas fehlt.
> *Noble is the simple life,*
> *And without compare are the glories of Nature,*
> Aber etwas fehlt.

Something is lacking. And so they dream, our five men, as we do, each of their versions of utopia.

For utopia-dreaming allows us to critique the present and imagine what else might be possible; it engages the imagination with so-called reality; it motivates us to engage in constructing a better world for ourselves, as needed, and for others. Like theirs, ours is a horizon time, a time for imagining something beyond the edges of the here and now: Possibility is not exhausted by the immediate. We can continue to count on hope, yearning, and—though sadly vestigial—a homing instinct.

Granted, our previous utopian experiments—ours and theirs—have left us unhappy, unfulfilled. We feel deceived. No wonder appetites for utopia have shrunk and many now long instead for apocalypse.

But hope for emancipation lingers. Even the neoconservative's self-serving rhetoric of "spreading democracy" echoes in its mendacious way the ideals that drove the eighteenth century, the Age of Enlightenment, both here in America and in the France of our five characters. "Marxism has many truths," Mao said, "but they all boil down to one: It is right to rebel."

Tell it to the police at Tiananmen Square.

And yet the watchword of the Cultural Revolution resonates here and today as much as in China and France at the times of their revolutions: "Fight self!" As another good doctor, William Carlos Williams, noted, a new world requires a new mind.

Now it is autumn; then it was dawn. All is still political. *Ça ira.* Let us proceed.

6.

THE MOWER AND THE SCYTHE

It was during a freezing January in 1755 that I had to officiate for the first time, and I am not proud of my performance. From the age of eleven I had assisted my father, but not too often, and never for torture, only for the pillory and once for a hanging. But Papa had retired in '54, and therefore *I* was Monsieur de Paris, the respected, the condemned, the feared—all at sixteen. You can imagine.

Some poor devil named Ruxton, I believe—I don't remember his crime—was my first client. I acted abominably, "officiating" as required but hiding from the sight of his being broken on the wheel by my assistants. I had to retain my official dignity while keeping myself from vomiting. A poor beginning.

Not long afterward there was a clockmaker, Jacques Mongeot, who had killed his mistress's husband. We—that is, they, my assistants—had to bludgeon him and then put him on the wheel. It took him two hours to die, while I stood there on the scaffold, as far as possible from the screaming behind me, freezing to death in the snow. And to make it worse, the mistress, Madame Lescombat, was brought by armed guards and forced to watch the scene and hear her lover's death agony. So beautiful she was, so heartbroken, I couldn't stand seeing her. Where was I to look if not at him, and not at her? I studied the façade of the Hôtel de Ville while my grandmother shouted at me from the crowd to do my job properly. *Comme il faut.*

But the worst was yet to come. If some children are traumatized by wolves eating little girls, consider *my* real baptism by fire. By club and knife and horse and fire. I—I!—at eighteen—was responsible for the execution of Damiens. People still talk about it today. I will remember it all my life.

Back in January of '57, Robert-François Damiens tried to assassinate the king. Louis XV. Robespierre was not even born yet! Damiens was an unemployed domestic, dismissed from the Jesuit college here in Paris for misconduct. "Robert, *le diable*" they called him.

It was the eve of Epiphany—some Jesuit symbol for him, no doubt. He wrapped himself in a big black cloak and walked right past the Swiss Guard on the steps of the Versailles Palace. At the time you could fairly walk in and out of the palace at will. Louis was just coming out, climbing into his coach on the upper driveway, and Damiens rushed at him, stabbed him, and did not even try to escape.

The king grabbed at his ribs, saw blood on his hands, and cried out, "Someone has touched me!" Was that some fencing language? What an odd thing to say. Yet many people have told me so.

The guards carried the king back up the palace steps to die. He had called for a Jesuit priest and quickly confessed his sins. But then it became clear that it was only a superficial wound made with a small knife unable to penetrate far through the two fur coats he was wearing against the cold. Not at all life-threatening. Embarrassing, in fact—both for the king and for his would-be assassin. At trial Damiens said he had only intended to frighten the king—but frighten him for what purpose? "To prompt him to restore all things to order and tranquility," he said. Oh, yes, now I understand.

But whether successful or not, gestural or not, symbolic or not, regicide is the ultimate crime, an assault not only upon the king, upon the people, upon the state, but upon God Himself, the ultimate sponsor of the throne. Repeated daily prayers were begun at all churches to exorcise the evil incurred by Damiens's attempt. God must have been amused.

Almost three months later Damiens was sentenced to death by the Parlement of Paris. Let me put this in the record. It was the court that prescribed this, not I. I was only carrying out my assignment.

The Court declares Robert-François Damiens duly convicted of the crime of Lèse-majesté, divine and human, for the very wicked, very abominable, and very detestable parricide perpetrated on the King's person: and therefore condemns the said Damiens to amende honorable *before the principal church of Paris, whither he shall be taken in a cart wearing only a shirt and holding a taper of the weight of two pounds; and then, on his knees, he shall say and declare that, wickedly and with premeditation, he has perpetrated the said very wicked, very abominable, and very detestable parricide, and wounded the King with a knife in the right side, for which he repents and begs pardon of God, the King and Justice; and further the Court orders that he then be taken to the Grève, and, on a scaffold erected for the purpose, that his chest, arms, thighs, and calves be burnt with pincers; his right hand, holding the knife with which he committed the said parricide, burnt in sulfur; that boiling oil, melted lead, and rosin and wax mixed with sulfur be poured into the wounds; and after that his body be pulled and dismembered by four horses, that the members and body consumed in fire, and the ashes scattered to the winds. The Court orders that his property be confiscated to the King's profit; that before the said execution Damiens be subjected to the* question ordinaire et extraordinaire *to make him confess the names of his accomplices. Orders that the house in*

which he was born be demolished, and that no other
building be erected on that spot. Decreed by the Parle-
ment on March 26, 1757.

Upon reading this, I must say I was horrified. No one had been quartered in France since 1610. I asked my uncle Gabriel, the executioner in Reims, to come help me—though actually it was I who assisted him, as he was so much more experienced in that sort of thing. My official presence legalized the proceedings.

The first order of business was to look for and purchase four equally strong horses, not an easy task as an emergency. It cost 432 livres! But this was an operation for which the crown would spare no expense—that is, if the crown chose to pay at all. Then I had to hire someone to administer the interrogation since neither Gabriel nor his assistants would have anything to do with it. Another 60 livres, and an unpleasant search among ruffians.

At 5 the next morning, Uncle Gabriel and I dressed in our official costumes and climbed into the cart which led the procession of the four matched horses and our fifteen assistants. We went first to the Conciergerie, where we witnessed the torture that was to make Damiens confess his accomplices. His arms were dislocated by *l'estrapade*, and his feet went into the much-feared boot. Yet through all that he revealed nothing and continued to insist that he had acted alone. Some kind of religious maniac he was, I think.

They wrapped his body in a sack, with only his head exposed. Then he was taken to the Ste.-Chapelle, where he was tied down on a bench and made to listen to a two-hour sermon. How much listening he did I don't know, though to my mind's eye, amidst the glorious color from the glass, it was a fair vision of hell.

In midafternoon we took him across the river to the Place de Grève. The torturer we hired—Soubise—regretted his decision to do the job and got so drunk he could hardly stand. And he forgot to buy the wax, the lead, the oil, and the sulfur, all of which were clearly specified in his orders. So Uncle Gabriel cursed him, and the public prosecutor cursed Uncle Gabriel, and the crowd roared with laughter, and Soubise decided to change roles to that of Court jester with all his drunken antics. He was having a great time while other assistants went out to buy the materials. I can't imagine what Damiens was thinking through all this entertainment.

When everything was ready, the prisoner was pulled, shrieking, from his sack, and a quaking Uncle Gabriel grabbed Damiens's right hand—in which we had placed the knife Damiens had used on the king—and held it over flaming coals until the skin was actively on fire. Then two assistants pulled pieces of flesh from Damiens's body with red-hot pincers while another poured boiling oil and melted lead into the wounds. His cries were unbearable for even the rough-est of us on the scaffold, but the crowd seemed to be enjoying itself immensely. Try to kill a king? The assas-sin deserves what he gets. I doubt they'd have been so happy to do the doing.

The quartering was horrendous beyond belief. The horses started off three separate times with Damiens's limbs tied to them. The arms were already dislocated; the legs became so—but they refused to be torn from the body. The horses couldn't pull hard enough—even though they were whipped. Finally the drunken Soubise took an axe to the joints. You can imagine the mess he made.

This time, unlike with Ruxton or Mongeot, there was no place I could turn away to: The blood lust of the crowd was as horrifying to me as the action on the scaffold or with the horses in the square. Every roof-top was covered with cheering people. And I tell you, there were more women than men, women of distinc-tion. In fact, they seemed to enjoy the show even more than the men, which fact is not exactly a compliment. Perhaps it has to do with their familiarity with pain in childbirth, or with the deaths that go along with it. Maybe their horror of Damiens's monstrous deed was just that much greater.

The spectacle went on for four hours, four hours filled with *le diable's* soul-shattering screams. Still, the most delicate of women and some of the daintiest ladies from the Court turned the event into a great holiday festival, as if they were watching some grand spectacle—which I suppose they were. None of the women turned away—but many men couldn't bear to watch.

I will never understand women, and I admit that after that day I became deeply wary of them all—as well I might. They take no active part in death dealing, but they are eerily capable of gazing at it directly.

Uncle Gabriel never recovered from the events of that day. His first day back in Reims, he abdicated his position and gave it over to his son. My *grandmère* Marthe tended to my emotional wounds by drumming her dictum into my head: Executioners are honorable men with a crucial mission. Your burden may be difficult, even painful, but your work is as vital to public order as that of any soldier or policeman. You have every right to hold your head high. The Sanson heritage must go on!

There's one more story I need to tell, as it has surely affected history.

Nine years after Damiens's execution, the Count de Lally-Tollendal, Maréchal of France, the general who lost India to the English, hated by his men and accused of treachery, was scheduled to be executed by heavy broadsword for his actions—or the lack of them. At the time, of course, a nobleman had such an option—not to be touched by the hands of a commoner like me, or worse by those of my assistants, but to be swiftly decapitated by a sharp, virgin sword, perhaps one of his own choosing. The gallows was for the rabble, the wheel for the scum, and the stake for heretics. But for those of rank, the shining sword of choice.

I had never used a broadsword before. I was by then a strapping fellow, like now, already well used to my role. But though I approached the task with aplomb, and though the *maréchal* was cooperative, as befitted his station, at the first blow I succeeded only in breaking his jaw. The crowd burst out into shouts of anger against me. Didn't they know how difficult the task was? Had they seen such a beheading before? Didn't they know it was my first time? My assistants ran forward to tend to old Lally, who was writhing and screaming on the scaffold flooring. I was too shocked and paralyzed to attempt a second blow. Jean-Baptiste, my old father, dashed up from the front row onto the scaffold, grabbed the heavy sword from my hand, and, even with his atrophied muscles, severed Lally's head with one blow. Then he fainted, with his mother screaming at him and at me and the crowd not knowing what to make of it. The police dispersed the mob, and the assistants cleaned up the mess.

This experience left its mark on the entire family, and especially on me.

7.
Two to Town, and Back Again

Nicolas Jacques Pelletier, now fifteen, walked out to seek his—and his family's—fortune. And fortunate he was, too, for several months before him, also headed for Redon, had come Gaele Loiseaux, making the far shorter walk into town from the north for the same purpose. She was sixteen and much wiser than Nico, both because of her gender and because of her impoverished upbringing in Brittany—in a one-room cottage packed with ever-sick siblings, all witness, of course, to the fights and sexual intimacies of their parents.

As she walked, she sang her favorite song in the mother tongue of Bretagne:

> *Jezuz ! Pegen bras eo*
> *Plijadur an eneoù,*
> *Pa'z int dirak Doue,*
> *Hag en e garantez!*

(Jesus! how deeply
joyous are souls
kneeling before God
in your love!)

What could the adult world surprise her with?
Very little.

Kenavo, paourentez,
Kenavo, gwanerezh,
Kenavo, trubuilhoù,
Kenavo, pec'hejoù!
(Farewell, poverty,
Farewell, affliction
Farewell, troubles
Farewell, sins!)

But still there was something.

She had come from Malestroit to Redon to take
a servant's job with a friend of her father's cousin, one
Joseph Auret, a successful merchant in chestnuts and
salt, recently widowed and needing more help.

Redon was the big city for both Nico and Gaele,
a town of six thousand souls, the "Venice of the West,"
the river port for Rennes, capital of Brittany, forty
miles farther northeast. Its large docks at the conflu-
ence of the Ouest and the Vilain were a gateway to the
Atlantic, and its canals, running right through the cen-

ter of town, with their towpaths and shaded avenues, were a thoroughfare combining urban busyness and rural charm. M. Auret's establishment and home were in the city center, on the Rue du Moulinet, a block from the waterway, and perfect for the movement, in and out, of his goods.

Venice! The Atlantic! The capital! The very words "maritime" and "merchandise"! Neither of these young people had ever been more than ten miles from home, and that rarely. The city was a source of wide-eyed wonderment for both, and Nico, too, wound up at M. Auret's, though only after several days of searching for work and sleeping in the streets.

But for Nico, beyond the wonderment of the city was something even more wonderful: Working in the same house as he, living in the same house as he, was—a girl. His words to Gaele were few, his glances sideways. He kept to his chores as the houseboy: running errands, loading and unloading crates, performing miscellaneous household tasks, doing everything right, never getting anything wrong.

He did get one thing wrong: He assumed Gaele might secretly feel about him as he secretly felt about her. But she was similarly devoted entirely to her work, her new position as *domestique*. One of the first luxuries M. Joseph had permitted his newly single self was a maidservant who cooked and cleaned, and carried loads of wash and washed them, and emptied chamber pots and privies, and worked from dawn to dusk without complaining—all in return for her keep and a tiny sum of money—all of which she sent back home.

It is fair to say that each of the three was starved of affection. Nico was entranced by the possibilities of an amorous conquest. He had brown, curly hair, and his eyes, he knew, were big and handsome. His mother had told him so. When in Gaele's presence, he tried to make them shine by blinking a lot, and to keep the hunger out of them. His older little sister had told him once that he looked *"hargneux."* He didn't know what *"hargneux"* was, and wasn't sure she did, but he clenched his big jaw and was determined to keep from looking so.

Gaele was excited to be away from her village, with a new world of possibilities swarming around her. And even though she sent all her money home, still, perhaps on one of her trips to shop or on an errand, she hoped to meet some nice young man who would buy her sweets or a ribbon. Perhaps in a few years, she thought, she would even marry, and she and her husband might help support her needy family. But Gaele, too, at least at present, was hungry for affection.

It was 1772, the beginning of a new decade, and M. Auret's business was growing. He was making more money than ever before. Farmers were doing poorly, yes, but the sea still made salt, and the *marronniers* still grew chestnuts, and he was still making connections and money. His neighbors pitied him the loss of his wife, and he was often invited out to dinner by business associates. But in the midst of the middle-class whirl, he was, he admitted, lonely.

And so he began to notice the beautiful sixteen-year-old who had been bringing his meals for the last few months. Yes, he was forty-two, almost three times as old as she, but he had much to offer her. There were new ideas in the air, even out here in Brittany, and the fact that Gaele was a peasant and he someone of the rising bourgeoisie—well, that would not matter so much any longer. And besides, who would know?

He asked if she'd like to hear some stories, to be read to at night. Her family had owned no books but the Bible and could not read that very well. He, on the other hand, read beautifully, and she found great pleasure in sitting at table with M. Auret—she now called him M. Joseph—and hearing those old stories her father had so struggled with reading, hearing them read not only fluently but with expression.

Would she like to hear stories from other kinds of books? She didn't know what other kinds of books there were, but of course she agreed. It would be part of her learning more about the world, she thought, the world out there, now right in here.

Nico listened jealously at the door as they cried together reading *Phèdre* and laughed together reading

Rabelais. He heard as they discussed the notion of *"Fay çe que vouldras."* What would it mean if all France were like that and not just the abbey of Thélème? What would it mean if only 12 Rue de Moulinet were to put that motto into practice? What might she want? She didn't know. And she didn't dare ask the same question of him. But some organ deep inside her blushed.

She washed his underwear daily, and emptied his slops, and in doing so felt *intime*, intimate enough warily to take in Milot's *L'École des filles, ou la philosophie des dames*, when he told her it was a famous book everyone knew about.

And so it happened. They both knew it would. M. Joseph's pupil became his lover; her employer her guide to a sensual world heretofore unknown to her. Their nightly classes went from *Histoires amourantes de la cour de Louis XIV* to Cleland's *La Fille de joie*, in special translation, and their howlings tortured Nico every night. Those two were no longer lonely.

Over six months, while she shared the monsieur's bed, the girl and the boy became acquainted, if only through propinquity and in service to the same master. Gaele discovered Nico and learned to like him deeply, so simple did he seem, simple-hearted, certainly, and simple in his thoughts, as she once had been. In Gaele's eyes, Nico was a connection, almost nostalgic, to her past. She told him of her dreams with M. Joseph, of her fears of the unaccustomed life, of her ambitions to improve and grow to be worthy of her lover. Nico listened, breathing shallowly, with his eyes fixed.

And one day she told him that she had missed two bleedings. And then she saw that Nico knew precious little about woman things.

"Are you a virgin?" she asked him then. He shook his head, more in wonder at the question than in negation. The only virgin he knew was La Vierge Marie, and that the only use of the adjective. And surely he was not she.

Ah, she thought, surprised, he was not a virgin, and so she said, "Tell me about her."

"Who?"

"You know, the one you . . . you know."

"What?"

"Did it with."

"Did what with?"

It was a hard row to hoe. And it wasn't mere curiosity, or worse, sadism or teasing. Gaele was only yearning to talk about something she had never explored before, to compare her new experiences with someone else's, to hear a man talk about it—all right, a boy—because she would never quiz her own Joseph.

It dawned too slowly on Nico what she was asking. And so things remained at a certain level of ambiguity, confusion, and tension until one night Gaele burst into his room and drenched him in bitter tears.

She had just told Joseph that she had now missed three bleedings and was with child. And instead of kissing her Joseph had gotten very upset and said that he would take her to old Mme. Trebuchet to get it fixed. What fixed? What was broken? "To get rid of it," he said. He had almost screamed.

"And how do I even know it's mine?" he had gone on, "that you haven't been sleeping around with the dock boys, like you've done with me? Or with Nico? How could I ever trust a girl like you?"

And now she was in Nico's huge arms, weeping inconsolably, her breasts pressing against him, and he didn't know what to do. So he just sat there with her, and that was exactly what she needed.

In the following weeks, as Gaele's condition became visible; Nico wondered how he might help—how he might help her now and later, when there was a baby. The master was talking about letting Gaele go, about not being able to feed an extra mouth or guarantee her health. Perhaps he could pay her a bit of money if she would leave and not say who the father was. And, the master said, she wasn't doing as much work as before, keeping up at her chores. He would have to hire someone to do the work she was no longer doing.

He had stopped reading to her at night, and Nico thought they had stopped doing it entirely, as he no longer heard their screams. Only her weeping, all the time weeping.

One morning she told Nico she would be leaving, that M. Auret had given her a little money to take care of the baby, and that she was going back home to Malestroit to live with her family again. Mme. Trebuchet had told her she would have the baby in September.

"I'll go with you," he told her. "I'll help you with the baby. I have little brothers and little sisters, so I know what to do."

Gaele smiled at him, laughed, and gave him a peck on the cheek. He knew he had said the right thing.

"You're nice, Nico," she told him, "but I don't need a servant. I'm sure I'll have plenty of help at home."

"I won't be your servant," he said. "I'll be your husband."

For Nico, there were two types of men who helped women. One was the husband, while "manservant" was what he did for M. Auret. He didn't think she would want that. So "husband" was what was left. And if that was anything like his mother and her husband, his father, he would get to sleep in the same bed with her, naked under the covers, and then . . . It was too hard to think beyond that.

Gaele did not laugh him off, as well she might. Going home to her parents bearing an illegitimate child was one thing, and a very bad and sinful thing it was. But coming home a grown woman with a husband, was quite something else—for her, for her parents, for the neighbors. Nico was not Prince Charming, but he was nice, he was strong, he doted on her and seemed sincere, he *could* help with the house and the farm, she could learn to read and teach him, and they could teach their children. And *this* child would have a father, not be *bâtard*, against the law. As if any child could be against the law. What law?

And so the next day she told Nico that he could be her husband, that they would get married, and that he would become the father of her child. And Nico wanted to believe that it would happen, that by some miracle during the wedding the priest could turn him into the father of this child just as every Sunday he turned bread into flesh and wine into blood. But whether such was possible or not, Nico was happy.

The large sixteen-year old husband and his small, distended seventeen-year-old spouse took a mail coach two hours west to Malestroit and a glorious, if surprising, arrival of bridegroom and bride to a stone-broke family of Loiseauxs. Nico sent word of his marriage to his parents and said he would send money when he could.

8.

CONCERNING SOME
EVENTS IN PARIS

About the time that Nico and Gaele arrived in Malestroit, some peculiar events were going on in Paris. In January of 1772, one Pierre-Marie Trespagne, a procurator of Parlement, suddenly succumbed to an unaccountable illness, which neither his physicians, nor those summoned by the city government could fathom. After a bout—mercifully brief—of distress and suffering, M. Trespagne was pronounced dead, presenting all the signs of the departed. His face exhibited the usual pinched paleness, the lips becoming a translucent purple. His eyes were dry and lusterless and did not blink. His temperature fell until there was no more warmth coming from his body. He had stopped breathing, and his heart no longer beat. Over the course of several hours his body assumed the expected rigidity. On the following day he was placed in a substantial coffin, appropriate to his rank, and was buried at the Cimitière des Innocents, the central cemetery of Paris.

Late that day a grave digger working on a neighboring plot sat down to rest on the mound over M. Trespagne and felt some small commotion of the earth beneath the seat of his pants, something, he said, like small animals scurrying in the earth deep down. His coworker razzed him about it, called him an alcoholic with heebie-jeebies up his ass—but then sat beside him and experienced the same sensation. They decided to explore. M. Trespagne's grave was shamefully shallow and carelessly, loosely filled, and the two men quickly exposed the coffin. Its top was partially open, as though by an effort made by the buried man's head, there was blood everywhere, and evidence the he had gnawed open his own right arm in desperation. Poor man. This was not right payment for his years of public service.

The story, complete with artists' renderings, filled the front pages of every Paris paper. The image of a "corpse" devouring itself because still alive was enough to drench the public in fear and set off cultural and political revolutions (much as the events of September 11th have done in our own time).

The 1770s initiated an era of *taphophobie*—fear of graves, especially of being buried alive. And certainly such insecurities had been prepared by the earliest demonstrations of mouth-to-mouth resuscitation and cardiac defibrillation. Bring someone back from death? Then perhaps they were not really dead in the first place.

Surely the suffering of one buried alive is of the most extreme kind. The frightening, increasing weight upon the lungs, the smell of earth and strangling garments, the inability to move more than a few inches in the coffin, the absolute blackness, the infinite silence broken only by one's screams and the scratching of one's fingernails on wood, the thoughts of grass and sky and rescuing friends so close above, unreachable— can any potential human experience be more intolerable, more appalling? This was the stuff of private nightmare—and mushrooming newspaper sales.

Ironically, such public fear was the price paid for medical progress. In earlier times dead had been dead, ashes to ashes, dust to dust. But now—who could know the subtleties, the shifting boundaries that divided life and death? Who could really say where the one ended and the other began? The doctors? The doctors who had discovered diseases in which all normal living functions ceased but where the leaving off was mere suspension, a temporary pause in the mysterious ways of life? Science was advancing. The world suddenly knew too much to know what it knew and what it didn't. And what it didn't know, it feared.

Fearsome too was the behavior of those very doctors. For whom, for what, did the numerous corps of grave robbers mine their wares at midnight? To what dissections were the corpses carted? To the laboratories of those very doctors who by day professed to serve the public and by night raped and devoured their remains! *Sapere aude?* The dark side of science.

In stepped the undertakers, their engineers and carpenters. Those who could afford it bought "safety coffins" at exorbitant prices, glass-lidded boxes rigged with periscopes for light, breathing tubes for air, and flags and bells controlled from within the coffin to call for attention above the surface.

And, on a side less practical, in stepped the psychical research societies to explore the mysteries of life, death, and the in-betweens. It was all the dance of science, and for many the hobby *du jour*, the defining activity of "the Enlightenment."

In 1778 Franz Anton Mesmer relocated his medical practice from Vienna to Paris. In the decade's pre-revolutionary upheavals of thought, there was much popular enthusiasm and support for anyone challenging the establishment, and the medical dignitaries played their role by rejecting and ridiculing proponents of Mesmer's "animal magnetism." If *they* hadn't been taught it, it couldn't possibly exist. Viennese physicians had already dismissed the idea that Mesmer could be channeling "magnetic fluid" through his body and curing his patients with its application. "Magnetic fluid," all right—the use of magnets was widely accepted.

But magnetotherapy without magnets? Absurd. They warned their French colleagues of his coming.

But the public greeted Mesmer warmly, especially the upper classes, and there were heated discussions and debates among the aristocracy. He soon established the Mesmerist Society for Universal Harmony for "the pursuit of education, justice, humanity, and generosity." His clinic was a haven of luxury, a studied calm in the midst of economic and social turbulence. Thick carpets graced the floors; tall mirrors, luxurious drapes, and tapestries hung on the high-ceilinged walls; zodiacal signs abounded in an ambience of music and soft light. Commoners could be treated for free, seated around one of Mesmer's magnetic tubs housed in less plush surroundings, holding conducting rods as he passed among them, healing. Many chose to be attached to a magnificent tree he had magnetized just outside his clinic. But the nobility made appointments as they could for the rooms with grander *décor*, where they became willing guinea pigs for new scientific discoveries and swapped among themselves their theories of the universe. Though the king was skeptical, the queen herself was treated.

In a short time Mesmerism was being discussed by commoners and intellectuals alike, in the cafés, in newspapers and broadsides, in the literary salons. Mozart would shortly satirize it in *Così Fan Tutte*. And for carping scientists, theories were all well and good, but how did they know the cures were not simply imaginings?

Still, Mesmer's practices were not irrational. Magnets were used to heal, were they not? and electricity even more. Electricity, the subtle fluid penetrating living bodies and subsisting in them, was diffused like magnetism. Electrotherapy, as practiced in court by Jean-Paul Marat—was that not being proclaimed? As Mesmer maintained, "When by an operation of art or nature, there happens to be a greater proportion of electrical or magnetic fluid in one body than in another, the body which has the most, will communicate to that which has least, till the proportion becomes equal; provided the distance between them be not too great; or, if it is too great, till there be proper conductors to convey it from one to the other." It was Mesmer's good fortune to be able to accumulate this greater proportion, and share it with his patients.

And speaking of Mozart, that strange young man had come to Paris, with his mother, in the same year as Mesmer, to seek his fortune. Twenty-two years old he was: emotionally perhaps fourteen, spiritually ten thousand, and more than halfway through his life. He was on assignment from his father, Leopold:

> *The purpose of your journey is twofold—either to get a good permanent appointment, or, if this should fail, to go off to some big city where large sums of money*

THE GOOD DOCTOR GUILLOTIN

can be earned. Both plans are designed to assist
your parents and to help your dear sister, but above
all to build up your own name and reputation in
the world.

If you could count on a monthly salary from
some prince in Paris, and, in addition, do some work
occasionally for the theater, the Concert Spirituel and
the Concert des Amateurs, and now and then have
something engraved par suscription, *and if your*
sister and I could give lessons and she could play at
concerts and musical entertainments, then we should
certainly have enough to live on in comfort.

The very recollection of all the projects which
since your departure from Salzburg you have formed
and communicated to me is enough to drive me crazy.
They have all amounted to proposals, empty words
ending in nothing whatsoever.

Wolfgang and his mother—with whom, unlike
with his father, he would trade filthy jokes—arrived in
Paris on March 23. On July 3 she died. The man-child
was most upset.

Nevertheless, he agreed that summer—for a
modest sum which he would forward to his father—to
play a recital at the home of the Duchesse de Bourbon
in the Faubourg St. Germain. Mozart was to be the
first of many to show off the newly designed heavier

piano the duchess had just bought from Johann Andreas Silbermann, Gottfried's nephew and most famous pupil.

Even in Strasbourg Tobias Schmidt was connected enough to Parisian musical circles to have heard both of the new piano and of his ex-neighbor's engagement to demonstrate it. He wangled an invitation, hired a seat on the mail coach, and attended the concert surrounded by his betters.

Perhaps it was *épatez la noblesse:* The young man played a set of original variations on a bawdy folk tune, *"Ah je vous dirai, Maman";* then, with a young player named André Badiarov, launched into a new sonata for violin and piano in E minor; and finally played a new piano sonata in A minor, which demanded everything Silbermann's machine could offer in expressiveness. Perhaps it was the tension with his father. More likely it was the death of his mother. But that evening minor was the major event, the dominant tool and emotion.

Schmidt wrote to a musical correspondent in Aix-en-Provence about the revelations he had experienced that night, about Mozart's diabolical strategy for the program, about how "in the middle of the unending C major of a trivial folk tune, Mozart had thrown himself and his listeners into a precipitous C minor variation which ripped open the pleasant, clever world, and exposed the darkest forces lurking in the background." The other two pieces were to Schmidt "even more sustainedly dark than the trap of the first, and that much more affecting."

Schmidt accosted the pianist after the recital and, leveraging their common past in Salzburg, was able to walk Mozart back to his shoddy hotel. Schmidt asked how the boy felt about being free of his family for the first time.

"Yes, I'm free," Mozart said. "But I have to go around paying visits to all the possible patrons on my father's list. And I must say the ruling class is not as genteel as they pretend. I go to people's fancy houses, I am made to wait around for hours before seeing them, even if I have an appointment, and then I have to play for them and their friends on their awful pianos. People talk while I'm playing, and there's no food left when I finally get to the table."

Schmidt was surprised. He mentioned how famous, even beloved, the young man already was in the world of music and musicians.

"Oh, yes," the boy averred, "people pay plenty of compliments, but there it ends. They arrange for me to come on such and such day; I play and hear them exclaim, 'What a genius—unbelievable, astonishing!' And then it is *adieu*. At first I spent a lot of money driving about—often to no purpose, as the people couldn't even be bothered to be at home.

"Those who don't live in Paris can't imagine how

annoying this is. Besides, Paris is greatly changed; the French are not nearly as polite as they were even fifteen years ago. Their manners now border on rudeness, and they are detestably conceited."

He was remembering his first tour, as a seven-year-old. And then, out of nowhere: "For twenty-four two-hour lessons in composition for the daughter of the Duc de Gines, I was offered 3 louis d'or—total! I turned them down. Such niggardly nobility. Not in Munich, not in Mannheim, and not here in Paris has any Court wanted me, the much-praised genius. No openings available, you know. Inferior men rule the scene, men who know how better to assert themselves."

The minor mode, indeed.

Schmidt left Paris the next day. Mozart left on September 26. Mesmer left six years later, in circumstances that will involve one of our five men. Paris marched forward toward what would come.

9·

FLIGHTS OF FANCY

The American Revolution was eight years old, and France was going bankrupt supporting it. Nevertheless, in the great Minister's Courtyard fronting the Royal Academy of Science at the palace of Versailles, a grandiose celebration was taking place. At 1 P.M., to the sound of a drum roll, a sheep, a duck, and a rooster rose up into the sky.

Attached they were to a forty-foot-high, forty-thousand-cubic-foot taffeta balloon, fireproofed with alum, painted sky blue with golden flourishes, signs of the zodiac, and suns. Along with the king, queen, and Court watching from the balconies, the doctors Guillotin and Marat were there, packed into the square along with more than one hundred thousand Parisians of all classes to witness the great event—the first living beings hauled up, against their nature, into the heavens. Would they survive, or were birds the only beasts allowed by the Creator to fly?

Marat, physician to the Comte d'Artois, brother of the king, provided inside information: "You know the king wanted the flight tried with two criminals he had chosen."

Guillotin didn't know.

"But Montgolfier was indignant. 'The king may be sovereign master of my life,' he said, 'but he is not the keeper of my honor!' That's good, no?"

"Good thing it was *our* Louis and not his father or grandfather."

Marat agreed the forebears might have had the balloonist executed for such defiance.

The two physicians watched the beasts, tethered in a basket below the balloon, rise to about 1,500 feet and drift two miles westward, a dot in the sky, to the woods of Vaucresson, where their aircraft fell gently between the trees. It might have gone much higher and farther had it not tipped upward on the ascent, spilling the fire-heated air over its lip. But the demonstration was good enough. The crowd later feasted on the various reports that the rooster's neck had been broken in the descent, or that its wing had been broken by a kick from the sheep, or that the sheep had been discovered nibbling on the straw in the basket while the birds cowered in a corner. In any case, it was likely all had survived.

It's difficult to imagine so many people, especially the poor, mixing it up, pouring out of Paris to Ver-

sailles. But the Montgolfier brothers were already famous. Six years earlier Joseph M. had had an idea while
watching laundry drying over a low fire. What were
those air pockets in the articles of clothing, lifting
them upward? He built a frame out of the lightest possible wood, covered it in thin taffeta, and lit a small
paper fire under its stand. The thing took off and col-
lided with the ceiling. He and Étienne built larger and
larger models and in June had demonstrated a ten-
minute flight to a group of dignitaries, including the
king. The selling point, of course, was the possibility
of military use.

Word of the brothers' success astonished all of
Paris: The crowd was preordained. Joseph Montgolfier
was too shy—and too unkempt—to be the public face
of their enterprise, but Jacques-Étienne, his younger
brother, "stylishly dressed in black," was able to make
all the necessary arrangements for the great and crowded
day, a prerevolutionary moment in more ways than
one, for complete mixing of social stations had never
before been seen at the palace.

The first human flight occurred only a month
later, in November, and Guillotin and Marat, much
interested, applied to be its attending physicians. In-
ventors, adventurers, and manufacturers had quickly
smelled the implications of manned flight, and a small
but industrious sky-rush was on. Would even religion

lose its grip when the assumption of virgins became commonplace?

It was another young doctor who stepped, center stage, into the picture. Jean-François Pilâtre de Rozier had always had an eagle eye for science and publicity and had become one of the major stars of the educational circuit, speaking regularly to Parisian crowds on scientific topics. His interest in medical gases had been piqued by a rotation at the military hospital of Metz, and his subsequent research involved various gaseous substances and respirators. In 1781 he had opened a popular museum of science on the Rue St.-Avoie, housing a collection of experimental equipment and ingenious instruments, where all types of people might come together to speculate and discuss. He wrote a book on electricity and magnetism and demonstrated, in a huge tub, his "dry suit" for diving.

He had been present in June at the first Montgolfier flight and had assisted at the raising of the three beasts. On November 21, using Montgolfier's balloon, he and a military friend made the first human free flight in history, attaining three thousand feet without harm and traveling more than seven miles in less than half an hour—from the Château de la Muette on the edge of the Bois de Boulogne to land among the windmills of the Butte-aux-Cailles, one of the prominent hills to the southeast. Guillotin and Marat followed as best they could on horseback and were there for the landing, medical equipment in hand, prepared for any untoward eventuality. But all was well. The balloonists had "seen the Sublime."

All did not go so well two years later, in June of '85, when Pilâtre de Rozier, age twenty-eight, became a martyr to science by attempting to cross the English Channel from Boulogne in a balloon that utilized hydrogen for a trip too long for hot air. Just beyond the starting point his balloon exploded, "enveloped in a violet flame," and he and a companion fell 1,500 feet in full, horrific view of the crowd below. From England, where he had gone to receive them, Jean-Paul Marat wrote that "all hearts are stricken with grief." Louis ordered a medal struck, commissioned a bust, and ordered a special pension for the scientist's family. A week later Rozier's fiancée committed suicide. Guillotin attended her funeral, too.

The kissing cousinship of science and death.

B esides Versailles, there was another palace that witnessed a flight of fancy—one original flight, and then tens of thousands of impregnated others. Their sum total? Perhaps "the French Revolution."

The Palais Royal stands on the right bank, just north of the Louvre, with a huge garden space behind it. Cardinal Richelieu had lived there, Moliere played and died there, and later the palace was given to the king's cousin, the Duc d'Orléans. In 1780 the *duc* gave it to his son, who, over the next few years, opened the gardens to the public and encouraged the most spectacular mix of pleasure and politics in all of Europe. The *palais*, belonging to the nobility, was a privileged area that the police could not enter except by invitation. And without police, what could not go on in its arcades and above and below them? It became an enchanted place, a small, luxurious city enclosed in a large one, lined with cafés filled with speechifiers, the gardens filled with swarming crowds, prostitutes low class and high, pamphleteers and pickpockets, a daily carnival of every appetite, the cultural and political antipode—even nemesis—of the stately Court at Versailles. There were singers and chess players, wig-makers and magic-lantern shows, billiard parlors and lemonade stands, and the miniature cannon, astronomically situated so that at exactly noon, sun rays would fall upon a lens to light a fuse, to make a boom. As someone remarked, at the *palais*, you might lose track of your morality, but at least you could set your watch.

All this was more or less fine with the police, since "mischief" would be confined to a predictable place, and if respectable citizens chose to frequent it, well, it would be at their own risk. Little did the authorities know the power of open space, free speech, and mixed populations parading, people-watching, window-shopping, reading, flirting, eating, stealing.

Order there was none, and Paris fed on the jumbling, got used to it, and wanted more. Anything could be said or heard at the Palais Royal, and crowds gathered eagerly around anything that was "a scene." The *duc*'s playground was a utopia where nowhere became somewhere, an empire of *Liberté*. That word.

The cafés were the heart and soul of the affair. Two dozen encircled the gardens and beckoned strollers into their arcaded interiors, often underground. Some of the most important of them—the Café du Caveau, the Café des Aveugles, the Café du Sauvage—suggested the kind of close, mysterious darkness with possibilities for abandon. The Café des Aveugles, directly downstairs from the straighter Café Italien above, offered twenty separate "caves" in which to exercise one's sexual or narcotic preferences. The verb "to politic" was born in these cafés, and "politicking" was not the sober, responsible discourse of Guillotin's National Assembly but rather a politics of dream and desire, lubricated by alcohol and drunk with exuberant talk.

Being the sober, upright scientist he was, Joseph Ignace Guillotin's favorite was the Café Méchanique (precursor of the Horn & Hardart Automat), in which food and drinks appeared from trapdoors and windows activated by elaborate levers, weights, screws, pulleys, inclined planes, and other devices illustrating various principles of Newtonian physics. Rube Goldberg would have loved it. Shortages had made the selection a bit sketchy, but what food there was was amusing to obtain, and not bad for the price. Guillotin often stopped there when in the neighborhood.

Nursing a cold coffee on a hot afternoon in 1786, he found himself staring at the blade of a slicer applying itself to a spring-advanced melon, released by the fall of a 5-sous piece onto a counterweighted lever. It was a good day for melon sales, and the surgeon watched with approval several precisely achieved slicings. To his horror, he found his mind wandering to the botched execution of the Count Maréchal de Lally-Tollendal, some twenty years earlier, which he had witnessed—against his preference—as part of a medical team.

"Anything the matter?" inquired a voice from a facing table.

"No—thank you," the doctor replied, and then, "Why do you ask?"

"All of a sudden you became pale. I'd even say deathly pale."

"Oh. I was just thinking of something unpleasant. Have you been watching me? Are you a doctor? From Paris?"

"No. Just observant. I'm from Strasbourg."

"What brings you to Paris?"

"An old ambition."

Guillotin moved over to the stranger's table, the better to hear him amidst the chatter, the mechanical sounds, and the resultant laughter.

"May I?"

"But of course. Tobias Schmidt." He held out his hand.

"Joseph Guillotin," the doctor replied. "And what do you do, M. Schmidt?"

"Carpenter. Cabinetmaker. And now, after many years, a maker of harpsichords and pianos—though it is the pianos I am most interested in." He handed Guillotin his card.

"'T. Schmidt et Cie., Keyboard Instruments, 8 bis Rue St.-André-des-Arts.' Why that's just across from Marat's print shop! Dr. Marat—a good friend. Do you know him?"

"I know the printer well. But his name is André, not Marat."

"No, no, it's not the doctor's shop. Just one he uses to put out his papers. And occasional broadsides."

"I see. Perhaps I'll run into him."

"Meeting you like this seems providential. My wife and I were just talking about buying a piano. She sings, and I play the violin, and it might be wonderful to have chamber music at our house instead of always going out to others'. Do you have any instruments to sell? Or might you build us one?"

"I'm interested in building larger pianos with more sound. Instruments that will be able to handle the new music, the greater personal expressiveness. Have you heard the latest works of Mozart?"

"I've heard of him. Quite young, isn't he? But I don't know any of his music."

"Really! Well, you must come to my place, and we'll play through some of his violin sonatas. He and I were neighbors in Salzburg, and I have fair copies of several."

They made an appointment for the following week.

HARD TIMES

It was the best of times, it was the worst of times. . . ." But for all Dickens's acumen, it is hard to see what was "best" about them. The sense of new possibilities for society? But that sense was driven by need, by the misery of increasing exploitation and the poverty of masses suffering under an increasingly assertive and psychologically hollow aristocracy. In such a situation, if power corrupts and powerlessness corrupts, then *all* was thoroughly corrupted.

Nicholas and Gaele Pelletier would not have said it was the best of times. The couple's arrival at her family's farm in Malestroit was greeted happily enough, but with an undercurrent similar, perhaps, to the C minor lurking under C major. Gaele's parents were heavier than she remembered but looked less healthy, more wrinkled, displaying a kind of gaunt fleshiness. Her siblings were simply gaunt.

The couple arrived on a Saturday and the next

day went *en famille* on the usual half-mile trek to St. Gilles Church, in the middle of town. The church was known for its portal featuring the traditional symbols of each of the four evangelists: Saint Matthew's winged man rides Saint Mark's lion, while Saint Luke's ox reposes under a pillar decorated with Saint John's eagle.

Gaele knew her young husband was known as "the ox," and she chose to interpret the sculpture in the most generous and hopeful way: as the image of a man who would sacrifice, even suffer, with patience and strength and would labor in silence for the good of his wife, her family, and her coming child. But she knew as well—and had been taught from childhood—that to the church, the ox was the symbol of Christ, the true sacrifice.

The legend of that church portal—a legend spawned by visitors from the city—was that if you looked closely and with great imagination at exactly 3 P.M., the shadows of the ox and eagle would combine on the wall behind them to cast a silhouette of Voltaire. Most Malestroitians did not know who Voltaire was, or if they did, they did not care.

Still, the ox at the door had different meaning for Gaele, a secret meaning which, like Mary, she pondered in her heart, and she clasped Nico's huge arm more tightly than ever as they entered the church to pray.

But three years later, she, four of her siblings, and both her parents were buried in St. Gilles churchyard, the one watched over by the angel, the eagle, the lion, and the ox. It was the cholera again, and this time a tenth of the town succumbed.

There was no "germ theory" in the villages, and no running water. People ate from the same plates and drank from the same glasses, scraping them and wiping them without washing; they ate leftovers from the sick and slept with them in the same beds, not changing the linen even after it had been soiled or its users had expired. The girls could not keep up with the laundry, nor could the fabrics. "The less washed, the longer lived"—so the saying went. One never bathed. Life at subsistence level bordered too close to death.

Gaele left behind her a girl-child, petite Armelle, to be raised by her father—putative, adoptive, real—and by her one remaining aunt, Gaele's sister, a young woman of seventeen who alarmingly resembled Gaele at that age, that young girl with whom Nicolas had fallen so deeply in love. The three of them lived together in a cottage not quite thirty by fifteen feet. Its one window allowed sometimes for a ray of dusty light, which lit a dresser and a crate set up as a dining table. Near the fireplace were two beds on planks, each mattressed with straw. Aunt Gwennaelle shared hers with petite Armelle, and Nicolas slept alone, ever and ever alone. The rest of their belongings? A few clay dishes, a few wooden spoons and forks, a cook pot, a bellows, one lamp, and two chairs. The humidity, the mud, the filth, the stink, the mold, and the mange can only be imagined.

Every day, for all three meals, they ate chestnut gruel and buckwheat porridge and, occasionally, watery soup made from some few boiled vegetables— worm-eaten cabbage or turnips, a rare onion, some greenery from the hedgerows for color if not for nourishment, the water thickened with old boiled bread. After summer droughts, hard winters, and spring erosions, God's downward spiral, they found themselves in a common boat with impoverished neighbors— with increasing debt to lenders and a portion of the next harvest already spoken for by creditors. And even if they could fill their stomachs with gruel and porridge, the supply of proteins and vitamins was grossly inadequate: Rickets threatened the growing Armelle, while scurvy threatened them all.

The cow died, and so they had to sell the pig and most of the chickens. Poverty crumbled into indigence. Beyond the farm, Gwennaelle and Nicolas worked at a declining number of other jobs—for their neighbors could afford no outside workers, and Armelle was too small to beg.

The Grimms' tale of Hansel and Gretel and its French variants were not quite fictions: When her milk had run out, Gaele and Nicholas had talked of abandoning petite Armelle on the coast or in the forest. Better the little one should die and they make another child—this time their very own—than that they all should die of malnutrition or starvation. Such thoughts were not unnatural but rather hopeful and realistic.

Gaele's own death—and her mother's, and her father's, and her siblings'—lessened the strain on subsistence, and so the three survivors carried on in their hovel, in filth and squalor, begging on Sundays or saints' days and at fairs, smuggling a little salt, selling the glass from the window and tearing up the floor for firewood. They saved every scrap of rotting vegetable peel, every harvested snail or slug, and used their own excrement for manure.

Little Armelle earned her keep. She begged acorns and dandelion leaves and made the rounds of more prosperous farms in search of food. She prowled the surrounding land for bruised or windfall fruit, gathered sticks to sell for firewood and sorrel to make a palatable if empty soup. Gwennaelle cooked and cleaned as best she could, fed the remaining chickens and sold most of their eggs, planted and harvested the dwindling garden. She also stopped menstruating.

In the late summer of 1786, when their plot of ground could no longer support them all, Nicolas Pelletier took to the road.

Armelle was twelve. Her father had sent her off

to Vannes the better to beg her existence. Whether she would stay there, he did not know. She was adept by now at making herself up and dressing to look younger and as wretched as possible. Her stories were heartbreaking: Her siblings had burned to death in a fire; her parents' farm had been robbed of all goods and livestock while they were out working the fields; her widowed mother had been raped, and there was nothing for them to eat. She sold things, too, anything she could beg or steal—pins, needles, combs, rabbit skins, mole pelts. For a while she worked for an old woman selling original concoctions to terminate pregnancy or poison rats.

That summer was unusually hot and dry, and fires kept breaking out in fields and villages. There were rumors of incendiaries roaming the countryside. Why they would set things afire no one seemed to know, but the rumors created a paranoid fear of strangers, making things more difficult for Nicolas as *he* roamed the countryside. Who was this stranger offering to work? He was strong, so maybe helpful. But he was big, so maybe dangerous.

The oldest child from a peasant farm, Nico had many skills, but in his case, all a bit too rough. He offered to repair pots; they cracked shortly after. Though he was good at mending clogs, his hands were too large for nimbly fixing rush-bottomed chairs, and his repairs soon failed their sitters. He stole a ferret and for a while put himself forward as a rat-catcher. But the ferret died, and Nico was out of business again.

Some things he could do: He was an excellent harvester and a passably skilled woodcutter. He could comb hemp if he could stay awake doing so. He was good at clearing fields of stones and a good assistant at burning charcoal, but he was hired and paid by the job only, and employers were put off by his strange comments. He hadn't the skills for cutting stone, building walls, plastering, or thatching, and clearly the social skills of hawking or sales were beyond him. He was too big to be a chimney sweep.

It wasn't long before he went from being simply poor, an itinerant laborer looking for work, to being a vagabond, *un mauvais pauvre*, a constant criminal, slow at rascality and often as drunk as he could get. He stole ducks and chickens and sold or ate them. They were hard to transport. He pinched bits and pieces from rag-sellers' stalls, or handkerchiefs from clotheslines. The cold came on. He begged for slops, for bones, for bread, for bruised vegetables and rancid butter. At night he sought alcohol for anesthesia. And with that came more drunkards, male and female, hasty trafficking and alliances in cabarets with others in his state, men and women to whom life had been equally unkind, creatures caught in the great trap, similarly driven to mischief.

He was deadened, but not completely dead. Yet, as he made his way eastward, as the forests opened in front of him and closed in behind him, he felt his death coming. The mists enshrouded the shapes of the hills. And one evening the world was so closed in around him that all Nico could do was run. And when he stopped, he gasped for breath, his hands on his knees, his eyes shut and his mouth open.

Why does it take so much time to reach the next hill when it is only a few steps away?

If I kiss the earth, will it behave? Will it forgive me? And bless me?

He stretched out, facedown, to burrow into the world so close. Spit he mixed with it, and tears, but all he found was dirt and darkness.

He could not imagine standing again; he could not imagine walking. He was alone, all alone, always alone. He stretched his arms out at his sides, those arms, once strong, now shrunken, which had held his wife, his child.

Gaele! Armelle! I can't remember what you look like!

And he was so lonely that the world might exist only in his imagination; perhaps there was nothing at all beside himself, himself and his tormenting thoughts. His life passed in front of him in a conceptual blur, and at blurring speed. "Yes, and then that happened, and then that . . ."

Stop!

He called to himself out loud: Nico!

And became terrified: He was not there. He cried out in a harsh, hollow voice, "Nico! Nico Pelletier!"

No echo. And an indescribable fear came over him. It was *all* the void, the *void* was what was close, *le rien*, Nothingness.

"Gód! You come down here. Come down, you hear? or I'll come get you—and smash you in the face!

Again, no echo. And Nico was again the void.

Darkness was the hardest, when the day collapsed in shadow and everything grew more threatening. As the wind came up, anxiety took hold. Despair. He wanted to chase after the sun. But he didn't have the strength.

Nicolas Jacques Pelletier made several attempts at suicide during the late-fall and winter nights. Perhaps they were not very serious, rather more attempts to pinpoint himself, in moments of greatest dispersion, symptoms of the intense fear that followed, of the sense of nonexistence. He had little hope in death, but where else could he rest? When a man can rest, what more can he need? Just to slow down, to slow down like the trees, no, the stones, to be admitted to deadness . . .

One night he left the forest for a nearby town. In the square he broke through the ice and washed himself in the public fountain. Through a window he saw a family: children sitting at the table, the grizzled father at the head, old women, girls, their faces bright, warm. Perhaps his family was once like that. He couldn't remember. Perhaps they were all dead. He knocked on the door. They let him in, his clothes torn and grubby but his hair slicked clean. As best he could, he told the family of his life, and everyone listened. Before he slept in his first bed in years, he felt he should say the Lord's Prayer. But this, too, he couldn't remember.

II

CROWDS AND POWER

Standing on the scaffold as I often do, six feet above the crowd, I like to look it over, study it, and consider it after the event.

First, let it be said that Parisians are always interested—fascinated—by anything, by the least novelty going on around them. When someone looks intently at something—up in the air or in a little alleyway—right away others will stop what they're doing and try to see what he's looking at. All of a sudden a crowd will form, with everyone asking the other what they are looking at. One little escaped canary on a third-story windowsill is enough for the whole street to be blocked with spectators. I guess people have nothing better to do. If a dog falls into the river, immediately there's a crowd on the bridge arguing about what to do to save the poor animal. And if two people get into a fight, my God, they are separated by dozens of men, held back, with throngs of women haranguing them on the virtues of peace and harmony. Crowds: They are always with us.

But the crowd that gathers at a pillory, or even more at an execution—*that* has an added dimension. What such a crowd does is bear witness to the legitimacy and power of the king, of France, and their witnessing shows their submission to the grand idea of the state. Royalty needs the crowd as much as the crowd needs the parade of majesty. Order, that's the thing. Order—its power—it brings a kind of peace.

So I watch them, all those people down there, out there, and I see many things. But under all those things I see a basic happiness that whatever is occurring is occurring. And I am a delegate of that whole community. They understand I am not responsible for what they are seeing or are about to see. I don't pass the sentences; I only carry them out.

Who is the real executioner? They are! The crowd! Those people out there are the ones who approve my being there. They gather from all over the city to watch me do my job. Some may be ambivalent, but they all want it to happen. "Crucify him! Crucify him! His blood be upon us and on our people!" Better the Roman executioners should do it than that they should have to stone Him to death. Let justice be done by others.

It's hard to know the truth about these things, but here's what I think: When the criminal is killed, that is the moment of the crowd's power, not mine.

Everyone's horror of death is transformed into a secret joy that it is someone else who is dead. He is lying there, says some small inner voice, and I am standing, I am strong, I have withstood the presence of death, I am alive, and the other is fallen.

How else to account for their malevolence? There's no risk to them, so they think themselves superior for the moment, immensely superior. The criminal is defenseless, shackled and given over to me and thus to them for destruction. No one need fear punishment for his death. Perhaps having him killed by me makes up for all the murders they would like to commit but won't for fear of punishment. At one time or another, most people would like to kill someone.

Besides, we are all vaguely aware that we will have to die. It is helpful—perhaps even healthy—to see others dying. In this way we take in death in small bites before it's our turn to face him.

Though at times I think just the opposite may also be true: It may be that after an execution, after its concreteness, the crowd may feel more menaced than ever by death. It's a complicated business being Monsieur de Paris, the Royal Executioner.

Sometimes I look out at them and wonder why the whole thing is made so efficient. Hanging takes but a few long seconds. Decapitation, if it goes well, is even faster. The crowd rushes to get there so as not to miss the whole event.

It used to be more of an unhurried, kitchen-type affair. My ancestors, peace be with them, put people into sleeves of moistened parchment, set them on fire, and leisurely watch the parchment shrink and burn and reduce the flesh to dust. Or they would drive wedges into the long bones and split them, and finally the skull. Or roll down the skin from the torso into a kind of hanging apron. Would that not prevent more crime than even breaking on the wheel? These civilized days, we usually strangle our criminals for mercy after the second or third blow. All is soon over. The Chamber of the Question? The thumbscrews and the boot? Those old boys could watch all that—the strappado, the roasting—with tranquil nerves. They'd be deaf to all the anguished screams, to shrieks you couldn't even spell. My forebears were mental sanguinaries. Stable. Not me. I'm more sensitive. I can barely perform our *modern* tasks. I think I was permanently scarred by Damiens.

I give my assistants the victims' watches or rings or lockets or any clothing they want to wear or sell while I myself have to look beyond my job to earn enough money. And yet I have become some kind of symbol of tyranny, the personification of royalty and the Court in Versailles, as suspect as any aristocrat—as if *I* were responsible for last winter's freeze or this summer's drought. What is my crime? I have decapitated, hung, and beaten the enemies of the throne, the enemies of *France*.

This year I was ordered, *ordered* to break the parricide Louschart. The crowd overwhelmed the Place de Grève, shouting its anger at me—*me*—who did not prescribe breaking, who believed the old man's death was an accident, who was only following orders. "Set him free!" they screamed, as if I could do that. I do not understand them. And they destroyed my scaffold and my wheel, and burned them—800 livres of wood, plus another 500 for carpenters to repair it. And you think the city has paid me back? You think I'll ever be reimbursed? I'm not holding my breath.

And they freed Louschart, just like that. Freed him. When he had been officially condemned and sentenced. What makes them think they can take justice into their sweaty paws? And our so-called monarch, Louis, *L'Oui*, Monsieur Yes, does he punish them? No. He abolishes the wheel as punishment! It does not bode well when the crowd can push around a king.

I am owed 136,000 livres by the Royal Treasury. I just want you to know that. I'm sure that at the moment they can't very well pay, but I will continue my petition.

12.
ÇA IRA

Ah! ça ira, ça ira, ça ira.

Nous n'avons plus ni nobles, ni prêtres,

Ah! ça ira, ça ira, ça ira.

L'égalité partout règnera.

L'esclave autrichien le suivra,

Ah! ça ira, ça ira, ça ira.

Et leur infernale clique

Au diable s'envolera.

Ah! ça ira, ça ira, ça ira

Les aristocrates à la lanterne,

Ah! ça ira, ça ira, ça ira

Les aristocrates, on les pendra.

Ça ira.

It will go. It will go well. Everything will go well. The song was spreading, and wags among the crowd added many, many topical verses. No more nobles, no more priests, equality for all. The Austrian queen will disappear, and her hellish clique go with her. The streetlamps will be hung with aristocrats.

The inspiration for the song? That old optimist Benjamin Franklin was interviewed in the early '8os about how things were going with the American revolution. He answered in his awkward French, *"Ça ira, ça ira."* Catchy title. He thought America would be fine.

"This land is your land; this land is my land," we have sung. There and then, the call was more violent. *Ça ira.* "Oh, you can't hurt me, I'm stickin' with the union!" we sing still. There and then, the union was eight-tenths of the population, and any strike would be general. *Ça ira.*

It was coming; it was known, though the powers that were didn't know it. They danced gavottes to other tunes.

13.

KING YES SAYS YES AND NO

Though he was far from autocratic, King L'Oui did not say *oui* to everything. He was highly suspicious, for instance, of Franz Mesmer's claim that there was "but one disease and one cure." And so, in 1784, he planned an official investigation of "animal magnetism" and appointed an official commission to pursue it.

Who was on the commission? Ben Franklin, of course, he who tracked electricity to its home in the sky. Also our Dr. Guillotin, and Antoine Lavoisier, the "father of modern chemistry," theorist of fire, whose head would roll ten years later. There, too, among others, was Jean-Sylvain Bailly, the great astronomer, and future president of the National Assembly, whose head would do a similar dance a year before Lavoisier's. An august group of savants.

They observed many sessions and interviewed many patients. They inspected all the tools and instruments, the tubs, the wands, the musical instruments (one of which, the glass harmonica, had been perfected by Franklin). They spoke at length with Mesmer and his assistants in their powdered wigs and lilac jackets. They took notes on the twitchings and convulsions of the patients, the trances and miraculous, sudden cures.

That there were cures was admitted. It was the *cause* of the cures that was the question. The commissioners challenged Mesmer and his assistants to magnetize them, but as far as they were concerned, nothing happened. They felt nothing, and they maintained that if the cause were physical—say, the alleged universal fluid passing into their nervous systems—they should feel it entering their bodies. Mesmer maintained that it was a force too subtle to be detected and that their conclusions should come from the results he obtained. But they wanted tangible proof, some agent that could be measured. Science.

Franklin was too sick to come to Paris for these investigations, but M. Deslon, a principle Mesmerist, went to Passy to magnetize him and the large group which gathered around him. The results were poor. Some subjects failed to react. Some in a control group reacted when they shouldn't, as when a commissioner impersonating Deslon "treated" a blindfolded woman, who went into immediate tremors and spasms of pain.

The commission's unanimous report was devastating:

The commissioners, having recognized that this ani-mal magnetic fluid cannot be perceived by any sense, and that it has had no effect on them or on the patients shown to them; having assured themselves that the pressing and touching rarely cause changes helpful to the animal organism, and often cause agitation harm-ful to the imagination; having, finally, demonstrated by decisive experiments, that the imagination without magnetism produces convulsions, and that the magne-tism without imagination produces nothing; they have concluded unanimously, on the question of the exis-tence and utility of animal magnetism, that nothing proves the existence of the animal magnetic fluid; con-sequently that this nonexistent fluid is without utility; that the violent effects that one observes in group treat-ment come from touching, from imagination provoked into action, and from mechanical imitation that makes us in spite of ourselves repeat that which strikes our senses. At the same time, we feel ourselves obliged to add, as an important observation, that the touch-ings, the repeated action of the imagination causing crises, can be harmful; that the spectacle of these crises is equally dangerous because of imitation, which na-ture seems to us to have made a law; and consequently that all group treatment where the methods of magne-tism are employed must have, in the long run, harm-ful effects.

The academicians and doctors of the Faculté de Medicine chimed in with a secret report containing matters too sensitive to be made public—the erotic effects of Mesmerism, especially that of male practitioners on female patients.

The man who magnetizes ordinarily sits with the knees of the woman between his. The knees and the lower parts of their bodies are thus in contact. His hand strokes the abdomen and sometimes lower down in the region of the ovaries. The touch is then extended over numerous areas and in the vicinity of the most sensitive parts of the body. Often while the man applies his left hand in this way, he passes his right hand around the woman's body. The tendency is for the pair to lean toward one another to make this double touching process easier. Their proximity becomes the closest possible, their faces nearly touch, their breaths mingle, they share all their physical reactions, and the mutual attraction of the sexes acts with full force. It would not be surprising if their feelings became inflamed.

Franklin himself had this to say:

As to animal magnetism, I must doubt its existence till I can see or feel some effect of it. None of the cures said to be performed by it have fallen under my observation, and there being so many disorders which cure themselves, and such a disposition in mankind to deceive themselves and one another on these occasions, and living long has given me so frequent opportunity of seeing certain remedies cried up as curing everything, and yet soon after laid aside as useless, I cannot but fear that the expectation of great advantage from this new method of treating disease will prove a delusion. That delusion however may, and in some cases, be of use while it lasts.

Thomas Jefferson, replacing Franklin as minister to France, though hearing of the investigations secondhand, wrote this to one of his correspondents:

The doctrine of animal magnetism after which you enquire is pretty well laid to rest. Reasonable men, if they ever paid any attention to such a hocus pocus theory, were thoroughly satisfied by the Report of the commissioners. But as the unreasonable is the largest part of mankind, and as these were the most likely to be affected by this madness, ridicule has been let loose for their cure. Mesmer and Deslon have been introduced on the stage, and the contest is now who can best prove that they never were of their school.

There were, of course, always true-believers:

If I owe the health I enjoy to an illusion, I humbly ask the savants, who see so clearly, not to destroy the illusion. While they enlighten the universe, let them leave me to my error and permit me, in my simplicity, frailty and ignorance, to make use of an invisible agent that does not exist and yet heals me.

But the Faculté de Medicine, as might be expected, outlawed animal magnetism as a medical practice and, though there were holdouts, effectively put the final nail in its coffin. Officially prohibited by the structures of power—though broadly practiced by amateur healers and swindlers—Mesmer's lucrative practice among the nobility declined, and he left France to retire quietly in Switzerland. His last word was to Franklin:

I am like you, Monsieur, among those men whom one cannot insult with impunity, among those who, because they have achieved great things, retain their integrity under humiliation as strong men retain theirs under authority. Whatever the test, Monsieur, like you, I have the world for a judge, and while they may forget the good I have done and prevent the good I wish to do, I will be vindicated by posterity.

I quote at length here not only because good Doctor G. was in the thick of this debate but because the Mesmerist movement, the Mesmerist moment, provides essential illumination for our story.

If King Louis XVI were unhappy with the Mesmer craze, if he were suspicious of Marie-Antoinette's
involvement, about her breath mingling with that of
Mesmer while his hand caressed her abdomen (and
certainly there were plenty of salacious songs and stories going around), he could simply have banned the
practice and had all practitioners arrested. But this was
the end of the eighteenth century, an enlightened time,
a time of science, a world that now contained the *Encyclopedie* and the *philosophes* who produced it. No arbitrary judgments for Louis, himself, like many in his
Court, an amateur scientist. Louis's setting up a study
commission was not, as it is today, a device for stalling
and obstruction; it was a genuine strategy for finding
the truth. Even in this one small action, largely forgotten, Louis displayed how the concept of kingship had
evolved. And Guillotin was for it.

A new battlefield of thought was beginning to
penetrate society: objective testing confronting subjective understanding and its unpredictable mirror of
body versus spirit. To wit: "If I believe I am cured, and
you were curing me, then I am cured, and you were the
agent." Versus "If a substance is dense enough to affect
material bodies, then material instruments should be
able to detect it." Faith versus science, to be sure, but
also a concentration on the material world that would
sully the controllers and their clergy.

"Poor? Concentrate on your spiritual rewards."

"*Va te faire foutre!* First let me eat, and then do your preaching."

The latter sentiment, once privately entertained, was now more publicly proclaimed, and its soundness was reverberating throughout the sanctuaries of Versailles.

Materialism is a two-edged sword, with an edge of people and an edge of establishment, like the diehard Paris Faculté de Medicine seeking to stem the tide of irregular, credulous medical pluralism and self-care. And doubly dangerous it was to a man like good Doctor Guillotin, who practiced medicine the way he once saved baby birds, an upper-class bourgeois who took his poor clients seriously, who tried to speak in their terms, to accept them as they were, with all their ancient beliefs, and at the same time to give them the gift of his care and modern science.

Fighting "old wives' tales" was supremely taxing to him, for on the one hand he loved to hear and ponder them, and on the other he knew what he knew, what he had seen during his training and tried throughout his practice. A turbulence of dimensions pushed him into politics so as to struggle for his baby birds, his poor, on yet another level. Dr. Joseph-Ignace Guillotin, statesman-physician, would soon make a dramatic debut.

Mass starvation is not good for public health. On July 13, 1788, hail rained down on much of central France, destroying the burgeoning crops. Perhaps a whimsical Mother Nature judged that that event had already filled France's water ration, so the rest of the summer would be baked in drought. One farmer wrote, "A countryside, erstwhile ravishing, has been reduced to an arid desert."

The following winter was more harsh than any for the previous eighty years. Frozen rivers refused to turn water mills, and thus what grain there was could not be ground to flour. And even if it could have been ground, it could not have been shipped into the cities. Mirabeau thought the country had had a visit from the Exterminating Angel.

"I have had the honor to fight tyranny all my life," he thundered to a group of friends sharing a bottle of his fine Bordeaux around a blazing fire. "And I assure you I will continue to do so!" The men, Guillotin among them, raised their glasses to his strength and ferocity. "But, gentlemen, the cold out there, cold as a nun, cold as a corpse, cold as the wait for the worm—this tyranny of cold is far worse than any emanating from Versailles!"

The good doctor loved such bluster. Unlike himself, his quiet, rational self, the barrel-chested, pock-marked count could call on the gods—above all Aeolus and Dionysus—to launch his diatribes and send them out into the world. What power, Guillotin thought, what potential to persuade.

But the thermometer was not easily persuaded. Bread prices doubled, and even then there was little to be had. Catastrophe piled on catastrophe: As the months progressed and the huge snowpack melted, spring brought devastating flooding. Migrant workers found no jobs; farmers were evicted and joined the class of the landless and workless.

King Louis, father of his people, along with his director of finance, Jacques Necker, their champion, attempted to assess the situation by calling for crisis reports from the towns, *cahiers de doléances*, describing the local distress.

Such a plethora of problems brought forth many possible approaches to solutions. Above all others, food was the key to freedom, and freedom the key to food. The cry of the people—*pactes de famine!*—parasites of the ruling class, they thought, had engineered the crises for profit, signaled the speculators to withhold supplies. Speculators. Hoarders. Possibly even ministers of the king. The people needed scapegoats. You would, too. Inadequate patriotism of the rich. Punitive overzealousness.

The king called upon the people to assemble locally and elect deputies to list their grievances and their hopes. The Court would relieve as it could the cry of the people. From February to April of 1789 a social-political event took place such as had never before been tried. Twenty-five thousand books of grievances were submitted to Versailles in an unprecedented act of mass representation for six million souls. Necker had pledged freedom from censorship, and free the elections and reportage were.

With many variations, the central themes were firm:

- The Estates-General—the assembled body of the nation, last gathered in 1614—should be recalled, and should sit whenever circumstances demanded it. Some demanded that it sit to establish a constitution.
- All taxation would have to be approved by the people's representatives, and no one would be exempt on account of rank or claims of privilege
- Liberty of person, thought, speech, and publication was to be guaranteed for the ongoing health of the nation.
- *Lettres de cachet*, authorizing imprisonment without trial, should be abolished.

- The national budget should be made public, as Necker had promised.
- If nobility were to remain, it should be an honorific matter only. (This from a surprisingly large number of *cahiers* of the nobility itself.)
- There should be, for all classes, equality before the law.

This was the collective vision of the *cahiers*: Rank would melt into citizenship; science would do away with ignorance, poverty, and sickness. Self-interest, enlightened by Rousseau's general good, would prevail. Patriotism and public service would flourish, led by a king of unsurpassed popularity. Out of current misery would be born a new epoch, for France and for humankind.

Tempted by the acclaim of his people, wary of its meaning, but standing before this vast mountain of documents, King L'Oui had no choice: On 8/8/88, the king announced that the Estates General would meet in Versailles on May 5 of the following year. Let all elect their delegates!

Now, here's a question: If there are three estates— the clergy, the nobility, and the common people, the Tiers-État—and if they are to have equal power, how many representatives should each group have? Equal representation, equal numbers, you might say. Ah, but if representatives from the two privileged, non-tax-paying classes voted together, they would outvote the delegates of the vastly greater mass of peasants and bourgeoisie. Would that be fair? More importantly, would that be tolerated?

Not if the bourgeoisie had anything to say about it.

In the fall of 1788 Guillotin authored his "Petition on Behalf of the Citizens Domiciled in Paris", which argued persuasively for doubling the allowable representation of the Third Estate to a number equal at least to that of the other two estates combined.

Good Doctor Guillotin. He who had already won the hearts of the poor nationwide with his essays "A Protest Against the Tax on Vinegar" and "A Plan for *Dessèchement* of the Swamps of Poitou and Saintonge." He would speak for suffering humanity. He would write for them. Good Doctor Guillotin, reasonable, benevolent, public-spirited gentleman, who cared indefatigably for young and old, rich and poor, at all hours, no matter where in Paris.

His "Petition" was immediately adopted by all six merchant guilds of the city, who printed and circulated six thousand copies. The current Parlement of Paris, upset by its radical potential, attempted to suppress it, and finally even the good doctor himself. On

December 8 he was called for arraignment at the Palais de Justice.

The crowds came flocking, those very crowds that flooded the Place de Grève for executions—in support of Guillotin, conspicuous member of a reform movement that sought to banish the death penalty, though he would take away their brutal entertainment. The press was there *en masse*, and the pamphleteers, and the metropolitan police whom he would enfranchise. The noise outside and inside the courtroom was so intimidating that his triumphant acquittal was both a foregone conclusion, and a spur to the cause of the "Petition".

Against the advice of the Assembly of Notables, on December 27 the government announced the doubled representation of the Third Estate. It did not, however, order that all deliberation be done in common and that decisions be made one man, one vote—thus taking back with the left hand what was offered by the right, a decision it would regret the following June.

Needless to say, Joseph-Ignace Guillotin was elected one of the ten deputies from Paris, and the doctor-statesman took his seat on May 2 in the fateful year of 1789.

Leave it to Guillotin, singular Guillotin, the good doctor. Was the meeting room—a large hall at Versailles's Hôtel des Menus Plaisirs—too stuffy? He would rearrange things for maximum ventilation. Could delegates not speak from the central table without turning their backs on half their colleagues? Overnight, Guillotin, sensible Guillotin, Assembly secretary, has rearranged the platforms, the lectern, the stands and chairs in a semicircle. Has King L'Oui said *"non"* instead of *"oui"*?

June 20, 1789. On that rainy Saturday morning, the king, wanting to take stock, announced he would call a Séance Royale on the following Monday and that there would be no meeting of the Estates General until afterward. By the time they heard the heralds, Président Bailly, with the National Assembly behind him, was en route to the usual meeting place. He found it locked, surrounded by National Guard.

"Why are we locked out?" Bailly demanded.

The captain showed the royal order.

"Workmen are busy setting up the platforms for His Majesty's *séance*, so unfortunately, I'm very sorry, I can't let you in. If necessary, M. le Président and his secretaries may enter to gather up any papers, since I can't guarantee they won't be moved or soiled or even lost."

Three men passed through the gate while the rest waited tensely in the rain. Inside, no patriotic eloquence, just sawing and hammering—*royal* sawing and hammering—and outside, six hundred angry deputies.

Indignant grumbling on the Avenue de Paris, becoming loud complaining. Courtiers looked out their windows, pointed, laughed and giggled. Some called out to the patriot rabble. Travelers paused, traffic backed up, and tempers flared in the raw, wet morning. What to do, what to do?

Guillotin knew of a tennis court—an indoor tennis court, right in old-town Versailles—a tennis court owned by a patient, a friend, a tennis court on the Rue St. François. And to there, in long, wet lines, in high dudgeon, the National Assembly angrily, soppingly trudged.

There is a famous David drawing of that day's extraordinary event. Four naked walls with a roofed spectators' gallery above. No sawing here, no pock of tennis balls, but an echoing racket of wrath-filled men, piqued, vexed, fed up with the people's business being bracketed off by royal whim.

A crowd of witnesses looks down from the gallery, from adjoining roofs and chimneys, shouting encouragement, adding to the now exhilarated din. The papers are unwrapped, and with his trusty hammer, Président Bailly opens the exiled Assembly.

The famous "Tennis Court Oath" of June 20. Guillotin was overjoyed with his good work.

Three days earlier—the most salient reason for the Séance Royale—the Third Estate, convening, as ordered, in the absence of the others, had voted itself "96 per cent of the nation," its "known and verifiable representatives," in Mirabeau's phrase "the Representatives of the People." On that night of the 17th, the meeting had decided by 490–90 to call itself, and itself alone, "the National Assembly," to invite the other estates to join it but to proceed without them if necessary. And, again following Mirabeau, this newly gathered Assembly voted that all present taxes be declared illegal unless approved by that body—one of the great moments of self-authorization in history, a dream of the future and its felicity.

It was expected that the king, egged on by the queen, would use his *séance* to annul the Third Estate's actions of the 17th. Saturday's lockout was likely the first step in the dissolution of the Assembly. But here the members were now, no longer guests in the royal realm but an independent power in an independent place. And here they swore an oath "to God and *la Patrie* never to be separated until we have formed a solid and equitable Constitution as our constituents have demanded." Wherever this group might gather would be the National Assembly.

The *séance*, when it came, was ominous. The refurbished *salle* was surrounded by soldiers. The Third Estate was made to enter through a side door after the other two orders were seated. Necker, the Third Estate's champion, was not there. After diluting or contravening all the reforms of the 17th, Louis announced that if the Assembly "abandons him" in his efforts at reform, he would be forced "to proceed alone for the good of my people, and I will consider myself alone to be their true representative. For now I command you, Messieurs, to adjourn directly and tomorrow assemble in your separate chambers to resume your sessions." The king and Court left in eerie silence.

Furious, the group continued to meet—as the National Assembly!—its numbers now augmented by 150 clergy and 47 nobles who had decided to betray their class and join in. They sat amidst the clatter of carpenters taking down the royal set and affirmed all the Assembly's earlier decisions. When asked to leave by the king's master of ceremony, Mirabeau boomed, "Go tell those who have sent you that we will not be dispersed except at the point of bayonets."

King L'Oui's reaction? "Oh, well, let them stay."

That was His Majesty all over.

L ate in the evening of the 28th of June, the good Doctor Guillotin was visited at his home by a guard from the Bastille. Breathless, bowing and apologizing elaborately, the guard reported that a prisoner— a noble prisoner—locked up by his family via *lettre de cachet* from the king—a noble prisoner, was deathly ill and was pleading to see him, asserting that only Dr. Guillotin might be able to save him.

The two men galloped the two miles, down the Rue de Rivoli, then the Rue St.-Antoine, the guard on his horse, the doctor in his fiacre, waiting for the drawbridge, then proceeding to the office of the governor of the Bastille, Bernard-René Delaunay, an upright, fierce-looking man of fifty who, half a month later, would not look so upright, his body torn to shreds and his head sawn off and paraded on a pike through the July streets.

"It's Sade again," the governor said. "An entertaining fellow, but he never stops complaining. His family is paying our highest rent, so we can't afford to lose him."

"I don't know him," the doctor responded.

"But he seems to know you. Or at least *of* you. Writer, self-styled philosopher," the governor snorted. "He's working on a novel, like all of them. He's extremely difficult. I cannot stand him, and he loves to provoke me."

"What's his complaint?"

"I don't know. Stomach something. Can't talk. Doubled up in pain. He wants you."

"We may need emergency surgery. I can't do it, but let's go see him. If need be we can have him transferred to someone who can."

Delaunay led Guillotin out of the office house and into the tower called "Liberty," one of two detention centers for upper-class and noble prisoners who could pay their way plus some. There was only one cell per floor, and Sade's was three stories up, higher than the prison walls, high enough to command a glimpse of Paris, the city of light. That, too, was billed and paid for.

The men entered an octagonal room, fifteen feet in diameter, with four large and four small sides, a twenty-foot ceiling, whitewashed walls, and a rug-laden brick floor. There was one window, curtained in velour. The cell was decorated with tapestries, portraits, and landscapes from the family collection and a sizable assembly of pictures more suitable to the surroundings: representations of the Savior's sufferings. There were shelves filled with books, a comfortable armchair for reading, and a writing table with a good lamp. Against the wall nearest the door was a bed, and in it, curled up under blankets in spite of the heat, lay a groaning figure, barely visible.

Delaunay lit the table lamp and carried his own over to the bed so the doctor could examine the patient.

"I . . . I . . . need to . . . speak to the doctor. In private . . ."

"Oh, so that's it," said Delaunay, giving Guillotin a wink. Just what he had concluded from Sade's comment was unclear, but it must have supposed the problem to be between the legs. The governor left his lamp and proceeded down the tower stairs, accompanied by a guard.

The doctor reached out to take the patient's

pulse. The patient grabbed the doctor's arm and, using it for leverage, sprang up, fully dressed, and sat up on the edge of the bed.

"Good evening, Doctor. Thank you for coming. What time is it?"

Guillotin, astounded, consulted his watch.

"Twelve fifteen." He wound the little golden machine.

"There! Exactly! Just why I called you. Do you know what time I asked to have you come? At 3 in the afternoon. Nine hours ago. What if I had been dying? What if it were a surgical emergency? What if I had just broken out into the most acute and contagious phase of the black plague or the king's pox, a threat to all the other prisoners—all seven of them?"

"There are only eight prisoners in this tower?" the doctor asked.

"Not in this tower! In the whole stupendous Bastille! Ask M. le Governeur if you don't believe me."

"But what about you? Are you sick?"

"Of course not. Do I look sick?"

"So . . ."

"So why did I call you? Because you are a doctor, a famous doctor with influence, a member of the Faculté de Medicine, a delegate to the self-styled National Assembly. . . ."

"How do you know all this?"

"My wife visits me every day with all the news."

"It's like some kind of grand hotel here, not like a . . ."

"Yes, this room is, well, endurable; I've made it so. And I have my run of the halls, the stairs. and the roof. But look, dear Doctor, there's a public health problem here, a question of life and death for some, and you are the one to solve it."

These were not words the good doctor could resist. He sat down in the armchair to listen.

"We have these two high-class towers, one cell to a floor. We nobles get to do what we want with them. But there are six other towers, presently, I grant you, not very heavily populated, but wait until Necker's moves are rejected by the queen and Artois, and the economy becomes even more catastrophic, and the famine increases. They'll be stuffing this place with rioters. So what I'm telling you will be important.

"Let's just start with today. Call at 3, arrival at midnight. It is almost impossible to look for any immediate help for transitory complaints or sudden attacks, especially at night. The guards sleep in a building entirely separate and at a considerable distance. No voice can possibly reach them. The only resource left to me is to pound on my cell door. But will someone with apoplexy or a hemorrhage have the ability to do that? It is extremely doubtful whether the guards would even hear the pounding, or whether once having re-tired, they would think it proper to hear it.

"Nevertheless, those whom the disorder may not have deprived of the use of their legs and voice have still one method left of applying for assistance. The moat that surrounds us is only 150 feet wide: On the opposite bank is a gallery on which sentinels are posted. Our windows overlook the ditch, so through them a sufferer might cry out for help. And if the interior grate does not extend too far into the chamber, if one's voice is powerful, if the wind is moderate, if the senti-nel is not asleep, it is not impossible that one might be heard.

"The soldier must then alert the next sentry, and the alarm must circulate from one sentry to another, till it arrives at the guardroom. The corporal then goes forth to see what the matter is, and when informed from what window the cries issue, he returns again the same way—all of which takes up no inconsiderable time—and passes through the gate into the interior of the prison. He then calls up one of the guards, and the guard calls up the lackey of the king's lieutenant, who must also awaken his master, in order to get the key, for all, without exception, are deposited every night at that officer's lodging. Do you get the plot of this comedy?

"The key is searched for: it is found. The surgeon must then be called up. The chaplain must also be roused to complete the escort. All these people must necessarily dress themselves; so that in about two hours the whole party arrives with much bustle at the sick man's chamber.

"They find him, perhaps weltering in his blood and in a state of insensibility, or suffocated by apoplexy. What steps they take, I know not—I am not a physician. If the prisoner still possesses some degree of respiration, or if he recovers it, they feel his pulse, ask him to have patience, tell him they will write next day to the physician, and then wish him a good night.

"Now, this physician, without whose authority the surgeon-apothecary dare not so much as administer a pill, resides at the Tuileries, several miles distant. He has other practice: He has a duty to be near the king's person; another to be near the prince's. His duty often carries him to Versailles, and his return must be awaited. He comes—finally. But he has a fixed annual stipend whether he does more or less, and, however honest, he must naturally be inclined to find the disorder as slight as may be so his visits be the less required. And the authorities are the more induced to believe the doctor's representations inasmuch as they are apt to suspect exaggeration in the prisoner's complaints: the negligence of his dress, the habitual weakness of his body, and the abjection, no less habitual, of his mind prevent them from observing any alteration in his countenance or in his pulse; both are always those of a sick man. Thus, the prisoner is oppressed with a triple affliction: first of his disorder; second of seeing himself suspected of imposture, and of being an object of the raillery and severity of the officers, for the monsters do not abstain from this even now; and third of being deprived of every kind of relief till the disorder becomes so violent as to put his life in danger.

"And even then, if they give any medicines, it is but an additional torment to him. The policy of the prison must be strictly observed: Every prisoner shut up by himself, by day and night, whether sick or in health, sees his turnkeys only three times a day. When a medicine is brought him, they set it on the table and leave it there. It is his business to warm it, to prepare it, to take care of himself during its operation.

"And when the prisoner is reduced to the last extremity, if he is able to raise himself from his worm-eaten couch, he is allowed a guard—some invalid soldier, stupid, clownish, brutal, incapable of attention or of that tenderness so requisite in the case of a sick person. But what is still worse, this soldier, when once attached to his patient, is never again permitted to leave but becomes himself a prisoner.

"Thus, you, the patient, must first purchase your guard's consent to shut himself up with you during your captivity, your possibly contagious disease, and if you recover, you must put up with the ill humor, discontent, reproaches, and vexation of this wonderful companion, who will be avenged on you in health for the pretended services he has rendered you in sickness."

The marquis strolled over to his window, looked for a moment at the glowering lights of the great city, and turned to his visitor.

"Dr. Guillotin, do you approve of this system? Do you think the populace of Paris would approve? Do you think the delegates to the National Assembly would approve? Do you think even the king would approve, if he knew about it?"

Guillotin was fascinated, not just by the public health problems involved but by the eloquence and animation of the extraordinary complainer. Though it was late, and he was tired, and though he was here on fraudulent pretenses, he was pleased that he had come.

"May I ask you something?" he said. "I'll tell you why in a minute."

"I am a prisoner. I have nothing I'm allowed to hide."

"What is your opinion concerning capital punishment?"

Sade returned to his bed, propped the pillows, lay back, crossed his legs, and put his hands behind his head.

"I have no objection on principle to capital punishment," he said. "Nature, my only mistress and my only instructress, certainly does not suggest that a man's life is of any value; on the contrary, she teaches in every way that it is of none. The sole end and object of living beings seems to be to serve as food for other beings destined to the same end. Murder is a natural right; therefore, the penalty of death is lawful on condition it is exercised from no motives either of virtue or of justice, but by necessity or to gain some profit thereby. To kill a man in a paroxysm of passion is understandable. In nature, desire and destruction are legitimate. But to have someone killed by someone else after calm and serious meditation and on the pretext of duty honorably discharged is incomprehensible.

"My hatred for the death penalty is a hatred for men who are sufficiently convinced of their own virtue to dare to inflict capital punishment when they themselves are criminals. You cannot simultaneously choose crime for yourself and punishment for others."

"You are familiar," the doctor inquired, "with Rousseau's writings on the death penalty?"

"M. Rousseau was not without talents, particularly in music, but he was a scampish fellow who professed to receive his morality, as he should, from Nature while actually deriving it from the dogmas of Calvin. Nature teaches us to devour each other, true? And gives us the example of all the crimes and vices which society corrects or conceals. We should love virtue, of course, but it is well to know that this is simply and solely a convenient expedient invented by men in order to live comfortably together.

"What we call morality is merely a desperate enterprise, a forlorn hope, on the part of our fellow creatures to reverse the order of the universe, which is strife and murder, the blind interplay of hostile forces. Nature delights in abusing herself unto destruction, and the more I think of things, the more convinced I am that the universe is mad.

"Theologians and philosophers who make God the author of Nature and the architect of the universe, show Him to us as illogical and ill-conditioned. They declare Him benevolent because they are afraid of Him, but they are forced to admit that His acts are atrocious. They attribute to Him a malignity seldom to be found even in mankind. And that is how they get human beings to adore Him.

"Our miserable race would never lavish worship on just and benevolent deities from which they have nothing to fear; they would feel only a barren gratitude for their benefits. Without purgatory and hell, your good God would be a laughable creature. So yes, the death penalty by all means, and let us dance the *carmagnole* around the gibbet, or better yet the lamppost, but only as a criminal act, a human attempt, not the state's attempt, to grab at human justice, Nature's plan.

"The state's justice is wholly dependent upon human conditions, upon the character, temperament, and psychological climate of a country, a silly attempt to oppose nature. Unjust things are *indispensable* to the operation of the universe. All the silly laws we have made, either to encourage the growth of the population or to punish destruction, necessarily oppose all her laws.

"But for servants of Nature—All refusal to participate in propagation through issueless eroticism, every time we cooperate in these murders that delight and serve her, like torture, we are sure of pleasing her, and act in harmony with her views. Nature desires the total annihilation of the creatures she produces, so she may enjoy her faculty of producing new ones. She destroys in order to create."

He sat back down on his bed. The good doctor was both amused and intrigued. He was glad he had come.

"For us?" Sade continued. "There are several ways of participating in this universal destruction. Capital punishment is good. Crime is excellent. The most abominable murderer is merely the instrument of Nature's laws. Everything that is violent in nature is always interesting and sublime. That is why the child, who is closer to the state of nature, spontaneously manifests a ferocity that society has yet to overcome. We see him cruelly strangle his bird and take pleasure in the poor animal's convulsions."

Guillotin flashed back to his youthful attempts to quash such behavior.

"Destructive violence," Sade went on, "is the chief characteristic of Nature and ensures her continuity.

Death is pure imagination. It exists only figuratively, with no reality. Matter, once deprived of the sublime portion of itself that gave it movement, is not thereby destroyed; it merely changes its form; it is corrupted. Movement is not eliminated in the cadaver. The transformation of the human into other forms of life goes on. Death provides nourishment for the earth, fertilizes it, and serves the regeneration of other kingdoms.

"So bravo, murderers, and let the gallows dance and swing."

This was not the response the doctor had expected from a man who had spent the greater part of his adult life being tormented by the state.

"Why do you ask?"

"I was going to ask you to write something against it—capital punishment."

"You are silly."

Their laughter bounced off eight feet of stone.

"For the Masons. My lodge."

More laughter, but only from the marquis.

"The Masons! The cult of Reason doesn't need secret rites. The only society I am interested in is the Society of the Friends of Crime. And the scaffold for me would be the throne of voluptuousness. Unfortunately, I sicken to see blood flow. But then again, if it were mine, I'd likely not see it."

On the way out Guillotin returned Delaunay's lamp to the office. The governor was still at his desk.

"So? Is he still alive? Late-night run to the Hôtel Dieu?"

"He'll be all right. Just acute intestinal cramps. Should pass by tomorrow."

"I thought it was nothing. They always feign illness to get attention. Make things sound worse than they are. Sorry to have gotten you out of bed."

"I wasn't in bed. Just reading."

In fact, Delegate Guillotin spent quite a bit of time in his study, reading, keeping up with speeches made in the various towns, petitions submitted to the Assembly, memos sent among his Girondin colleagues, the men who gathered together at Mme. Roland's salon to talk, dream, and strategize.

Night after night—all those papers dancing in front of him by candlelight.

He believed men's words to be a poor exponent of their thought. And the Mason in him judged their thought itself to be a poor exponent of the inward, unnamed mystery whence both thought and action have their birth. "No man," Carlyle wrote, "can explain himself, can get himself explained; men see not one another, but distorted phantasms which they call one another; which they hate and go to battle with: for all battle is well said to be misunderstanding."

Though he didn't know it at the time, the good

doctor would exemplify such distortions better, perhaps, than any other.

W hile he sat musing thus in the evening following his visit with the Marquis de Sade, his
servant brought to Guillotin a letter, sealed with a
thumbprint.

My dear doctor,

Your question about capital punishment——in answer to
which I ranted on——diverted me from our public health discussion
which I believe to be——through you——amenable to improvement.
Allow me to detail for you what I have learned in my peripatetics
through the prison, and in my talks with inmate colleagues. The
information might come in handy for a most striking speech at the
Assembly.

Yes, my cell is luxurious——for a cell. But aside from the
towers Liberty and Bertaudière, all the other cells are contained in
towers of which the walls are at least twelve, and at the bottom
thirty or forty, feet thick. Each has a vent-hole made in the wall,
kindness itself, yes, but crossed by three grates of iron, one within,
extending into the chamber, another in the middle, and a third on
the outside. The bars cross each other, and are an inch in thickness;
and by a cruel refinement of the invention, the solid part of each of
these meshes answers exactly to the vacuity in another; so that vision
out is quite compromised.

Formerly, each of these homey caves had three or four open-

ings, small indeed, and ornamented with the same gratings. But this multiplicity of holes was soon found to promote the circulation of the air; they prevented humidity, infection, etc. A humane governor therefore had them stopped up; and at present there remains but one, which on very fine days admits just light enough into the cell to make the darkness visible.

In winter these quarters are perfect icehouses, because they are lofty enough for the frost to penetrate; in summer they are moist, suffocating stoves, as you yourself experienced the other night, the walls being far too thick for the heat to dry them. Several of the cells, and mine was of the number, are situated upon the ditch into which the common sewer of the Rue St.-Antoine empties itself; so that whenever it is cleared out or in summer after a few days' continuance of the hot weather, or after an inundation, which is frequent enough both in spring and autumn in ditches sunk below the level of the river, there exhales a most infectious, pestilential vapor; and when it has once entered those pigeonholes they call rooms, it is a considerable time before they are cleared of it. Last night, again, was a good example.

Such an atmosphere a prisoner breathes daily, throughout the summer; in order to prevent total suffocation, he is obliged to pass his days, and often his nights, with his face up against the interior grate, which keeps him from approaching too close to the breath hole of a window, the only orifice through which he can draw his scanty portion of air and light. His efforts to suck a little fresh air through this narrow tube serve often but to increase around him the fetid odor with which he is on the point of being suffocated. Fetid I love, but . . .

My very best wishes for success in improving this inhuman dungeon and threat to public health. But now that I have written you this summary, I have so fired up my choleric phlogiston that I may very well try to do something about it myself. Stone walls do not a prison make—for Lovelace or myself.

You may be hearing more from

Your most obedient servant,

Donatien-Alphonse-François Sade, Marquis et Comte

III. Allons, Enfants de la Patrie

HISTORY, WORDS, AND VIOLENCE

Man at War with Time

The whole race is a poet that writes down
The eccentric propositions of its fate.
—WALLACE STEVENS, "Men Made out of Words"

The End advances upon us. We are hunted and cornered and ever more desperate. We seek out what threatens us; we embrace our maledictions, inviting catastrophe; not for anything, it seems, would we give up the nightmare. We advance *en masse* toward unprecedented chaos, thrashing out against one another like convulsing epileptics, like inebriated robots, because— everything has become impossible and unlivable. It seems the sole passion we are still capable of is a passion for the end.

History is now so jittery, so unbalanced, so delirious, that it is hard to see how it can keep from exploding. We are exhausted and likely to succumb, a just punishment perhaps for so much arrogance and stupidity. Having violated every natural law and crashed through all of wisdom's checkpoints, the realization of human history, like catastrophic climate change, is now inexorable. Inevitable. It is now our program.

Oh, we still dream of Paradise. But something whispers that the future will contain none of it. Our history has been a gradual negation, a progressive distancing from Edenic utopias, even those of the mind. Our history is the history of our excesses, our repeated inclination to go demonically astray. As we thirst for Destiny our history unmakes us. And even as it moves to checkmate, we love it because it is ours, *our* history, and because we feel incapable of imagining any other. We have not understood the deadly direction of our progress and prosperity, of this, our errand in the wilderness.

Great men, Heidegger said, are capable of great errors. He ought to know. The eighteenth century was filled with great men, with great new ideas, doing great new things. Consider the Freemasons, perhaps the most prominent social force of the era. The French Revolution was to a large degree a wild Masonic experiment. By 1780 there were over two hundred lodges in Paris alone, with sixteen thousand members—noblemen, priests, politicians, administrators, businessmen, apothecaries, surgeons, goldsmiths, merchants, and master artisans, a coalition of *grands seigneurs*, intellectuals, and bourgeoisie—a new force that one day could be a formidable challenge to the government. Guillotin was a Mason, as were Franklin and the Duc d'Orléans.

Since 1700 such men had been preparing the revolutions which from 1775 to 1815 broke out all over the world, planning and preaching a great change of mind concerning the largest subjects. Masonry gave birth to the essential metaphor all revolutionaries use to understand their mission: that of an architect building a new and better structure for human society, re-creating in its lodges the natural cooperation of the artisans who shaped stones for a common building. Beyond the Masons' architectural goals was an overriding alchemical one: to unite the inferior with the superior so that, through the fire of knowledge, in the vessel of Masonry, the human self might be transformed, irradiated by the all-seeing eye atop a pyramid over the words *Novus Ordo Saeculorum*. Anacharsis Cloots, the self-styled "orator of the human race," idealized Pythagoras as the model intellectual-turned-revolutionary, and praised the Pythagorean belief in prime numbers, geometric forms, and the higher harmonies of music.

Talk about heads in the clouds: Not human discussion but the music of the spheres was the highest form of discourse, expressing the harmony of creation, the world as it should be. The most spiritual of the arts, music would be the highest language of liberation, of the realm of freedom, releasing emotion yet creating order in the dimension of time, freeing humankind from spatial and material limitations and loosing a new sense of boundless expectation. Through music, infinite striving could infiltrate classical forms of space and time, and the language of hope shape that of the future. Mozart was a Mason.

Eighteenth-century Freemasonry was the apostle of science and progress and thus the enemy of tradition. Revolution per se was not its aim; far beyond such worldly considerations, eighteenth-century Freemasonry hoped to spur an underlying evolution of humanity to usher in a Golden Age envisioned by Rousseau. But still, it led to the complete intellectual upset of the time and paved the way for social and political revolutions.

From the beginning, French Freemasonry was a melting pot where a new mix of elements was brewing. Like the air-balloon events and the crowds at the Palais Royal, the lodges were places where people, whatever their rank, trade, or religion, might meet on an equal footing, infused by a spirit of unity. It was thrilling to be present at meetings where all men were equal and carried the sword and where all were brothers called "chevaliers." The Masonic spirit went far to explain the success of the Third Estate in shaping the National Assembly.

America, Masonic America, led by George Washington, Benjamin Franklin, and other master Masons, America was a source of inspiration, the most cherished topic for the French intelligentsia, the only contemporary instance of a "rational and natural government." Frenchmen watched over it with anxious enthusiasm, always fearing that Americans would make some idiotic move that would deprive the universe of its only respectable republic.

America. The Philadelphian Fantasy was the name of the game—a vast plan of universal regeneration and subversive internationalism, peopled by citizens of the world, forming an immense circle whose center would be Paris but whose rays would penetrate everywhere. France entire was to become the fraternal city whose circumference embraced the entire human family wherever it might be.

Enter history. Or rather, enter the "fall of man," that great downward trajectory currently hovering at abysmal approval ratings from the gods. Rousseau and Washington wouldn't have thought well of the present, either.

Liberty, Equality, Fraternity

> Life consists
> Of propositions about life.
> —WALLACE STEVENS, "Men Made out of Words"

"Liberty, Equality, Fraternity!" There is something inspiring about the call. And yet something depressing and even tragic reverberates within it. The French Revolution, and revolution in general, was and continues to be necessary because of the ongoing state of the world. The three-word slogan is a distillation of much that could be—and of all that is not.

Any yearning for Marx's "total redemption of humanity" is a tragic one, born in pity and terror of a deep, systemic disorder in which the humanity of some people—and thus of humanity itself—is denied. The thought of redemption springs from the actual suffering of real people, and from all the consequences of this suffering: humiliation, brutalization, fear, hatred, envy, greed. It is born out of evil made the more intolerable by the sense that it is not foreordained but stems from particular actions and choices. Yes, our experience has shown that an instinct for submission, a desire to obey and be ruled, is also prominent in human psychology, and politically, perhaps, more relevant than a will to power.

We have seen that all past revolutions have ended in disappointment. Ernst Bloch notwithstanding, dreams rarely, if ever, come true. Nevertheless, the revolutionary spirit still inspires hope, a hope that includes the utopian belief that we can control our future, the idea that effective thought and action do still exist, and the faith that we might finally understand the true nature of humanity. Tragic is this striving, for tragic is our world, tragic on a scale far beyond commonplace pity and terror.

"In 1789," Tolstoy wrote in *War & Peace*, "a ferment arises in Paris; it grows and spreads. . . . During that twenty year period an immense number of fields were left untilled, houses were burned, trade changed its direction, millions migrated, were impoverished or enriched, and millions of Christian men professing the law of love of their fellows slew one another."

All in the name of liberty, equality, and fraternity.

The only consciousness that seems relevant to our world is one that takes in the actual disorder, participates in it—in an attempt to end it. But it seems also true that a commitment to revolution can end in a kind of hardening that may even negate the revolutionary purpose. Under real-world pressures—isolated, under fire, suffering life-threatening scarcities—this hardening and negation show up again and again in revolutionary activity. Supporters of the status quo then seize on the evidence of hardening and negation, either to oppose revolution as such or to restore the convenient belief that humankind cannot change its condition, and that aspiration brings terror as a logical companion. TINA. There is no (acceptable) alternative, so give it up, they say.

The revolutionaries in France were beyond such thinking. Society had not yet dedicated itself to human liberation or even to the simple recognition of the humanity of all. And *that* the revolutionaries would have—by any means. Given the forces arrayed against them, any means meant revolutionary violence.

Trampling out the Vintage Where the Grapes of Wrath Are Stored

> *Denn das Schöne ist nichts*
> *also des Schrecklichen Anfang*
> *(For beauty is nothing*
> *but the beginning of terror)*
> —RAINER MARIA RILKE, "First Duino Elegy"

Violence is not only cathartic, it is definitional: We fight, therefore we are. As Israel demonstrates daily, there is no propaganda like "the propaganda of the deed"—violence against political enemies to inspire the masses. Complex analysis is easily cut through with the sword. "The practice of violence," Fanon asserts, "binds men together as a whole, since each individual forms a violent link in the great chain, a part of the great organism of violence which [in any revolution or revolt] has surged upward." Do all our various "surges" know what they are doing? They know only this: that they choose to make choices other than those offered by their society's here and now.

All that has gone before is in principle worthless, activity bent on social suicide—and then on surviving it. Can revolution be justified as right, as good, and justified not merely in political terms but in ethical terms? The answer has always come down to the text of the great drinking song in Daumal's *La Grande Beuverie*:

You know, there's times you just don't know;
Nothing's what you think, not anything, not a thing.
But comes the dawn, you start to crow
As how you know 'bout everything.
But you don't know nothing,
Nothing's what you know,
The whole world's simply nuts.

So much for the Enlightenment. Political action can be rational only in relation to an articulated what-ought-to-be, that is, only if there is some end in view; only the end or goal of an action can determine whether an action is to the point.

But for violence? A goal for violence? Organization of violence? Despite the best laid schemes of mighty men, confusion is inevitable and par for the course. As the good Doctor Guillotin would discover, the world is nuts.

A Strange Kind Of Love

Gee, I wish we had one of them doomsday machines.
—GENERAL "BUCK" TURGIDSON, *Dr. Strangelove*

In the 1950s Herman Kahn, thinking the unthinkable, proposed a doomsday machine consisting of a computer linked to a stockpile of widely buried hydrogen bombs and programmed to detonate them at any sign of a nuclear attack against the United States. As Kubrick's Strangelove pointed out, "because of the automated and irrevocable decision-making process which rules out human meddling, the Doomsday machine is terrifying and simple to understand . . . and completely credible and convincing."

Attend the irrevocable decision. The resistance to human meddling. The bureaucratic processes unleashed, eviscerating freedom, empowering Nobody in cascading decisions and effects. The rule of Nobody is not no-rule, and tyranny without a tyrant is no less tyranny, tyranny passionately courting doomsday. In this light, was not the good Doctor Guillotin's machine also a kind of doomsday device, mechanizing and bureaucratizing a hands-off kind of death, a production line for corpses, a cutoff of dialogue and thought?

The device was the result of a strange kind of love, embraced temporarily by a man who loved his patients, who wanted to see them treated equally regardless of their social station, who wanted their deaths, if deaths there had to be, to be instantaneous, painless, and immune to bungling.

If deaths there had to be—therein lies the issue. Guillotin, for all his enlightened medical authority and progressive persistence, could not think through the consequences of his suggested improvement. The Terror was not on his screen.

First came the "kind" decapitation of unfortunates such as Nicolas Pelletier. Then the decapitation—real, if meant to be symbolic—of the king and queen. And hard upon those, the decapitation of counterrevolution and all counterrevolutionaries. Quick, mechanical, without further thought—the electronic battlefield now and in the future. Quick, mechanical, doomsday-directed. The application of Guillotin's humanitarian idea to the mechanical production of death is central to the path we tread today. As we contemplate the two arms rising perpendicular to the earth, the Masonic square and circle of the yoke, the triangular blade accelerating according to Newton's law of gravity, we have to question whether Kahn's doomsday machine is not one more example of enlightened good-doctoring.

14.

SPARKS ON TINDER

July 2, 1789. Something was up. The marquis could smell it. His privilege to walk on the terrace atop the Bastille towers had been canceled. This was not to be borne. He summoned Delaunay and threatened to make a scene if the directive was not rescinded. Delaunay laughed and left. All right. You want a scene? You'll get a scene.

The prisoner- and public-health complaints that de Sade had shared with the good doctor were rational and well taken. But history often turns not on well-founded themes but on the merest of whims of critically placed individuals. Take away my walking privileges, will you? Sade's aborted strolling was an odd but important seed of the Revolution.

Sade picked up a long funnel normally used for emptying his chamber pot into the moat, placed the improvised megaphone in his cell window, and, getting his cacaphilic kicks, began to shout at the top of his lungs to all below who might hear him:

"Parisians! Attention! Emergency! M. Delaunay and his barbaric guards are, at this very moment, cutting the throats of innocent prisoners! Help! Immediately! Storm the prison! The government murderers are cutting our throats!"

Spectators gathered along the Rue St.-Antoine and in the surrounding streets, their heads tilted upward, while the marquis screamed in his big funneled voice; a small crowd assembled.

"Lay siege to the fort! Bring cannon! Set fire to the gates! Call the . . ."

Five turnkeys put an end to his broadcast. The crowd, having little to go on, shrank away as quickly as it had grown. Just some imprisoned maniac, they supposed.

But Delaunay had had enough with this particular guest. The income was not worth the trouble. A decision had already been made to close down the prison, for at this point it was nearly empty of prisoners, housing only seven besides the marquis—four forgers, two "lunatics," and one "deviant" aristocrat. The cost of maintaining an entire medieval fortress and garrison for so limited a purpose was, given the current economic conditions, more than excessive.

So at 1 the next morning, six armed men snatched Donatien-Alphonse-François de Sade from his bed without allowing him time to dress or take anything with him, hurled him into a coach, and drove him, "naked as a worm," to the mental hospital at Charenton, where he was to be locked up indefinitely and restrained as one would a madman. But the head-shaking and tsk-tsking about the Bastille, that symbol of royal tyranny, had begun.

Murmuring. Grumbling. Spreading westward, northward, southward from St.-Antoine toward the Palais Royal and beyond. The sultry weather didn't help: Along the quays the air was heavy from the discharge of the great sewers that oozed into the Seine between the Pont Notre-Dame and the Pont-au-Change. Even in the Tuileries gardens, the terraces were unapproachable because of the stink as the city's defecators lined up beneath a yew hedge to relieve themselves. Everywhere things smelled worse than usual. Horse shit in the streets, dog shit on the shoes, human shit to be avoided. The reek of fish out of water too long, of vegetables, wilting, rotting in the humid heat. It made one testy, and wary of stink in relationships, in society, perhaps in God's creation.

On Sunday, the 12th of July, the sky was especially heavy, and the heat wave burning on, depressing, enervating. The pavements were scorching, the sun an unrelenting volcano. Sweltering humans sought whatever relief they could find.

The Palais Royal, with its iced drinks, spreading trees, and arcades, was especially crowded that day, but the shade and the ice couldn't cool the rumors. There had been extraordinary troop movements the evening before, with the king's Swiss Guard and German battalions massing at the outskirts of the city. Was some royal plot afoot? What was it? Whispers. "I heard the king dismissed Necker last night to appease the queen." Anger. Agitation. Paris besieged by her own troops because someone had asked for bread? A spreading general commotion. By noon groups were forming under the arcades to determine what to do.

Sunday being their day off, Guillotin and Schmidt, respectable men, were seated in the garden at the respectable Café de Foy tables, nursing cold-brewed coffee and discussing the doctor's week in the Assembly, the bills offered, the rhetoric, the tone. People all around, murmuring, rumoring. The phrase *"aux armes"* could be heard here and there. As the many bells of Paris chimed many 3 o'clocks, a breathless young man climbed hesitantly onto a café table, pushed and encouraged by the crowd around him, nervous and obviously unused to public speaking. Guillotin and Schmidt had a ringside seat.

"Citizens . . ." the speaker called, his voice too soft, and cracking.

"Louder!" the crowd yelled back at him.

"Citizens," he cried, his voice gaining on itself, "there is not a moment to lose. I've just come from Versailles. M. Necker is dismissed, recalled."

A hundred people howled their alarm.

"This is a signal for massacre of patriots." He just knew it. He could predict it. "This evening all the Swiss and German troops will leave the Champ de Mars to cut our throats."

His listeners were in an uproar. The crowd grew ever larger. He shouted over them, his courage spurred by their reaction. They yelled out their support, and absorbed his exaltation as he spoke with tears in his eyes, made eloquent by an unfamiliar energy, throwing out ideas in no particular order.

"There's only thing left for us to do—to arm ourselves and adopt some kind of badge, something to identify one another. What colors shall we use?"

"Let's pick a color," yelled someone in the crowd.

"Do you want green," the speaker asked, "the color of hope? Or Cincinnatus's blue, the color of American liberty and democracy?"

Two shouted back, "Green, the color of hope! Green for hope! The hope of France!"—voices from the several thousand now drawn to whatever was going on.

"Yes, green," many yelled. "Green for hope! The hope of France! The hope of the world!"

The speaker looked around the crowd. Perhaps he was acting; perhaps he had seen someone he knew; perhaps he was really afraid. He added with vehemence, "Friends, there are spies here, right among us, police agents staring at me right now. But I won't be taken by them; I won't fall into their hands. At least not alive."

And pulling two pistols out of his waistcoat, "*Aux armes, citoyens!* To arms!" he yelled.

What power in those words! The signal had been given—the signal for Revolution. How else to understand it? It was the voice of the people of Paris, the voice of the entire French nation. It was in the name of all that Camille Desmoulins protested; it was all of France he called to arms. His feverish appearance, his voice trembling with passion, impetuous, boiling, handsome he was in the light of the flame burning inside him, the flame embracing all.

Cheers continued to mount, vociferations from a crowd telling its heart, roaring its enthusiasm and its anger. Now that the unknown young man had spoken so well, had shown them the way, the crowd was ready to follow him wherever he would go.

As Desmoulins jumped down from the table, he was overwhelmed with hugs. People drew him to their hearts, bathed him in their tears, lifted him to their shoulders.

"No," he cried, "the people can have no leaders. The People is one brain, one heart." They put him down.

"Friend," the people yelled, "we will guard you. We will not abandon you. We will follow where you will."

He said again that he wanted to be but one more soldier for France. Someone brought him a green ribbon. He cut from it a piece which he put into his hat. The rest he gave to others, though there was far too little for the thousands of hands that beckoned. Someone in the crowd had a happy inspiration and plucked leaves from the surrounding chestnut trees. The crowd went at it until the lower branches were completely bare. They had their green for hope.

"The chestnuts may not survive such enthusiasm," Schmidt observed. Nevertheless, he accepted a leaf from the hand of a pretty maiden. Guillotin did not.

Despite Desmoulins's protestations, a great crowd adorned with green ribbons or leaves followed at his heels. Where were they going? No one knew. They followed their hero, who didn't himself know where to go. No matter. A parade through the streets of Paris was the first response to the firing of Necker, a peaceful demonstration that gathered other patriots en route and allowed them to express their consternation, indignation, and grief.

"Are you up for a parade?" Schmidt asked his companion.

"For a while," Guillotin responded.

They followed the crowd out of the courtyard and onto the street.

A thousand people wrought-up, more, seeded

with bits of green and shapeless hopes, wound down the Rue de Richelieu and descended the Boulevard du Temple, where Curtius had his wax museum. Someone commandeered a bust of Necker, gladly offered up by Curtius himself. And agents of the Duc d'Orléans, beloved proprietor of the Palais Royal, liberated a bust of their prince to be paraded along with Necker's. The two heads, wrapped in black crepe, as if for mourning, were carried at the head of the crowd. Orléans, Necker, and Desmoulins, the people's heroes—those bodiless heads an unconscious image of things to come.

The cortege followed the Rues St.-Denis, St.-Martin, St.-Honoré as inhabitants of those streets stood in doorways and peered out open windows to see it go by. Many joined its ranks, including members of the National Guard making common cause with the people. The parade had grown to a multitude following Desmoulin's hesitant steps.

"Hats off!" cried voices from the crowd, and marchers and spectators doffed their hats and held them over their hearts. Guillotin and Schmidt went along so as not to offend. From some inchoate directorate, a project arose: "Close the theaters! This is a day of mourning!"

Groups detached themselves from the great stream and scouted the center of town to achieve the goal. The Opéra, in the midst of Grétry's *L'Aspasie*, brought down its afternoon curtain. Other theaters closed their doors, cafés emptied, storefronts were shuttered. A day of mourning was born—even if late in the afternoon. Life stopped, and activity was limited to the funeral cortège expressing the revolt of the people.

At the Place Vendôme some demonstrators threw themselves on a group of German troops who tried to disperse them with unsheathed swords. Shots rang out. Guillotin and Schmidt left the parade, a cortege no longer, and headed for their homes. Neither was comfortable with violent mobs.

The first heads to be smashed were those of Necker and Orléans as their wax busts broke to pieces on the ground. A furious crowd pelted the horsemen with stones, and the horses bucked and retreated toward the Place Louis XV, pursued by the crowd. Strollers on the Champs Élysées ran for cover.

Several squadrons of foreign troops were gathered at the Place Louis XV. The crowd yelled and cursed and threw stones, but the horsemen held their ground. Baron de Bensenval, the officer in charge, had that very morning received a note written by the king himself: "You will reply to force with force." The Prince de Lambesc's men pushed their horses against the crowd, driving it back at the risk of trampling the front ranks. Some of the crowd spilled over the bridge leading to the Tuileries. Lambesc was foolish enough to chase those fleeing into the garden.

On that hot summer Sunday, the lanes were full

of peaceful walkers. Seeing the soldiers, the women and children screamed with fright and ran under the trees, while the men faced down the soldiers, arraying themselves among benches and chairs for protection. Some threw stones and bottles from the terraces. Fearful horsemen struck out left and right with the flats of their swords. People were caught under the feet of the horses. Lambesc thought it prudent to withdraw.

But there were victims, victims. The wounded were taken away, some perhaps dead—a member of the National Guard who was marching in the cortege, an old man who Lambesc thought had a saber in his hand. It was a cane. The Prince de Lambesc, henceforth "Butcher of the Tuileries."

The fleeing crowds spread out over the city, decrying the acts of brutality they had witnessed: A peaceful cortege had been attacked. An unarmed national guardsman had been killed. German horsemen had charged French women and children. An old man savagely cut down . . .

Indignation. Anger. Huddling groups. Heading homeward, Guillotin and Schmidt could everywhere hear the words "To arms!" The jobless, the homeless, the thieves, the wretched, the thousands of vagabonds and beggars from Montmartre all gathered and swarmed as if rising up out of the very earth. Only a minority of the population, still they were most unsettling as they had no scruples and nothing to lose. In two days they would reappear as "conquerors of the Bastille." At the end of that Sunday, July 12, they were among the most excited, most ardent to cry, "To arms!" and to demand them.

Calls for insurrection sounded from one end of Paris to the other. The entire city was boiling, bubbling. People assaulted the gun shops, forced the doors. They armed themselves with everything that fell to hand—rifles, pistols, swords, daggers, knives. There weren't enough weapons for everyone. To be armed, to be able to repulse foreign troops was the first concern. Citizens must be armed! Alarm bells sounded, meetings were called. To the Hôtel de Ville! Noisy, excited groups from all quarters converged on the municipal building.

No officials were at their posts. The crowds invaded the vast building and stayed to demand city arms. Toward 6 P.M. a few electors arrived, full of goodwill, devoted to the popular cause, but inexperienced and powerless, intimidated by the responsibility the people demanded they assume. They spoke with the crowd in vain, trying to appease it. The armory was pillaged as other groups continued to arrive. The crowd grew, swarming outside the building onto the Place de Grève. Cries and curses arose from the surging mass. The electors called for the convocation of sixty districts of Paris.

Tumult and confusion at the Hôtel de Ville and elsewhere, more violence. The National Guard depot was overrun by a detachment of the Royal Allemand.

German soldiers were taking the guns, disregarding their officers, burning with vengeance for lost comrades. There was shooting and death among the horsemen, while others pulled back. Bayonets mounted, the National Guard charged the Place Louis XV. On the Champs Élysées, foreign regiments were advancing, received with rifle fire, and given the order to attack.

But the French National Guard refused to fire on those foreign soldiers who had been their comrades. Both had entered into the service of the king to fight against the enemies of the state, not to take part in a civil war they didn't understand. The Swiss were the first to refuse to march. Their furious officers had to order a retreat.

Disorder continued into the evening and through the night. All the city's gates were burned. Before thinking of the Bastille, it was against the gates, these overpowering symbols of the law, that the people turned their fury. The wretched had other objectives, and sacked the stores and bars in a monstrous drunken party. Guillotin and Schmidt heard shouts and shots throughout the night.

15.

LE QUATORZE JUILLET

Gouverneur Morris, author of the famous sentence, "We the People of the United States, in order to form a more perfect Union . . ." was in Paris that month. He wrote in his journal that the city was being heavily patrolled by a citizen militia (*milice bourgeoise*), and that the morning of the 13th was the first since the troubles had begun that he felt safe walking the streets—though he did take the precaution of ornamenting his hat with a green ribbon. What he didn't know was that one of the sixty town electors was sitting in an office in the Hôtel de Ville doling out gunpowder rations to a threatening crowd drunk with power and alcohol, who might very well blunder into blowing the building sky-high. But then, most of the city's gunpowder was not *there* at City Hall. It was known to be stored in the Bastille. Two hundred fifty barrels—thirty thousand pounds.

The governor of that formidable fortress, Bernard-René Delaunay, having dispatched M. de Sade to the asylum, had spent the next ten days with his ear to the ground. By the 14th, he was most apprehensive. He had not many men at his disposal, and worst of all, in the event of a siege, his fortress had only a two-day food supply and no internal water supply at all.

Outside the gates were nine hundred Parisians, including defecting soldiers and National Guard—they, too, apprehensive, since there were rumors of troops about to march on and crush the Paris insurrection.

The crowd's initial aim was to take possession of the powder, and emissaries were sent into the prison to demand this of Delaunay. Over a lengthy "lunch," the prison governor made it clear that he could do no such thing without permission from Versailles. The people outside began yelling, "Give us the Bastille!" and they broke into the undefended outer courtyard and shot down the outer drawbridge chains. Defending soldiers threatened to fire; a shot was heard (each side claiming it was the other); and the fight was on, too quick and courtyard-concentrated for negotiations.

Cannons lugged by the besiegers faced those of the defenders. A desperate Delaunay considered igniting the whole store of powder, destroying himself, his men, the invaders, and much of the Faubourg St.-Antoine, and he threatened to do so to force an honorable evacuation, handing a note to this effect through a chink in the inner drawbridge wall. Refused, he was prevented from carrying out his threat by his own men, who demanded he surrender. The drawbridge was lowered, and the crowd rushed in. The Bastille was taken.

They searched for, found, and liberated the seven prisoners and dealt harshly with those they considered the defenders. A Sergeant Béquard, the soldier who had dissuaded Delaunay from detonating the powder, had his hand sliced off immediately after opening the gates to the people. The crowd paraded his hand—still gripping the key—around the streets to hoarse cheering. That evening he was again misidentified as one of the defenders who had begun the shooting and was hung by the crowd on the Place de Grève.

The citizens had lost one hundred fighters, the Bastille only one. A sacrifice was demanded to address the imbalance, and the hated Delaunay was chosen. He was marched through the streets and covered with curses and spit. At the Hôtel de Ville, he struck out suicidally against his captors and was stabbed multiple times by the crowd, who finished him off with pistols. A man Delaunay had kicked was offered a sword to decapitate him, but he turned it down, and sawed through Delaunay's neck with his pocketknife. The Bastille governor's head was stuck on a pike, which was carried, bobbing, dipping, and swooping above the laughing, cheering, carnivorous mob, precursors of storm and destruction.

"Kill any man without a hole in his jacket!"

"Kill any man who reads and writes!"

"Kill any man who doesn't blow his nose through his fingers!"

Dr. Guillotin saw Delaunay's head pass by the second-floor window of his study. He was not encouraged by the possibilities for *fraternité*.

He was even less encouraged when, a week later, enraged over rising prices and putative plots to starve the people, a crowd lynched an official named Foulon and paraded his head on a pike with hay stuffed in its mouth for presumed complicity in the plotting. A band of rioters then marched his son-in-law through the streets with his father-in-law's head in front of him, shouting, "Kiss your papa, kiss your papa." They murdered him, too, tore his heart out, threw it at the Hôtel de Ville, and resumed their parade with the young man's head beside the older one's. This, they proclaimed, was how traitors would be punished.

On the night of the 14th of July, many in Paris danced and sang in the torchlit streets around the Bastille. They danced and sang the *carmagnole*. Some of the words went like this:

Marie-Antoinette promised herself
To cut everyone's throat in Paris.
But this she never could pull off
Thank you to our cannons.

> *Let's dance the Carmagnole*
> *Long live the sound*
> *Let's dance the Carmagnole*
> *Long live the sound of the cannons.*

Antoinette had thought she would
Drop us on our asses.
But her plan was no damn good
She fell, and broke her glasses.

> *Let's dance the Carmagnole*
> *Long live the sound*
> *Let's dance the Carmagnole*
> *Long live the sound of the cannons.*

Her husband, the great big conqueror,
Does not know our power.
Go, Louis, you blubbering babe,
Off into the tower.

> *Let's dance the Carmagnole*
> *Long live the sound*
> *Let's dance the Carmagnole*
> *Long live the sound of the cannons.*

The handwriting was on that rugged wall. The spirit of '89 was determined to build a new world from the ruins of the old regime. These were moments of madness, of disbelief suspended. The world was a tabula rasa, wiped clean by a surge of popular imagination, a universe ready to be redesigned. Anything seemed possible, except perhaps continuing to be ruled by a bumbling king and his despotic wife. The present could be destroyed if necessary, but the future seemed without limit.

Even chess pieces were renamed to do away with kings and queens.

16.

THE GREAT FEAR

They're coming, they're coming!"

Who's coming? They!

For the countryside in the apprehensive weeks following the taking of the Bastille, "they" might have been anybody: British marines already landed, they say; the Swedes gathered—did you know?—in the north-east led by Artois, or the thirty thousand Spanish troops gathered, I hear, outside Bordeaux.

But the "they" most often feared were putative gangs of frightening "brigands," relishing rape, dismemberment, and the wholesale burning of houses, farms, and crops, starving peasant bands gathered to devour their own, financed by Artois and other aristocrats to take revenge on the French people for their theft of the National Assembly. "The brigands are coming!"

The tocsin is rung, village militias are gathered,

armed with pitchforks and scythes. People are sent to warn the next village.

The children are hidden in haylofts and given bread, cheese, and milk for a multiday siege. The brigands, we hear, have already murdered all the men and boys two towns over. The mayhem never arrives. But the breathless band sent out to warn is understood as evidence of the approach of the brigands.

And then again: Nobles out to attack us? Let's fire the castles. The nobles, the landlords, the judges—they're always preying on us. Do they know what we're thinking? Do they think us capable of thought? Do they even know we're here? We'll show them.

All over France, estate owners were attacked, their cellars and larders looted, their legal documents—those mysterious orders written by lawyers and enforced by the police—destroyed, and their chateaux burnt.

In fear of retribution, they, too, were coming, the landlords and their armies, didn't you hear? They've been meeting. Soldiers have been seen. Cottagers drove their cattle in from the fields, shuttered their windows, and barred their doors. Townspeople armed themselves, locked the gates, manned their walls. Rumor was cheap—but decisive. *"La grande peur,"* "the great fear." As the illiterate and unpropertied majority rose up, paranoia reigned, and the countryside feared even itself in collective psychosis.

This was not a good time for Nicolas Pelletier to be wandering the countryside, hungry, homeless, pillaging to survive. He was sleeping at night in hideouts of stolen logs, thatch and straw, branches and ferns, roaming the woods by day and living off random poaching and the theft of wood.

He lived in the forests, clad in skins and stinking rags, his feet wrapped in sacking, suffering agonies in the bitter winters, a prisoner of the heartless horrors of rural poverty.

His days were spent in ceaseless scavenging for food. In the woods he ate weasels and foxes, when he could snare them, snakes, rabbits, and badgers—easier to catch. At the outskirts of towns, he raided chicken coops, milked untended cows, stole laundry drying on hedges, cut off horses' tails for selling to upholsterers, and sometimes lacerated his body in order to pass as an invalid wherever alms were being given out. He joined and deserted three regiments as a false recruit. The army was not for him—nor he for it.

Hey, what are you up to?" said the farmer with the gun.

Nicholas was not fast on his feet or clever with

his mind. He just stood there. The chicken flapped away, squawking.

"I am poor," he said.

"So am I," said the owner of the chicken, putting down his gun. "Want some wine? It's hot."

He offered Nicolas a swig from the wineskin in his hand.

"Oh, yes, monsieur, thank you, monsieur. It's us poor people that . . . you see . . . poor people . . . We're flesh and blood, too."

They sat together under the shade of a great sycamore.

"*Ouay, ouay.*" The old man puffed on his pipe. "I follow the ox that's pulling my plow, while M. de Cre-vant up there follows me, gathering up the grain, and leaving me the stubble. I know what poor is."

"I know what ox is," Nicolas replied. "People I work for . . . God created me for their use. Like an ox. You see, monsieur, sometimes a person's got a certain kind of role. . . ."

"I have no work, if that's what you're asking."

"And I have no work, too. This is an evil world."

"Evil if you are poor," the farmer said. "At least until your reward in heaven."

"Our kind is miserable forever, I think—in this world and the next. If we ever got to heaven, we'd be washing and stoking and hauling the stars around. I'm just a poor ox, but it frightens me when I think about how things are. When poverty comes in the door, love flies out the window. So fast I think I might die of fright."

"Oh, the rich aristocrats are not so different. They speak in the name of His Unassailable Holy Sovereign Royal Highness. But get near these children of man and you can see through their princely pretense. They, too, eat when they're hungry, and sleep when they can't keep their eyes open. And you know— they crept into this world as naked and soft as you and me, and will be carried out as stiff and cold as you and me . . . and yet for some reason they have their boots upon our necks. Why is that, do you suppose?"

"Why. Why. Do I ever think of anything else? Every minute all us poor people ask God, 'Why? Why?' And all these years we've had no answer. The Heavenly Father created us out of a little earthly clay, so who are we to ask Him anything? Still, even a worm can fall in love. There's no law against it, is there? An ox. Is the Lord my shepherd or not?"

"*Ouay, ouay.* But it's the fat paunches that make the laws and count our harvests and our heads. They're our shepherds, maybe, not God. But it's mean shepherds they are. Want some more wine? They tax the ground under your feet and the morsel in your mouth and sit around in dress coats while we stand before them naked and humiliated. They take stock of your thighs and shoulders and figure how much more you can bear up under. Your daughters become their maids and whores, and we their lackeys and soldiers."

Nicolas took another long swig.

"My wife was someone's maid and he made her his whore."

"Who?"

"I can't remember his name. Did you ever see anything with two sides, two different faces?"

"Where is your wife?"

"She died long ago. In the Revelation, the angel swears there will be no more time. She was a good person, though."

"*Ouay, ouay.* We know little enough about one another. You have to crack open people's skulls and drag thoughts out by their tails. But you look like a good man. Sorry I don't have work for you."

"I look like what they think of me. An ox. Strong. In the Revelation there is a mighty angel that can lift up a great millstone and casts it into the sea. I do the best I can."

"*Ouay, ouay.* We poor have no leisure."

They sat in silence for a long while. Then Nicolas offered, "I hear that at Nanterre a woman had a baby born with a serpent's head, and that lightning struck the church at Rueil and melted the cross on the steeple, and that a werewolf was seen in the woods of

Chaville. Jews are poisoning the springs and throwing plague powders in the air to cause diseases."

"*Ouay, ouay.*" The old man got up. "Take a chicken with you when you go."

"Oh, thank you, monsieur. Thank you. May the Lord's blessing be upon you, sir. Sometimes I am ashamed to still be alive. The world . . ."

The farmer waved good-bye and trudged off to the farmhouse.

Pelletier took the largest hen from the henhouse, and seeing the old rifle left under the tree, he stole it. Perhaps he didn't mean to, but he did.

Within an hour he was apprehended and thrown into the prison at Dreux to await trial. This small town of barely twelve hundred lay on a slope descending into a ravine crowded with willows. Around it were blighted fields of potatoes and beets bounded by cankered chestnuts. Nicolas could see them from the window of his cell.

The prisoners were thrown together at random. A child of seventeen at a bench next to a man of seventy, a six-month detainee next to a convict due to be sent to the galleys for life, a smooth-cheeked youngster who had filched some apples alongside a highway killer soon to be hung. And here, in cramped and filthy workshops, the near-innocent with the near-damned worked side by side in semidarkness at vile and dirty tasks, deprived of air and daylight, forbidden to speak, barely able to see, mindless, like hideous human husks, some appallingly old, others appallingly young.

First time caught, first conviction, for him there was no room at the hateful inn: After six days awaiting his hearing, Nicolas Pelletier, now with a prison record, was set loose once again upon the world. Or rather, the world was set loose again upon him.

He felt no remorse for the crimes he had committed. At every step he heard a voice that whispered at him, "Condemned to death." No more than all of us, he thought.

At Chartres he witnessed the execution of a beautiful young woman in the square fronting the cathedral. Was she a witch? Had she cheated on her husband? He was too timid to ask about her crime. He watched her spasm, hanging there, watched her nipples grow beneath her thin shift, watched her body dance and twitch. He felt aroused and felt ashamed. In an alley he faced the wall and beat at his codpiece to force himself down.

"What will come of it all?" he thought. "Anything is possible. The poor must pay for everything."

By owl-light, on a hillside off the road to Paris, he watched the sun go down. Look how it makes my shadow lengthen, even if I have nothing to eat.

That is the sun, the fire sailing round the sky, and I am a little insect, a worm who can't stop his shadow from running away from him. Everything moves away, clocks tick, bells peal, water flows, people run.

I'll sit on the ground so maybe things will stop, and nothing go any more, so nothing moves.

He knelt as the sun sank and watched his shadow taking his head over there to the next hill. "The world is too close," he muttered. "It shouldn't be allowed to come that close."

The Enlightenment didn't mean very much to someone like him.

Dreux was the first of his several arrests. Drunkenness, brawls, poaching, vagrancy, theft—many of his activities were threats to the established order. And the order so established was equally a threat to him—making his way through treacherous territory on foot, sleeping at night under haystacks and bushes when he could not get hospitality at mistrustful farms, he stood a good chance of having his throat cut or his few goods stolen. Honest poverty is thinly sown, and penury brings much trouble.

And thus he slid down the banister of crime toward the scaffold. When he was in anyone's company at all, it was that of rogues and rascals, petty crooks, smugglers, pickpockets, prostitutes, receivers and dealers in stolen goods. They would pick pockets, filch from poorboxes, commit highway robbery and assault—with or without battery. They took vast amounts or not so much, shared the booty with each other or kept it for themselves. The booty? Money, handkerchiefs, medals, snuffboxes, food. In the end most of them would go down in pestilential workhouses or else crawl into a bush or a hayloft and die.

When sleeping under the stars, this is what he thought: What is it that makes the stars shine? They look like a million teardrops. Maybe they are all the tears God has wiped away. Or maybe all His. How sad He must be to make so many tears.

His second arrest was for trying to bribe an officer with a stolen watch to allow him to beg undisturbed. He had been impersonating a leper. The bribe seemed permissible, but the policeman's wife had died of leprosy. One week in the prison at Bonneval.

When taking shelter from the midday sun, this is what he thought: Can the sun be angry with a worm if the worm should address it? The world is hot as coals in hell, tormented by the sun. God can do it—He should blow out the sun.

He tried it himself. His cheeks puffed up. The sun ignored him.

We poor people have mouths, he thought, and guts with teeth at one end and skin around them, and if we can, we eat and shit things out, and the shit piles up. Sometimes I just want to crawl on all fours. Who is like unto the beast? Even the kennels aren't safe.

His third arrest was in Orléans for transporting a wagonload of books that had been banned for breaching moral and religious standards. He was let go when he testified—believably—that he had been hired for one day by a man he didn't know, whose name he wasn't sure of, that he didn't know what was in the boxes, and in any case, books? he couldn't read. The court confiscated the material for its own uses.

He was let out under a hard, gray sky. Like the world is dead, he thought. Strange how still it is. When God goes, everything goes.

He slept that autumn night at the edge of a forest. The wind came up.

Bad, he thought, it's the wind.

And now it rains, though there's no sky. Why is

that? Why? Everyone thinks, and then thinks of something else, but I think of only one thing over and over: Why is God tormenting me?

Alcohol anesthetized.

Poverty pursues the poor. As autumn turned to winter, he was always cold. The sorrows of the earth stopped flowing and coagulated around him, a slurry of life-sucking ice. His cheeks were sunken on his huge skull; his hair was streaked with gray. His skin had turned the color of frozen earth and was lined with wrinkles not of age but, mysteriously, of death.

His road led inevitably toward Paris. On the outskirts he was fingered as a "thief without morality, of no fixed abode and sleeping in the limekilns of Belleville, committing many kinds of damage in the countryside of which the peasants had complained." He *had* been sleeping in the limekilns, but as for "committing many kinds of damage in the countryside," he hadn't. It must have been someone else.

They asked him, "What are your political opinions?"

"I don't have any," he said.

"What is your country?" the city guard wanted to know.

"I don't know."

"You don't know what your country is?"

"My country. Ah. Yes. Les Herbiers."

"What did you say?"

"Les Herbiers. My country."

"Les Herbiers is not a country."

"It is my country. And after that, Malestroit."

"Is your family from there?" the guard continued.

"Yes. My families. They were poor. They are dead. I have no family anymore. No friends."

Now, approaching his end, he was a Vendée peasant once more: somewhat savage, serious, and strange, his clear eyes fading, his hair long. He had once lived on milk and chestnuts and lived close by his thatched roof, his hedge, and his ditch, distinguishing each neighboring hamlet by the sound of its bell. He drank only water and on feast days and Sundays had worn a leather jacket ornamented with arabesques. Speaking only his own language caused him to dwell in a mental tomb, remembering his ox, and the cow he had cared for, and whetting his scythe, and hoeing his grain, and kneading his buckwheat bread. He believed in the Blessed Virgin and loved his king—whoever that was—and his priest. He could sit perfectly still for hours, listening.

And now he was a wild beast of the woods stalking the edge of the city.

Un brigand.

Un pauvre.

17.

FELTING

K *nock, knock, knock.*
Knock, knock.

Guillotin entered the room. But it wasn't he who was knocking.

Knock, knock.

Knock, knock, knock.

"Good evening, my love."

"Ah, it's you at last, dear Joseph."

Marie-Louise jumped up from her table to give him a kiss.

"So late again," she teased. "You must be exhausted."

"What are you doing, pounding away like that?"

"Thinning this piece of felt. See? I want to try an embroidery on felt, not linen. Of my last flower etching."

"The peonies?"

"You like that one, so I thought I'd see if I can make it more colorful this way."

She returned to her worktable.

Guillotin slumped wearily in the one armchair in his wife's studio and stared at her swept-up hair and the long, elegant neck beneath it.

Knock, knock.

Knock, knock, knock.

Marie-Louise Saugrain, now Guillotin, his sweet wife of fifteen months, that doe-eyed, majestic, and full-bosomed beauty he had fallen in love with, fallen in love finally, at last, at forty-nine. He, who had been ever celibate, who had never hidden his scorn—or possibly his terror—of women, married at last, happily married to a woman sixteen years younger than he.

This was what being a lover of books had brought him. A bookish daughter of a bookish family, her father, Claude-Marie Saugrain, the owner of one of the most prestigious bookstores in Paris. "Clientele by Invitation Only," said the sign in the window—a younger, first-in-Paris Joseph would often peer in jealously through the glass. "After all," he thought, "this man's family were booksellers to Henri IV, and M. Saugrain is now the bookseller to the king's brother, Artois. Who am I to . . . ?"

But Claude-Marie Saugrain, like many intellectuals, was a high Mason, a good friend of Franklin's, and though all three belonged to different lodges, the

American had gotten Guillotin through the door. Once inside, and constantly browsing, the doctor discovered, behind the counter one day, the daughter.

It was embarrassing, all the sprucing up he thought he needed: the new coat, more colorful than black, the faintly rakish hat, the shoes unscuffed and the new silk stockings. *Sapere aude* gave way to a more subversive challenge, and this late-middle-aged man discovered that great revolutionary—Love. When thinking of Marie-Louise, his mouth went autonomically dry, his heart rate increased sympathetically, and his second through fourth pelvic splanchnic nerves pulsed away. It was embarrassing to be human. But so be it. And after fifteen months of sharing a table, a bed, and a life, he felt substantially the same. But he was tonight exhausted.

Sensing his eyes on her, she turned to him, wooden hammer in hand, looking for all the world like a lenient magistrate.

"Look at you," she said. "You look tired as a tomb. What's going on?"

"Tired as a tomb is right. I spent the day arguing in vain for abolition of the death penalty. 'Don't push too fast.' 'The nation isn't ready.' 'The votes aren't there.'" He did his best to imitate the regional accents involved.

"I thought you said Robespierre was with you," she said.

"He is, but even he can't move that mountain.

We've got a few voices—Estaing, Duplessis, Laborde, Simoneau—but they're timid and too few. There are probably four or five hundred votes to continue state slaughter. Of course they don't call it that. They call it justice. An eye for an eye, a life for a life. Some skewed version of equality and fraternity. They can hardly claim liberty, except the executioner's. Really, the arguments are predictable, disgusting—and exhausting to listen to all day. You'd think killing its own was the highest duty of the state. But at the root of their arguments, you sense only hardness of heart, cruelty, barbarity, boot-licking, and fee-grubbing."

"Can't you proceed more slowly, individually, convince each one otherwise?"

Joseph laughed. "Today Anacharsis Cloots . . ."

"The Prussian?" she asked. "The orator of humanity?"

Guillotin nodded, lips pursed in irony. "The Prussian exhorted us to 'cure ourselves from individuals!' There was great cheering."

"I see," she said. "All right, then." She pulled up her stool directly in front of her husband. "Here's what we have to do—*you* have to do. Penal-code reform can't really be about liberty, can it, but it *can* be about equality, and to some degree about fraternity. Why not propose—for now, till they come round, till the country comes round—at least that all punishments—including death—be applied the same across the classes. Same crime, same punishment, regardless of who commits it. Equality. They'll understand that, or at least pretend to."

"But we're still killing people to demonstrate people shouldn't kill."

"For the moment. That will change. When things become calmer."

"So where is the fraternity in what you are proposing?"

"I don't know." She shrugged. "Murderers have families. Legislators have families. Would they want their *families* punished if they committed crimes?"

"No, of course not."

"Would they want their families to have their bodies if they *were* executed?"

"Yes, of course."

"*Voilà*—fraternity. Realistic demands."

The good doctor chuckled at his wife's strength and her good reasoning. "But capital punishment is still at the heart of things. Watching executions, cheering at them, encourages so much violence. Look at what the crowd did to Delaunay at the Bastille, or Foulon's son-in-law—what was his name?"

"Berthier de Sauvigny."

"Yes, Foulon and Sauvigny, their heads sawn off and dripping on pikes, their bodies dismembered. We hear reports from the provinces even more terrifying. Where does such behavior come from? What nourishes it—the insane furor of the crowd? The awful examples constantly before them. At executions they're whipped up to applaud the suffering of the miserable wretch on the scaffold. An execution becomes a kind of circus act, starring Sanson in his fancy costume."

"They see it as part of the judicial procedure."

"What judicial procedure? The procedures are secret. The evidence is secret, and the accused can never see it or challenge his accusers. At the last moment some poor man, in the middle of a fearful night, is dragged out of bed to see his judges for two minutes— just long enough to hear himself condemned. Justice! Executions! We don't dare recall Damiens. This is not justice, my sweet. It disturbs the people's soul deep down, frightens it, makes it crazy. It turns justice inside out. Who is guilty are the judges!"

"Calm down, dear, calm down. Equality, fraternity—that's your strategy for tomorrow. You meet tomorrow?"

"We continue debate on the new penal code."

"All right, then: equality, fraternity—like this felt here."

She picked her project up off her work table.

"How like felt?" Joseph asked, amazed.

"Solid and supple, all the brother and sister

fibers hammered into a mass, not exactly homoge-
neous but still smooth. Infinite, open, unlimited in
every direction . . ."

"The Philadelphian Project."

"Exactly. A new society with no warp, no woof,
no center, no top, no bottom. Equality. fraternity.
Continuous variation. Like this . . ."

She held up her fresh piece of felt. He was delighted he had married her.

"Try to rip it." She held it out. "Go ahead. Try
to rip it."

Suspecting the result, Guillotin shook his head.

"To square this up, I'll need to cut it with the
sharpest knife," she said.

"Like a man's head," her husband observed.

"What do you mean?"

"That's another gift of fraternity: kindness. The
kindest way of death—decapitation. With the sharpest knife. So quick as to be painless."

"Sanson makes a mess," she observed.

"We need some machine even he couldn't bungle.
I've seen drawings, plans from England and Italy. It
would be over so quickly, the crowds would have nothing to goggle at. They'd stop coming. . . ."

He stared off into some inner space. She took
him by the arm.

"Do you want something to eat?" she asked.

"No. Thank you. I'm too worked up."

"We should go to bed, then. It's past midnight."

"Let me write this down. I'll be up in a few minutes."

"You never stop," she said in her mellifluous voice, and looked into his bloodshot eyes.

A new silence united the couple.

18.
EQUALITY, IF NOT FRATERNITY

"Fifteen glorious years," the inmates sing in *Marat/ Sade.*

"Fifteen glorious years," they sing at Charenton, the mental institution now boasting the Marquis de Sade.

> *Fifteen glorious years*
> *Fifteen glorious years*
> *years of peace*
> *years of war*
> *each year greater*
> *than the year before.*

Well, greater in blood, maybe; greater in murder and trepidation.

But surely the most glorious of the years was that one, 1789, when in the face of famine the nation rearranged itself to make new norms and a new constitution to express them, when Paris rose up, and when on

August 4 all feudal immunities and privileges were abolished.

Amazing—the self-beheading of a nation, when in a competition of effusive patriotism citizen-nobles demanded the end of "feudal barbarism" and a government that would be a light unto the nations of Europe. *Ducs, marquis, vicomtes,* bishops, and archbishops on parade at the Assembly, stripping themselves down to the joy of being simply *"citoyens,"* enthusiasts of self-dispossession.

Seventeen eighty-nine, when on August 26 the National Assembly passed the Declaration of the Rights of Man and all Frenchmen were understood to be born free and equal—equal!—with social distinctions, liberties, and rights to be founded only on the general good. Its seventeen articles remain inspiring today and might well be studied by world leaders, especially our own.

Seventeen eighty-nine, when on October 5 the women of Paris rose up en masse and marched the fifteen miles from Paris to Versailles, some riding on horse-drawn cannons, demanding relief and bringing the king and National Assembly back to Paris to be permanently present at, and not outside, the problems crying to be solved.

Seventeen eighty-nine, October 10, when, on the second day of debate about France's penal code, delegate from Paris Dr. Joseph Guillotin proposed six articles to the Assembly:

- that all criminals receive equal punishment without regard to social status,
- that their disgrace should in no way extend to their families, who were not to be punished in any way,
- that the state not be permitted to confiscate a condemned man's worldly goods,
- that the bodies of executed men be delivered to their families if requested, and if not, that they be buried without mention in public records of the kind of death suffered,
- that citizens not be reproached for the execution or loss of civil rights incurred by a relative,

and finally,

- that a method of capital punishment be found, the same for all, which would be both quick and painless: decapitation effected by a simple mechanism.

Once again the overwhelming feeling among the deputies was that the country was not ready for the frank abolition of the death penalty. Marat had called for "penalties at once lenient and certain." With regard to capital punishment, he was quite clear: It should be infrequent.

"Life is unique among the benefits of this world in having no equivalent; justice therefore requires that murder be punished by death. But execution should never be cruel. Even for the most serious crimes (parricide, fratricide, murder of a friend or benefactor), the machinery of execution shall be fearsome, but the death shall be an easy one." So argued Marat.

Fearsome machinery and easy death. Guillotin's proposal was right in line with the enlightened intellectual and philosophical thought of his time. "Decapitation effected by a simple mechanism" would be humane to the victim, minimizing his pain. It would be humane to the spectators, who would no longer be assaulted by the dehumanizing spectacle of torture. Finally, it would be humane to the executioner, who, freed from his monstrous duel with the victim, had only to trigger some flawless mechanical process.

An enlightened doctor proposing the humanization of justice, Delegate Guillotin was tasked with detailing the method.

Contrary to popular belief, the good doctor was not the "inventor" of the guillotine. The basic design for a decapitation machine was well known before Guillotin: primitive versions had been used to execute aristocratic criminals in Germany, Italy, Scotland, and Persia, and their use was known as early as the fourteenth century, especially in Scotland, where they were used until 1710. There is a record of an execution by a decapitation device in Milan in 1702 and paintings of a guillotine-like machine used in Nuremberg in the mid-1500s. It was thought, throughout the ages, that aristocrats, even at their deaths, should not be contaminated by the hands of commoners.

Guillotin himself had in hand a manuscript of *Travels to Spain and Italy* by the Dominican Father Jean-Baptiste Labat describing in detail a machine that might be both fearsome and easy:

> *The* mannaia *is used for decapitation. The device is entirely reliable, and, where an unskillful executioner sometimes requires two or three strokes to detach the head from the trunk, with the* mannaia *the condemned man is not kept waiting. This form of execution is for gentlemen and ecclesiastics. It is rare for such a person to be put to death in public, whatever his crime. The sentence is carried out in the prison courtyard, with the gates closed and in the presence of very few.*
>
> *The instrument named* mannaia *is a frame 4–5 feet high and some 15 inches across in its operational state. It consists of two uprights some 3 inches square, slotted on the inside to allow movement of a sliding cross-piece. The two uprights are connected by*

three mortice-and-tenon-jointed crosspieces, one at each end and one some 15 inches above the lower cross-piece. In this the kneeling victim rests his neck. Above this crosspiece is the sliding crosspiece which runs in the slots of the uprights: Fixed to its underside is a wide blade some 9–10 inches long by 6 inches wide which cuts well and is finely honed. On top of it, firmly attached, is a lead weight of 60–80 pounds. This deadly crosspiece is raised to within 1 or 2 inches of the top beam, to which it is attached by a short length of cord. At a sign from the chief of police, the executioner simply cuts the cord and the crosspiece, dropping vertically onto the condemned man's neck, cuts it clean through without any danger of the stroke mis-carrying.

The Dominican friar must have been a carpenter in an earlier life.

Guillotin's thoughts about a humanitarian "simple mechanism" were already revolving around such a device, one upon which the condemned man was laid prone between two uprights surmounted by a crosspiece from which the axe was made to fall onto the neck by means of some trigger.

Citizen Guillotin's six proposals were debated in October, but only the first of them passed while the rest were debated at length; most of the others did not pass until the following January. But the "simple mechanism," egalitarian though it may have been, was tabled repeatedly and not debated for almost three years—until March 1792. Why was that? What was so radical about this, the most "humanitarian" of all Guillotin's proposals? What was the issue?

Dr. Guillotin had argued that his mechanism would make for an easier death. But hanging was also considered an easy form of death—easier, certainly, than torture and breaking on the wheel. By Guillotin's own argument, hanging might also serve as a uniform penalty. As one deputy, Verninac de Saint-Maur, argued, "Beheading, which has in our country been the preserve of the high nobility, has acquired a certain social standing, a cloak of respectability which makes it all but an honor. Rather than elevate the masses to the dignity of the block, we should reduce the nobility to the modesty of the gibbet."

Equality and fraternity notwithstanding, the framing of issues remained the same, bound by class distinctions even as classes were to be abolished.

Doctor and philosopher though he was, Guillotin's skills as a legislative debater did not help advance the issue. He was variously quoted as saying, "The mechanism falls like a thunderbolt, the head flies off, the blood spurts forth, the victim is no more." Or "Gentlemen, with my machine, I can have your heads off in the twinkling of an eye and you will feel not the slightest pain." Or "The form of death I have invented is so gentle that, were one not expecting to die, one would scarcely know what to say of it, for one feels no more than a slight sensation of coolness at the back of the neck." The statement, whichever it was, had met with gales of laughter.

And some were laughing at him, and not with him. The Goncourts cite "a satirical novel" parodying the good doctor's speech to the Assembly:

> *My dear fellow countrymen, so many of my patients have died of my attentions that I may reasonably claim to be among the best informed of men as to the ways of departing this world. I have at last invented, with the help of my machinist, the delightful machine you see before you. Under the platform there is a bird-organ, set up to play the jolliest tunes. The chief protagonist being once mounted on the rostrum, shall stand between the two columns and shall be requested to place his ear against this stylobate, the better to hear the ravishing sounds that the bird-organ pours forth; and his head shall be so discreetly chopped off, that it will itself, long after its truncation, be in doubt as to this event. Only the applause that shall doubtless resound through the square will suffice to convince it of its state.*

Reading such pamphlets and hearing such talk was painful to the good Doctor Guillotin, for the seeds of truth contained in the fiction. He was indeed seeking to make death more friendly. With a friend like this, said the world, who needs an enemy?

Nevertheless, he persisted, and lobbied, and sketched.

19.
RESTLESS IS THE HEART

"Crybaby!" they called him, though it hurt too much for the fifth of our five to really cry.

Le bon petit docteur he was no longer but rather the long-suffering patient. Clutching the ghost of Saint Pantaleon to his heart, twelve-year-old Pierre-René lay sick in his bed in the dormitory of his training college in Toussaints, not far from home but in another world entirely.

His body was burning up, in full-blown aching torment. His head pounded against his eyes, and his neck was bloated, puffed to immobility. But worst of all was his throat, flaming red and covered with whitish spots. He couldn't swallow. But he *had* to swallow—his pharynx acted on its own, against him. And every involuntary swallow provoked a spasm of pain flooding into his fevered eyes, into his forehead and beyond his skull, illuminating the room in jagged red and yellow every thirty seconds. He wanted to die. He wanted someone to chop off his head so that the rest of him might be rid of the recurrent torture. The days were long, and the nights were longer. His groans kept his roommates awake. "Crybaby!" they called him, though his tears were silent.

Three days of anguish, and then the miracle of pain passing away. Swallows came more easily, limbs ceased to ache, his head no longer pounded and burned. He lay there, exhausted but lightened, annealed by fire, saved by Pantaleon the all-healer.

But then came the rash, first on his ebbing neck, next on his chest, then on his arms and legs, hands and feet. Clawing at his groin, his armpits, his throat and sides, scratching the scratching hands—they had to tie his arms to the bedposts. And with relief the flaking and scaling, skin peeling off his arm in sheets. He was not a lovely sight. His heart beat fast, he found it difficult to breathe, and deep one night an invisible hand grasped him, he was blinded by a dazzling light, and heard a voice speaking to him. It was God! He knew it. God had entered into him so that he might take his fate into his hands and know what he must do. This experience, eternal Heaven here on earth, here in Châlons-sur-Marne—he would live in God. He understood the Holy Scriptures for the first time.

It all made sense—why he had been born here, why his family didn't have enough money to send him away. This town of canals and streams, with its narrow, winding streets, its avenues and promenades—this was his town, this was his abbey. Pilgrims came to Ste. Pudentienne—his church, and he was already there. The local beer industry, the champagne, was nothing compared to the fermentation in this one little soul. He would stay in the diocese of Châlons, he would stay in school, go on to the seminary. He would become a priest, so much more glorious than being a doctor. He would heal not bodies, but souls.

Two teachers shaped him in the shear of their worldviews. The pious Father George Fouché was a man right out of the Middle Ages. For him, as for the sculptors of the thirteenth century, the Christian church was peopled by a multitude he considered perfectly real: saints and prophets, martyrs and doctors, apostles, angels and archangels, dominations, virtues, powers and thrones, sacred personages of every kind, surrounding the Word made flesh and His holy family, the race of whom, in low or high relief, crowded the porches or filled the naves of the cathedrals.

The other was Father Jean-Robert Riard, *un homme modern*, who thought that in this age of unfaith, Christianity didn't require a lot of goody-goodies. We of the faith, he thought, can't shrink from sores any more than a doctor. We must be able to look wounds right in the eye. And they all give out pus; pus is what we must work with. A priest should pay attention only to suffering. And so, he thought, should the state.

Old Father Fouché lived high above the earth, where all confusion disappeared, and the broad lines God intended came into sharpened focus, and the distant din of earthly wailing revealed its underlying harmonies. For young Father Riard, the grand work was to interrupt the opera of human malice, arias and choruses that all who are fallen sing to the powers of evil, right under the nose of God Himself.

When Pierre-René would come crying to the older man, his stomach twisted and burning after lessons with the younger, Fouché would calm him, and call him "little muddler," and exhort him simply to mind God and pray to Him. "Remember," Fouché said, "that in all Father Riard's catalog, there is only one sin—the lack of love. Hell is that lack of love, eternal punishment is not to be able to love anymore— ever again. I know that sounds unimportant to a young man. You love, you fall out of love, you go love elsewhere. But that's not what I'm talking about, no— stewing in your own juices, only your own, no. God is the opposite. God not only loves you, and every one of Father Riard's villains, but He is the love, the connection, you have with them. You are all sons and daughters of God, connected by and through Him, and that is the great miracle. Make those strands the basis of everything as you muddle along in all your habits and customs, when you work hard and when you relax, and when you just sit there, crying or smiling. And then, you know what? You will have torn from life, right from the heart of Adam, the great loneliness. And you can pray to everything, absolutely everything. See that spider crawling on the wall? You can pray to him and thank him for his crawling."

The boy laughed and reached out, and let the spider crawl on his hand.

Which didn't stop Father Riard from continuing to spin webs in his brain with all his warnings of the great Darkness and the shakings of the world, the unceasing and too-often-successful attempts of Satan to get hold of the mind of God. "The world is a huge mass of Evil," he taught, "rolling and swelling with lust, and it is you, my lad, who must free the Good from its prison, direct it toward victory, and make ours a faith which deserves the tithing we ask for. You can catch your parishioners to save them from Adam's fall. The abscess of sin can be lanced and cleansed from the human heart. Human happiness is possible, and it is up to you to lead your flock to that promised land. God's universe is not Belial's; His truth is not a lie. Find it. Share it."

Two paths converging at a point. But for Pierre-René treading them was like trying to straddle two horses at once, when each might veer off in divergence. He would kneel before the crucifix hanging on the dormitory wall and ask the Wounded One which truth his heart might best embrace. Was one truth truth and the other abscessed infection? At times his head would drop to his knees, and he would sob at Christ's feet, rise up to shake his fist at the Lord, and fall down weeping again. He couldn't believe that God would answer him, much less employ him to achieve His holy ends. And in fact, there was silence from the wall. God was silent. In his soul he heard no answer. He felt the worst was yet to come.

But he muddled along, excelled at school, became *le bon petit docteur* once again, and as he grew taller simply *le bon docteur*, as he ministered to his classmates' bodies and their souls. He passed from training school to seminary and remembered the day he was forced to put childish things behind him.

Seventeen, he was, when Henri-Émile, a twenty-year-old seminarian, accosted him in secret, late at night. Could he come with him immediately to a rough-cast shack on the outskirts of Châlons?

As they entered the room, dark but for one small candle, a groaning came from the blankets of a cot: "I don't want to die, I don't want to die!" Henri-Émile bent over to pull back the filthy covers.

"Marie . . . I brought . . ."

"Leave me alone!" a young girl screamed. "I want to die. I can't stand this anymore. I want to die!" Her disheveled blond head rose up, her eyes great with pain and horror.

"Her baby is here. You can see its head," the older seminarian told the younger. "Can you save us?"

"Save *us*? Save *us*?" the girl screamed, laughing, spiteful, hysterical, shaking like a flame. She sat up straighter as the pain became more fierce. "Raaaaaaaaa. Are *you* going to die? God damn, God damn, God be damned! And you be damned. And may this baby be damned! Damned!"

"Mademoiselle!" Pierre-René stepped quickly to her side. "Mademoiselle, you must relax. Please!" He had seen delivered only two calves, and once a sheep. He had never seen between a woman's legs. "Don't be angry at the baby. It hasn't done anything to you. . . ."

"Hasn't done anything?" Again that frenzied laugh. "Except this, the worst pain in my life. Except make my parents kick me out. Except make me go into hiding. Except make me lose my job and make my so-called-friends call me a slut. Except to ruin my whole life . . ."

Henri-Émile broke down weeping.

"And you, M. Holy Man," the girl snarled at him, "Not so holy with your pants down, are you? Think you can absolve your sins by bringing this kid around to sniff at my cunt? Aiii, aiii, it's coming! Not so fast! Push it back!"

She grew more frantic. Her groans became dreadful animal cries, incredible, unbearable to the seminarians. Pierre-René tried to stop up his ears, but nothing could keep out the sound. He fell to his knees at her bedside and said Ave Marias while she tried to hold the baby's head inside her with her hands. But her leverage was as nothing compared to the force of her uterine thrusts. She opened wide her legs.

"You, asshole, keep it from popping out too fast."

Pierre-René, frightened, confused, horrified at the mess and smell in front of him, tried to grab the baby's head.

"Don't pull it out, idiot; you want to pull its head off? Get that, whatever it is, shoulder out of me. Careful, you moron. Ain't you ever had your fingers in a cunt before?"

One shoulder coming free, the other slipped on through with the next contraction, and Pierre-René held half a baby in his unaccustomed hands.

"Should I get it out of its, what do you call it, wrapping?"

"Sac, asshole. Rip it open, else how is it supposed to breathe? Don't pull, don't pull, I told you."

Out it came, slippery as an eel, an amnion-draped little boy with a banana-shaped head. Pierre-René thought it might be some kind of monster, a fish thing, but with arms and legs. And huge blue testicles and a penis.

"You got some cord? A rope?" the new mother yelled.

Henri-Émile began to search the room.

"And a knife. Get a knife. Wipe it clean."

"I have a pen-knife for sharpening quills . . ." he said.

"I knew there was some use for that stupid seminary."

And then there was the sound of a cry, some new sound, the sound of an infant child, weak, discordant. Pierre-René crossed himself. The tiny crumpled thing began to howl, beat its pygmy arms and legs, fanning itself pink like the amphibian it looked to be, screaming now, asserting itself as if it had every right to live. Pierre-René tore two strips from his nightshirt.

"Tie it tight about a handspan from the child, and you tie it about two inches beyond that. The cord, the cord, you idiots."

The seminarians tied off the cord with shaking hands.

"Now, cut it."

Henri-Émile handed his penknife to Pierre-René. Pierre-René handed it back.

"Are you the father?"

Henri-Émile nodded ruefully.

"Then you get to bring your son into the world."

The cut was made, and the seminarians stood up, one to pace the room with his screaming newborn, the other to separate himself from this soul-shaking event. How much sin was here? He was afraid to think. Was it her fault or his? Why had God allowed this to happen? Was he now an accomplice? Pierre-René looked at Henri-Émile, and glanced between the girl's open legs.

"Wait a minute, godlets, you're not finished," the new mother yelled. "What about this, hanging out of me?"

"Do you want me to pull it out?" Pierre-René asked.

"Just massage my belly. It'll come out by itself. Here, gimme the kid. If he sucks it helps it come out."

"What?" Pierre-René asked.

"My womb. It'll come out. What was attached to him."

Henri-Émile handed her the baby. She pushed it away.

"On second thought, no. Let it die. Just you stroke my belly like this."

And she took Pierre-René's hand and stroked her sweating abdomen with it, right down to her gaping, hairy triangle. He tried to pull away, but her grip was like iron, and though exhausted, her strength was fierce. It made him afraid.

Henri-Émile looked at the child yowling in his arms, this new, fierce spirit, whole, complete, demanding, but dreadfully helpless, like a speck of dust at the mercy of any puff of wind, this object no human hand could fashion, this new thought on the earth, and he thanked his God for bringing it to birth.

"Marie-Odile," he effused. "Look!"

He held the boy up to her.

"There's nothing more wonderful in the world, even if . . ."

"Yeah, yeah," she said. "For you, every fly is a mystery. But excess people shouldn't be born until they change everything so there ain't no excess people. Here, gimme him. You can take him to the foundling home tomorrow, or leave him on the abbey steps."

The two seminarians watched the mother take her babe to her breast. The mystery of all this was inexplicable.

As a young priest, Father Pierre-René was haunted by the birth and early death of this never-named child, carrying it with him as a heavy burden of sadness about his flock.

Once ordained, he was assigned to the parish of Conques, a small hillside village of six hundred souls in the Massif Central. His was the abbey-church of St. Foy, the remarkable building to which pilgrims flock even today to see the carving of the Last Judgment over its door. It was a region of wine-growers, farm-workers, and a large contingent of beggars. At his retirement, shortly before his death, the previous priest had written to his young successor, "There is no trade because of the lack of suitable roads. . . . Two-thirds of the families do not eat any bread half of the time. . . . There are approximately eighty disabled persons including numerous children and one hundred beggars in the parish. Nowadays, to be starving, to live on chestnuts, to sell our own land and work for another: Here are our incomes, here is our plight!"

To Conques the young Father Pierre-René Grenier carried three nights of the soul. The first was his memory of that night of a birth and of the death of unnumbered suppositions. The second was the night of his idealized connection with the poor, with women of stinking thighs and vulgar tongue, women—and their men—prepared to kill their "excess" children without a second thought. But most blackening of all, he carried the night of self-doubt concerning himself as priest, and the idea of priesthood itself.

He would stand for hours, his hands gripping the church's wrought-iron grills—forged, it was told him, from the manacles of prisoners released at the intercession of Sainte Foy, a young girl martyred in 303. There he would meditate on prisons and prisoners, and on human freedom.

There was, granted, much of the absolute in him:

He felt he had no right to leave a thought alone until he had worked it through to the end. Years of incessant study had left him chaste and austere: He felt he knew everything and knew nothing. But to the voice within he was all attention: He had admitted—once and for all into each moment of his puny life—the terrifying presence of God.

Yet that voice spoke with a forked tongue. On the one hand, Father Pierre knew that while he was the lowliest of men, simple and even too simple, he was filled with passion for the work of bringing to pass the Kingdom of universal justice, especially for those with wretched, unfortunate, and ignominious lives. While the nobility might propose itself as an object of adoration, his vision was fixed on the immortality of the poor.

He understood the power of the illogical in life and attributed to it both an inability of the poor to cope and the possibility of their overcoming the merely rational, of making a great leap of faith, both soaring and profound.

On the other hand, who was *he* to lead them there—to the leap, to the Kingdom? He felt he was playacting the part of a priest. He was afflicted with a gloomy nervousness when he uttered certain prescribed ecclesiastical phrases, fearing mockery for being trite, professing the rule of hope, teaching optimism by force of habit. Had those words—so enormous in their implications—become so hackneyed and worn over the centuries that they were simply accepted and easily swallowed, like warm gruel? Was there any relevance in his noble phrases? Nobody made fun of him—were they just too bored by what he said to bother?

My poor. What is my message to them? Poverty! Don't they want something other, different, more? Aren't they hoping for an *end* to their poverty? But no. Blessed are the poor, I tell them. Poverty is your dignity. Take it by the hand, honor it, be faithful to it. What a disappointment, what a blow! I wouldn't mind preaching rebellion to the poor, not at all. But I don't. What hypocrisy!

I can bring them joy, he thought; they have only to ask. Joy is the gift of their church—or whatever joy is possible in this sad world.

Sanctimonious cant. They don't want joy; they want two good meals a day. And am I, myself, joyful? I could never achieve that kind of grace.

And yet, as soon as the ice was broken, his people took him into their confidence, looking to him to help them discover who they really were. You must not expect an answer from me, he thought. God has granted me neither eloquence, nor insight, nor force of intellect or spirit. There could be no forgiveness for his imposture.

The boys at the school were antagonistic, that

was sure. They scorned him for going to dinner once at M. Leclerq's. "When we are starving, a priest shouldn't go to dinner at a rich man's house," one yelled as he was coming home. That was so. He had no right. But he had to be priest of *all* the people, didn't he?

He was often short of breath, and had increasing difficulty walking Conques's steep hills. There seemed to be a dark something working inside him which he was sure could not be God.

The boys in his communion class. By the time they were old enough to speak it, the word "love" had already become something to mock, a dirty activity to be taunted with laughter, or stoned, like a toad. He felt for those poor little souls as he watched them at play, his heart clenching with a pain almost too dreadful to bear. Look how energetically they fought, how joyfully, how full of pride, entirely carnal, with some carnal form of hope. Love? For them? No, *lust* was their transformation, and Father Pierre was terrified of lust, especially in children. Lust, the first of the deadly sins, a tumor at the very source of life. The doctor in him shuddered. His own faith, he thought, was likely no greater than theirs, or no less, but their confident security appalled him.

The girls, he felt, were not so tainted: He had to admit he favored the girls. One especially, Marie-Claude, a nine-year-old with long black hair and great dark eyes, the best in his catechism class, bold yet innocent, those eyes with all the answers. He would single her out for questioning from among her less attentive friends and explain things for her special benefit. She often got the weekly prize, a religious picture to put into her prayer book.

"Won't it be wonderful to have your first communion?" he once asked her.

"No. Maybe. Who knows?"

He was surprised, perhaps a bit nonplussed.

"But you'll get to welcome Our Lord Jesus, personally. You understand what that means. You always listen to me so carefully."

"I listen to you 'cause you're a good-looking man."

From that time on it seemed to him as if she were flirting with him, playing a grown-up woman in a way he found not so much comical as vile. The way she lifted up her skirt to fasten her shoes. Even if children were only children, it made him clench up inside.

"I had a dream about you last night," she told him after class. "You were so miserable that I woke up cryin'."

He took her hand, then dropped it.

"It's not 'cause you're good-lookin' or nothin' like that. I just want you to be happier."

She took back his hand, kissed it gently, and then, in a gesture shocking and surprising, began to lick it like a cat. The young priest pulled his hand away.

"I'm sad," he said, "because many people don't love God enough."

After she left the room, he wiped his hand on his cassock.

The impenetrable secret of peasant lives. Would he ever know anything of the world? All those people who came to confess—he couldn't understand what it was that enabled so many of them to divulge their inner lives, but only as a mere convention, some kind of formal offering without any connection to their core. "Forgive me, Father, for I have sinned." It felt to him that God, for some mysterious reason, had not allowed them seriously to offer themselves up to him. As if they were children …

What then remained of the sacrament he was offering? Confession that barely skimmed the surface of the soul? Confession bathed in dust so fine it didn't even cause a sneeze? His parish was rife with Christians without real conscience, without even consciousness of conscience. It wasn't so much mildew as petrification. So many were merely clinging to old habits, communicating in parrot speech, in formulas so worn by use as to justify everything and question nothing. Weeds take root, and good needs luck to flourish.

His chest often felt tight and occasionally hurt him when he was stressed, or when he walked the hills to visit his parishioners. Sometimes he thought the village had tied him to some cross to watch him out of curiosity, to watch him twitch, to watch him die. Most times, he thought it must be gas, or indigestion.

On July 12, 1790, the National Assembly—Guillotin included—passed the Civil Constitution of the Clergy. Little did it imagine the forces it would thus let loose. At the end of November, the Assembly voted to require all clergy to sign an oath of loyalty to that constitution, which rejected the pope's authority over the church in France.

This might not be so bad, the young priest thought. He didn't usually look to Rome for legitimation or even opinions and didn't really know what the pope thought about much of anything.

Under the Civil Constitution, he was to be paid by the state and not from tithes, which had been abolished the previous August. As a "public official," he would eventually have to be reelected as a priest by the people of his parish, as simply "a magistrate whose duty it is to maintain and carry on public worship."

In December he learned that he would be required to sign an oath. Or what? Or no more salary, no more permission to perform administrative church functions or mysterious ones, like celebrating mass—he would need state permission to turn wine to blood.

He would be cut off from his flock, toward which, although ambivalent, he was already bound by so many ties, and the flock itself would be cut off from government approval and aid.

Who better than he, so honest, so fresh, understood the insufficiency of the infinite? His people *needed* support from the secular power: Impoverished as Paris might be, his peasants were even more so. He didn't think they'd care if he swore or didn't. They rated priests according to their personal likes and dislikes, and not according to their support of the revolutionary cause.

The oath required that he "be loyal to the nation, to the law, and to the king, and uphold with all your power the Constitution decreed by the National Assembly and accepted by the king."

Father Pierre thought he could take the oath "with reservations," if necessary. He could write those reservations on an accompanying sheet, and submit them along with his signature. It wouldn't be so hard to adhere to the constitutional church.

After all, Christianity had let loose a truth that nothing could ever stop because it was already there, down in the depths of human consciousness, and humankind had instantly seen itself mirrored therein. It was invulnerable to governmental whim. God saved everyone in the blood of His son. God and the new patriots must surely have the same plan.

He could get no articulate opinion from the farmers and beggars of Conques. But from M. Messier, the town's main wine merchant, an educated, widely traveled man, he got an earful: "Don't do it, Father," the older man insisted. "This is all about stealing from the church."

"Well," the *curé* said, "the country has to get money from somewhere. The church isn't going away, no matter who owns it."

"I'm not talking about money," Messier said, "or land. I'm talking about expropriating your spiritual primacy. All the mystery gone. You, a civil employee! The 'refractory' bishops are being replaced by citizens, laymen. Do you know who is voting in these elections? Unbelievers, Protestants coming from miles away, even Jews—Jews voting who are to be our priests!"

"But the priests are still priests, they chose to be priests, were trained as priests, blessed as priests, ordained. They are not Jews and Protestants even if Jews and Protestants voted for them."

"*Naïf!* How long do you think people can revere as carriers of divine power those men they chose themselves, whom by their own votes they put into office like any mayor or tax collector?"

"The people understand that priests are the voice of God. And their voice is the voice of God."

"Last week in Paris, Father, I saw a mob sack the Church of St.-Jacques. They smashed or stole all the emblems of the Holy Truth they could reach and stuck a convicted felon's cap on a statue of Saint Paul."

"They must have wanted to sell them. They're hungry for bread. Hungry for justice and bread. Their world is like Job's, dressed in filth, covered with ulcers and sores."

"So?" the merchant asked.

"I love poverty as equal loves equal. I cannot judge them. A priest cannot judge, only forgive. We must keep God's word: 'The poor you have always with you.' It's the most melancholy utterance in the gospel, the most burdened. It implies that there will always be rich, hard, grasping men out for more possession and power. Jesus knew this. So he blessed those inevitable poor, the 'publicans and sinners,' whatever they had to do to survive—but to the rich he held up the eye of a needle."

"Grasping and hardness are not restricted to the rich, Father. The thug vomiting up his whiskey in the gutter is likely drunk with the same dreams as Caesar in his featherbed. Poverty is neither here nor there. It's an illusion. We'd do better to look at ourselves, whoever we are."

The young priest nodded. "Poverty is the emptiness in our hearts. That's why our Lord has crowned her and taken her as His bride."

"It's the *church* that is His bride. When they ransack churches, or pillage your spiritual authority, they are raping the bride of Christ. Of course," the merchant waved his hand, "if the church is just a landlord, a property-holder, a target to be taxed, if the patriots get their way . . ."

"Why not try to improve things?" the young priest countered, unconsciously raising his voice. "After eighteen centuries of Christianity, should the poor still be despised? They are the living image of Jesus there, in the front row, displaying his misery, his bloody, sweating face from which after almost eighteen hundred years no one has seen fit to wipe away the spit."

He took a deep breath and apologized for getting upset.

"Father, you should think more with your head and not so much with your heart," Messier said. "What's their plan? Get rid of poverty, that is, get rid of the *poor*, the poor man who bears witness to Jesus Christ. That is still their plan. Turn the poor into little stockholders or even into low-grade government officials. Quite the easiest mind-set to manage, the most orderly and submissive. A social utopia. *Ça ira!* Subduing half the French people to the level of cattle—the best cattle, mind you—just happens to be the price to pay for the advent of the enlightened, the supermen, the real Kingdom on earth, the new holy Word—the *Encyclopedie.*"

Father Pierre paced the floor of his study—and so did his adversary in opposite directions, an inauspicious dance.

"God made us in His image," the priest said. "But an image is not God, my friend. When we try to build a Kingdom, some social order to suit ourselves, it's bound to be a clumsy copy."

"Father Grenier," the other said, "you will not be with us long."

If the young priest was a republican, his was more the *res publica* of poverty than the bourgeois ideal of Lafayette and Mirabeau. He espoused humanity. He believed in the uprising of the poor, of the women of the humble classes, who remained deeply attached to their religion. A kiss on the lips, a lick on the hand, so what?—he was passionately fond of them.

Frock or no frock, he thought, I am the same at heart. I can serve the nation more generously than I can serve my little flock in Conques. But of Thy cross, O Lord, may I not be ashamed.

It was the sunrise of the Revolution, and Father Pierre Grenier was not afraid of the new day. But his chest hurt more, and the pain lasted longer, and it didn't go away after sitting down. At times he was tempted to finish off his life.

The Civil Constitution scattered the twenty-two churchmen of Conques, all but one of whom refused to sign the oath. The town was no longer able to cope, since these men and their organizations were crucial to the maintenance of the church, the school, the hospice and the distribution of food and clothing to the destitute. An early casualty of the Revolution, Conques did not think highly of its one juring priest or wish him well in his move to Paris.

20.

LIEBESTOD

In this time of national rebirth, deaths were starting to accumulate.

Emperor Joseph II of Austria died on February 20, 1790, and a period of official mourning closed the Viennese theaters until June. This was bad news for *Così Fan Tutte*, which had premiered at the Burgtheater three weeks earlier. Singers and musicians had been signed for the original run and were in demand elsewhere at its end. How would the producers pay them with fewer performances? Mozart was terribly unhappy. In this, his penultimate year, he was debt-ridden and penniless. But he did have connections to the court: Although relations between France and Austria were more than strained—largely because of Austria's not-so-covert support for the *emigrés* and the likelihood of an Austrian attack on the Revolution—still, "the Austrian bitch" was queen, and the queen's request for a court performance of the new work by her countryman was grudgingly honored and duly appreciated by the unemployed company. The incoming performers were vetted for bona fides and spies, and their luggage and papers were assiduously inspected.

On the evening after the court performance, the queen, in a let-them-eat-cake gesture to her antienthusiasts, permitted a smaller performance—no chorus, reduced orchestra—"for the people" at the theater in the Palais Royal, the hall in which Molière, no *malade imaginaire*, had coughed his last. Dr. Guillotin attended on opening night.

The story of *Così Fan Tutte* concerns a rather nasty bet by two Venetian young men that their beloved women will remain faithful to them no matter what. They feign departure on a mandatory military journey but return to Venice disguised as two "Albanians," each of whom undertakes to woo the lover of the other. At the end of the first act they pretend to take poison to show their devotion to the indignant, frightened, confused young women. A crafty servant, in on the plot, pretends to be a doctor who cures them using a Mesmer magnet,

> *that mesmeric stone*
> *which, come from Germany,*
> *became so famous in France.*

The revived "Albanians" beg for kisses to help them recuperate, the pitying women feel tempted, but refuse, and the act ends in a polyphonic whirlwind of tension.

Like everyone else in the audience, Guillotin was swept away by the brilliance of the music and the pressure of the plot. But his intermission, unlike that of anyone else there that night, was filled with musings and misgivings about having driven M. Mesmer from practice.

He thought of Mesmer's house, and the great room in which he had achieved his often wondrous cures. He remembered that chamber, set up like some divine temple, with its allegorical paintings, stars and planets, and horoscopical diagrams, their mystical lettering, a temple in which all the social orders converged in postrevolutionary *fraternité*. That was fine, was it not?

He pictured the magnetizing bars, the wands and tubs, the magnetized trees, the musical instruments, including Benjamin Franklin's Armonica, whose sound might stir one guest, cause rambling in another, and incite twitching, hysteria, or tears in a third. For a violinist, so curious!

Thomas Pynchon describes the sound of Franklin's invention thus: "If Chimes could whisper, if Melodies could pass away, and their souls wander the Earth . . . if Ghosts danced at Ghost Ridottoes, 'twould require such Musick, Sentiment ever held back, ever at the edge of breaking forth, in Fragments, as Glass breaks."

Guillotin, too, had been enchanted—as was Mozart himself, who that very year wrote a short adagio for Franklin's instrument. Add to this acoustic background a blend of cries, gasps, sighs, songs, groans, and even the committee had been forced to agree that this new form of practice, Mesmer's, was most seductive, requiring a great genius to produce.

Among Guillotin's ruminations floated lines from da Ponte's *Così* text: *"A face that both delights and threatens"*— was that the face of the Revolution, lit by lampposts swinging with men? *"Fate cheats mortals of their hopes."* And what would be our fate in this great undertaking, what the fate of our hopes? Would they *"plow the seas and sow the wind"*? The poisoned men reminded him of Mirabeau, of the potentially disastrous rumors that swirled around his death and still were not settled.

Just as the bell was to ring to bring the audience back to its seats, a great commotion was heard in the lobby.

"Shut the spies and traitors down!"

"Kill them all!"

The shouts penetrated the theater. The doors burst open, and upward of fifty demonstrators ran down the side aisles and up onto the stage, filling the theater with furious execrations against the Austrians and the queen. The orchestra members fled from the pit to protect their instruments while the attackers sliced the painted backdrop to shreds with swords and knives and destroyed the painted wings with axes. Who knew what was happening to the six singers in their dressing rooms?

There was bedlam in the audience, and spectators poured out any exit they could reach. Guillotin escaped with the crowd and, several blocks away into the night, saw detachments of the civil guard galloping toward the theater from two directions. Something had died here more important than Emperor Joseph II of Austria. He could not name what it was, but he understood its death to be gloomily prophetic.

In this time of national rebirths, death was beginning to smell. And a good thing, too, for Nicolas Pelletier in his wanderings. That poor man had now reached Paris and obtained a job so repulsive that even in time of starvation there were openings.

Many died daily within the walls of Paris; most had no money to be buried. The bodies of the poor were placed in huge pits, one of which was opened every six months to accommodate the latest entries. The open pits were sprinkled with lime, but in the summer months a putrid smell bathed the working-class neighborhoods surrounding them. A British visitor to Paris remarked of one such pit that "of all the places I ever saw in my life, the most shocking to mortal Pride and Vanity, [it is] the most stinking, loathsome and indecent. It is inconceivable what a stench issued from such an aggregation of mortifying and putrefying carcasses; enough to give the plague to the whole city."

Led by Dr. Guillotin, chair of the Commission on the Cemeteries, most doctors thought the pits a serious risk to public health. With no germ theory to explain the spread of disease, the commission hypothesized that "some of the diseases that afflict mankind, which corrupt their blood and product putrid fevers, arise from the fact that the air we breathe is infected with the smell of decaying bodies. Such smells can cause death." And so, five years before Nicolas Pelletier's arrival, in November 1785, the Royal Council had ordered the rotating pits exhumed and the bodies and remains removed at night to the exhausted limestone quarries out past the southern gates of the city.

Nicolas was one of the diggers and carriers helping to move an enormous volume of corpses, earth, and bones. He joined a gang of largely drunken louts— for who else could bear the work?—in digging down twelve feet into cadaverous debris, opening vaults and common graves from which over forty thousand bodies, with their coffins, were taken. They worked at night by torchlight with bonfires burning to promote the circulation of the air. They gee'd and haw'd two thousand carts of bones and stinking flesh to the quarries. They came home, reeking themselves, and threw themselves on reeking mattresses in reeking rooms and hovels to sleep away the day before nightfall.

The rise of science had come just in time for Nicolas Pelletier, and the enlightened government would now employ him—in a last chance, he thought, to escape his life. "I can't explain myself. I never went to school. I'm just a poor man, a creature as God created it," he told his colleagues. "I wear a coat and pants. What is everybody after me for? My only fault is that I am too much like a human being. But all these smells might turn even me into a wise man." They laughed at the dumb ox—but he could outdrink them all.

They didn't laugh when he told them about the ghosts he'd seen rising up with the smoke of the fuming earth, or when he imitated the noises they made, even if the others couldn't hear them.

"What do they say?" one asked.

"They say this place is cursed. Listen . . . can you hear them? They say, 'We rise up over a field of corpses, and we look up at the stars, and we say that life is good.'"

In the tense quiet, several broke out in nervous laughter. They rolled their eyes and pointed fingers at their heads.

Pelletier sniffed the air like a bloodhound.

On March 16 the National Assembly officially abolished the *lettres de cachet*: "Arbitrary orders resulting in exile and all other orders of the same nature, as well as all *lettres de cachet* are abolished, and none will be issued in the future. Those who were affected are free to remove themselves to whatever place they deem suitable."

And thus, on Good Friday, April 2, 1790, the Marquis de Sade walked out through the gates of the Charenton Asylum for the Insane, where he had been transferred from the Bastille as incorrigible.

Two weeks later Benjamin Franklin died in Philadelphia. Like Mirabeau's, his funeral attracted the largest crowd of mourners his own city had ever seen. Paris, too, wept. The National Assembly decreed a three-day period of mourning.

Guillotin used his time to walk the city and think. What kind of a city is this? he thought as he passed by corpses fished out of the Seine and hung by their feet along the riverbank to dry. Each day he had to clean his shoes of the blood coursing through the streets. Out at the Porte St.-Denis his ears were attacked by the agonizing cry of a young steer thrown to the ground, its horns tied down, a heavy mallet used to break its skull and a huge knife plunged deep into its throat. On that cool April morning, bloodstained arms plunged into its smoking entrails and its body was hacked apart like Damiens's and hung up for sale. Guillotin, himself a surgeon, watched in horror and fascination.

The "cattle hall," the death tribunal, animals smelling you-won't-get-out-of-here-alive, bloodstained men swinging sledges and hatchets. Hogs 11,543, beef 2,016, calves 920, mutton 14,450. A bang, a blow, and down they go. Hogs, oxen, calves—the dying of animals. Now the twitching stops. Now they are still. Physiology and theology are done; now chemistry and physics begin. There was no reason for passersby to concern themselves.

But what happened then was truly unnerving: The next steer in line, dazed but not killed by the first hammer blow, broke its ropes and fled furiously through the early-morning crowd. The butchers chasing their escaped victim were equally dangerous, fierce and bloody, with their beefy arms and swollen necks, their legs covered in gore. They carried massive clubs and were ready for any fight, the blood they had already spilled inflaming their tempers. Guillotin thought he might prefer to be gored.

The chase disappeared around a corner, out of sight. In the street a dreadful odor hung heavy, and fat prostitutes sat and aired their thighs in the morning sun.

In spite of everything, the month of June had come to Paris, and in that year of 1790 the city was divided into forty-eight sections and the Hôtel de Ville was superseded by a new form of popular government: the Commune of the Paris Sections.

There was scuttlebutt in the Palais Royal that the king was planning to flee France by assuming masked disguises or by digging a secret canal to St.-Cloud, to the west of the city.

On November 27, the constitutional oath was imposed on clergy, and the first religious riots broke out in Pelletier's Vendée, bringing the first religious murders of the Revolution.

After a hard winter and a spring of disastrous flooding, in June the National Assembly approved a law providing that "every person condemned to the death penalty shall have his head severed."

21.

THE LION ROARS NO MORE

The giant Mirabeau was dying—this was obvious to his physician, friend, and fellow delegate from the Paris section, Joseph Guillotin. Honoré Gabriel Riqueti, Comte de Mirabeau. The great baritone voice had changed to a chesty growl. His face was often white, greasy with sweat, and his frizzy hair hung lank with sickness. He seemed a phantom of his former self. "When I am gone," he told the good doctor, "they will realize what I was worth." They—his opponents in the National Assembly.

In spite of his worsening health, Mirabeau threw himself full force into the Assembly's great debates and contestations, and he raised his growl concerning the Civil Constitution of the Clergy. "If the Assembly thinks the resignation of twenty thousand *curés* will have no effect on the kingdom, it must be looking through queer spectacles. Their persecution will turn the faithful against the Revolution." He denounced the creation of a religious schism alongside a political one and described the practical problems that would arise if thousands of priests chose to resign rather than submit to the decree. The Assembly, he argued, had no right to force the clergy to take the oath. Any priest who refused it should be considered simply as having sent in his resignation without incurring any other sanction.

"A moderate," some hissed, and cursed his terrible head.

"I am not afraid of unwashed mobs outside the doors," he said, "or of the washed mobs within."

He had, for a while, shown signs of chronic ill health—recurrent swelling of the legs, rheumatic pain in his arms and chest, and daily intestinal disturbances. Before the Assembly had moved to Paris, Mirabeau had been more active—walking, riding, and swimming—but in the city there were few opportunities for exercise, and this most robust of men now seemed susceptible to the slightest thing. Political and physical frustration brought on fits of depression. He brooded on death and knew he would not live to complete his work.

But he threw himself into Assembly fights on mine ownership, on education, on the death penalty, concerning the extradition of criminals, freedom of travel, and the structure of any future regency. He fought for equal rights of inheritance, regardless of sex or primogeniture, and was passionately concerned with the welfare of the old and needy and the necessity for state-assisted pensions. Thereto, he proposed that every deputy should have five days' pay deducted from his salary to be deposited in a pension fund for the poor. This was not a popular measure and was quickly voted down.

The most devastating of his trials was his going blind from ophthalmia, a severe, chronic, agonizing inflammation of the eyes. He would go for leech bleeds between afternoon and evening sessions of the Assembly and return bandaged to stanch the flow of blood. The linen around his neck was red. As he mounted the podium, Guillotin watched him with concern: He had never seen a sick man so obviously forecasting his death.

On Sunday, March 26, 1791, the great man fainted at an after-theater party in the company, it was said, of two young actresses. Helped to his home in the Chaussée d'Antin, by the next morning he was feeling better—well enough to visit the theater again that night. But as he sat at the show, his chest and abdominal pain returned so badly as to force him to leave. He couldn't find his carriage, insisted on walking, and though breathing with difficulty, afraid of creating a scene, refused to rest at a café until his carriage could be found and brought. By the time he arrived home, he was groaning with pain and sent for his physician, the young Pierre Cabanis, an enthusiastic revolutionary replacement for the famous Bagnières, who had nearly killed his patient in '88 when Mirabeau had caught cholera: twenty-two basinfuls of blood in two days was more than even that giant could spare.

Arriving at the house, Cabanis found him prostrate on his bed, coughing up blood. Just what was wrong the young doctor didn't know. Like everyone else, he tended to blame Mirabeau's libidinous lifestyle and sybaritic habits—intensified, of course, by overwork—for his failing health. His patient's debauched and recklessly gorgeous life repulsed him, and dazzled him, too. Was this the first acute strike of sexual disease?

The patient's own diagnosis: "If I believed in slow poisons, I should have no doubt that I have been poisoned. I feel myself wasting away, being consumed by a smoldering fire."

Cabanis bled him and bathed him in cool water, and the patient then felt well enough to continue a political discussion broken off several days earlier.

"The people have been promised more than can be promised," he alleged. "They have been given hopes it will be impossible to realize."

It is hard not to see the parallel with his medical condition, and his doctors' pledges to cure it.

By that Tuesday evening Mirabeau was able to discourse on the pleasure of returning from the edge of the grave, but during the night the symptoms returned and would not respond to the remedies of the previous day. Cabanis gave purgatives to clear the stomach and bowels—with some success, according to his notes—though the great man's pulse continued to fluctuate wildly, his shooting chest pain was increasing, and his breathing became ever more constricted. The young doctor applied leeches.

The next evening, Wednesday, Mirabeau's condition was judged "reasonable." The blistering agents Cabanis had tried seemed to have taken effect, the breathing passages were open, and the pulse was steady and unremarkable. But at midnight there were signs of an approaching crisis. Mirabeau's pulse was racing, and he breathed with great difficulty. At daybreak early Thursday morning the pain was unbearable, accompanied by whole-body spasms and a feeling of suffocation with its terrifying emotional side effects. The upcoming day would be a cruel one.

The young doctor panicked. Who was *he* to have the sole responsibility of treating a national idol in this acute state? He didn't know enough. He didn't know what was really going on. He didn't know *anything*. None of his treatments had gotten to the underlying cause, whatever it was. Rumors of poisoning were circulating, and if that were true, and it were proven to be true, and if he had failed to realize it and treat for it, his career was finished.

It was time for a second opinion. More than a second opinion. It was time for Mirabeau's medical reports to be signed "we"—"We feel that . . . ," "We administered. . . ." He needed full-time, responsible, share-the-glory-share-the-blame help. At the risk of having his incompetence exposed, he called on one of the leading physicians of Paris, acclaimed doctor of the poor as well as the nobility, Mirabeau's colleague of the Paris section of the National Assembly, Dr. Joseph-Ignace Guillotin.

And Guillotin was there for him. When he arrived, Mirabeau's spasms and pain were rapidly increasing, and the two doctors decided to repeat the bleeding from the foot, to apply blistering plasters to the legs and thighs, and to administer six grains of the stimulant musk every half hour up to thirty or forty grains. Musk is also an antispasmodic. Despite all this, Mirabeau's condition remained dire.

The modern reader might well wonder why these two practitioners, young and old, freshly trained and widely experienced, had only such gross—and, to us, bizarre—methods to call upon. A short digression on the state of medical knowledge in 1790s Europe might be advisable, lest these two worthies seem like bumblers.

Until well into the nineteenth century, medical practice was firmly anchored in Galenic theory. Galen, the Greek physician, anatomist, physiologist, philosopher, and lexicographer, was surely the most influential physician of all time. Physician to Marcus Aurelius, he adopted Hippocrates' notion that the balance of four humors was essential to the health of the body, with heat playing a central role. Any sickness—such as fever or inflammation—that caused the patient's skin to become red must arise from too much blood in the body. Similarly, any person—like Mirabeau—whose behavior was boisterous and "sanguine" was thought to be suffering from an excess of blood. Over the centuries, bloodletting was used to relieve pain, difficulty in breathing, and high temperature.

Well after the promulgation of the germ theory of disease, many physicians regarded bleeding as the appropriate treatment for almost every affliction, including hemorrhage and fatigue. Our own Benjamin Rush, signer of the Declaration of Independence, physician, patriot, and humanitarian, a man in many ways resembling Dr. Guillotin, and the epitome of the versatile, wide-ranging physician in America, a doctor who insisted on a theoretical structure for medical practice, Benjamin Rush in 1790 advised his students, "There is but one disease in the world, a morbid excitement induced by capillary tension, and it has one remedy—to deplete the body by letting blood with the lancet and emptying out the stomach and bowels with the use of powerful emetics and cathartics." Great skill was needed to determine how much blood should be taken, which vein should be cut, or how many leeches were to be applied, and when.

For these doctors, there was much proof that nature prevented disease by discharging excess blood.

Women, for instance, because of their menstruation and lactation, were immune to many of the diseases that afflicted men—gout, arthritis, epilepsy, apoplexy, and melancholy, for example—and men with hemorrhoids or frequent copious nosebleeds were noted to be similarly immune. In terms of Galenic humoral theory, bleeding rid the body of its toxic, putrid, or corrupt elements. Thus, what Cabanis and Guillotin brought to their patient, likely dying from purulent pericarditis, was not a course of life-saving, yet-to-be-discovered antibiotics but rather a complex medley of bleeding, purging, cupping, blistering, and, if possible, starvation diet.

These remedies were to be used with courage.

The doctors reported that from Thursday, March 30, 1791, on, Mirabeau's appearance "took on an aspect which it never lost thereafter; it was that of death, but of a death full of life, if one can use that expression. Despite the improvement in the pulse, the lessening of the breathlessness and spasm, we found it impossible to think any more of him as living. He himself felt that he no longer existed. And our assistants remarked that from then on we spoke about his life in the past tense, and about him as one who had been but was no longer alive."

Guillotin and Cabanis agreed that at the very least, their patient was suffering from an "intermittent, malignant fever," and they administered quinine, "at first in a weak dose, in combination with gentle laxatives; next in a very strong dose."

There was no improvement.

For four days Mirabeau was constantly purged and bled. As a result, his pulse was almost imperceptible, and his arms and hands were icy, though he could still move them. His breathing weakened minute by minute. When he asked for a frank statement of his chances, they told him they might be able to save him but "could not guarantee it."

Crowds packed the Chaussée d'Antin outside his house, number 42. "It was glorious to dedicate my life to them," Mirabeau said. "It is good to die in their midst."

At dawn on Saturday, April 2, he was too tired to speak and made a sign that the doctors should fetch writing materials. He wrote one word: *dormir*—to sleep. When Cabanis did not respond as he desired, he wrote sarcastically, "Don't you think that the death which is approaching me might have some dangerous effects?"

When later in the morning he regained the strength to speak, he said, "My friends, I will die today. When one has come to that, all one can do is be perfumed, crowned with flowers, enveloped in music, and wait comfortably for the sleep from which one will never wake." But by the time Guillotin sent a messenger to the apothecary Mirabeau was in agony. It was 8 in the morning. He reproached his doctors for not keeping their promise to spare him such pain. "Ah, doctors, doctors!" he murmured. At 8:30 he died. His last words: "More opium . . ."

Regardless of the ample autopsy results, many Parisians thought his death to have resulted from a Saturday orgy the week before. Such is the medical thinking of the crowd. A note in Guillotin's diary is relevant in this regard: "His passion for women was to some extent involuntary, or rather, entirely physical, the effect of a congenital form of satyriasis which tormented him all his life and still showed several hours after his death—a strange fact, certainly, but true."

All of Paris turned out for Mirabeau's funeral, and it was for him that the Church of Ste.-Geneviève was converted into the Panthéon, a burial place for the greatest of Frenchmen. But in 1792 a cache of secret letters from Mirabeau to the king and queen was discovered in an iron chest in the Tuileries Palace. In his machinations to create a constitutional monarchy, he had secretly colluded with the Court, entered its pay, and dispatched to Louis and Marie-Antoinette a series of advisory notes concerning how best to handle and limit the work of the National Assembly.

On September 21, 1794, so as not to pollute the

resting place of the recently murdered Marat, his remains were removed from his casket by order of the Convention and carried by night, without form or ceremony, to the graveyard of Clamart, the burial ground for those killed by execution. No stone marked his whereabouts. A nineteenth-century attempt to find the giant's bones was unsuccessful.

22.

UNFORTUNATE ENCOUNTERS

Five months after arriving in Paris, his soul smelling of corpses and brandy, Nicolas Pelletier was putting away a little money for the first time in his life. He had moved into a room near the Palais Royal—near, too, to the centers of gambling and prostitution, an underworld of uncertain borders. He had a night job. It gave him money. He thought to get a day job, too. He would make more money. He would buy clean clothes and get a girl.

But who would hire this odd-looking, odd-thinking, odd-speaking man? He didn't look honest enough to run errands. He was too frightening to work in stores with customers. The Parisian workshops were tied up in craft-guild schemes of apprentices, journeymen, and masters, sticking hard by the rules of sclerotic corporations and wary of scabs and competition. Besides, he had no working papers or letters of commendation.

When the weather was good, he hung out on the Champs Élysées, another amusing oddity among the conjurers, jugglers, sword-swallowers, tightrope walkers, palmists, and hucksters who plied their trades in the booths and tents that populated this frontier zone of the capital, in its gardens and in undergrowth off the wide paths. Could he be a pickpocket? Not with those great hands.

One warmish evening in mid-October, he thought he saw his daughter, little Armelle, last seen at twelve and not so little at eighteen or nineteen. She was beautiful, thrillingly beautiful to his vague eyes, as beautiful as her mother was when Nicolas had first seen her at M. Auret's. She was her mother's ghost arisen before him. But . . . she was calling out to men, hissing at them, approaching them, one after another. He ran toward her, then walked, and closer saw her broken teeth, her patched and muddy dress, her dirty cap, a scar or burn above her featured bosom.

"Armelle," he called.

She didn't answer.

"Armelle, it's me, Papa!"

She eyed the huge man approaching her with thick neck and outstretched paw.

"You ain't my papa," she countered. "He's deader'n a nail in a coffin."

"But I'm not dead, God loves us and . . ."

"And you ain't him." She looked the mark over.

"An' I ain't Armelle, neither. I'm Fanchon, Fanchon la Gaillardise. You wanna take a walk with me?" She took his arm and led him toward a trysting spot she knew— for dogs—in the bushes.

He was walking in the Champs Élysées, walking with a beautiful young girl! He could feel the side of her breast pressing through his coat against his muscled arm. Maybe she would like him.

"You have nice hair," he said. "Can I touch it?"

"Sure. Just be gentle with those big, dirty grabbers of yours. You got any cash?"

He searched his pockets.

"Yes, I do. Lots." And he may have meant it, for he had just been paid for a week of exhumations.

"How much?" Fanchon asked.

"Yeah, how much money does pretty boy here have?" added a voice from behind them. "How much money for the lovely, dirty girl?"

Two elegant young men in silk jackets had come up from the rear on this semiwild path in Elysium. They carried swords and moved alongside the couple, one to Pelletier's left, the other to Fanchon's right. They stopped when the couple stopped and moved on when they did, keeping pace with them, occasionally jostling them, sidling closer and closer, poking Pelletier in the arm and tripping Fanchon with their feet.

"What will it take to annoy you, sir, madame?"

The couple looked stolidly ahead, trying to avoid

a confrontation. Pelletier might be able to handle one, possibly even two, but they had weapons, and what if one grabbed his new friend? Better to wait things out.

After a few more yards, with the four still walking abreast, one of the young men, picking up a dog turd with the end of his swagger stick, lifted the offering to Pelletier's nose. "Will this annoy you, sir?" he asked as his friend guffawed.

Nicolas broke away from the girl, scooped up a heavy stick lying by the path, and began to beat at the pair with it. One fled, along with Fanchon, while the other was caught by a great blow to the side of his head and fell with his face in the mud. Nicolas the Ox watched the brown turn red, watched him twitch twice and then move no more as chemistry and physics began.

It had grown dark. No one had seen, he thought, and no one had heard or they would have come running. He grabbed a pouch drooping at his victim's side. There was something in it. Money, he thought, I found more money. And he walked quickly, farther to the west, toward the Bois de Boulogne, where he spent the night.

Early in November, having gone into hiding, having disappeared from his cemetery job, having moved into a slum dwelling near the Hôtel de Ville, now sharing a room with twenty others sleeping in shifts, he was arrested one midday in bed and imprisoned in the

Conciergerie. Fanchon had turned him in for a small, but necessary, reward.

Two days later, by final verdict of the third provisional criminal assizes, Nicolas Jacques Pelletier was declared "guilty in fact and in law of attacking, on the 14th of October 1791, toward 9:00 P.M., on an unnamed path of the Champs Élysées, an individual whom he beat to death with a cudgel, and of having stolen from him a wallet containing 800 livres in assignats, in reparation for which, he is sentenced by the court to be conducted, dressed in a red shirt, to the place de Grève, and there to be executed in conformity with the provisions of the Penal Code."

The following month, on December 5, 1791, Wolfgang Amadeus Mozart died, probably of typhoid. It is a legitimate question which death would be more significant.

23.

THE AGE DEMANDED . . .

. . . an image
Of its accelerated grimace.
Something for the modern stage,
Not, at any rate, an Attic grace.

—Ezra Pound

"But *foutromanie*, my dear doctor, *foutromanie* is all the rage."

The Marquis de Sade and his onetime physician Guillotin were drinking Bordeaux at the Café Le Grand Véfour in the Palais Royal.

"Pornography is *à la mode* and meeting with unheard-of favor. Sex has never sold so well. Please, allow me to pay! The streets are flooded with the filthiest of pamphlets, our presses are endlessly restocking the locked rooms with '*curiosa.*' People are wild for lascivious scenes and lubricious bodies. I can't find debauches outrageous enough, lovemaking furious enough, or perversions new enough to slake the public appetite. And mind you, M. le Delegate from Paris, that the erotic and the political have never meshed so tightly. Those pamphlets mocking our king's impotence, our queen's 'uterine furies,' the pederastic Jesuits . . . the public is not mincing words these days."

Forty minutes earlier the doctor had followed the playwright out of the Théâtre Molière from an abbreviated opening of *Oxtiern*, Citoyen Sade's first production. The risk of being branded an ex-nobleman, a *"ci-devant,"* was now too threatening, and Donatien-Alphonse-François had had decided to get his first job, to become a working man, a working literary man, a working public literary man. His pornographic output was bringing in much money, but such an achievement did not fit the image of the robust new patriot, the embodiment of cleanliness and health.

This best laid of plans, his appearance as a respectable "classical" playwright, had alarmingly backfired. The language of the play conjured up memories of the *ancien régime.* The second balcony crowd began to yell, "End it! Enough, enough!" The first balcony crowd: "Sanctimonious hypocrite!" The orchestra swells grumbled quietly among themselves concerning the pious sentiments and reassuring platitudes. Too respectable Sade had become.

The actors soldiered on as the atmosphere grew more tumultuous. Guillotin feared another *Così Fan*

Tutte. And he wasn't far from wrong. One spectator stood up and yelled in a huge Mirabeavian voice, "Lower the curtain!" One of the stagehands felt called upon to obey this unexpected order, and did so. The more proper half of the audience then shouted down the protester and called for his ejection from the theater. But when the curtain was raised the other half of the audience shouted for it to be lowered again. A terrible row broke out between partisans for and adversaries of the play. The guard and the constable were called for public safety. The hubbub grew steadily louder as the play progressed. And then—yes, *Così* encore: A band of patriots wearing curious red wool caps with forward-curving peaks burst into the theater, and Parisians took their first gander at the new "Phrygian bonnet." One of the revolutionaries climbed onto the stage and shouted at the public, "Citizens! All patriots must now rally behind the red bonnet. The friends of liberty will fight plays by aristocrats in every theater!" They broke into *Ça ira!* and were joined by half the audience. The author fled the theater, followed by Guillotin.

"All right, then, '*foutromanie.*'" The good doctor forced himself to pronounce the word but preserved the quotation marks in his intonation. "So why then such stiffness in your play?"

"M. le Docteur, I am fifty years old. I weigh three hundred pounds. I suffer from wheezing, eye aches, stomachaches, headaches, rheumatisms, and I don't know what else. All this wears me down and does not, thank God, allow me to think of anything else, and I am four times happier as a result. All this fuckomania disgusts me now as much as it used to set me on fire. I denounce this avalanche of obscenity. None of it is worthy of interest—these miserable brochures, scribbled in cafés or bordellos—what do they prove? Only the vacancy in the minds of their authors."

"But I hear that your *Justine*, for instance, is . . ."

"Lust, my friend, is the daughter of opulence and superiority. It cannot be treated except by people of a certain stamp, individuals blessed by nature to begin with, who are also sufficiently blessed by fortune to have *themselves* tried what they trace for us with their lustful pens. This is quite beyond the reach of the rogues who are flooding us with the contemptible brochures and ambient vulgarity I am speaking of."

"You seem sad," the doctor said. "Sadder than at the Bastille."

The playwright twirled his wineglass in his white, pudgy hands.

"I have lost my taste for everything. Nothing pleases me. This outside world that I was insane enough to miss so intensely does seem sad—and boring. At times I am seized by a desire to become a monk, and perhaps one fine day I may disappear, never to be heard of again. Never have I been as misanthropic as I have

THE GOOD DOCTOR GUILLOTIN

become since returning to the society of men, and if I seem strange to them, they can be sure that they have the same effect on me. Let us drink to that symmetrical association."

Guillotin reluctantly raised his glass to Sade's.

"However," Sade declaimed in the middle of a gulp, "back to fuckomania. Liberty! Equality! We need a language that will allow equal dignity for words as well as for men. Why should any single word will be vile? *Foutromanie*, dear doctor—say it. Say it!"

Guillotin whispered it into his wineglass, mentally apologizing to his wife and mother as he did so.

"There are sexual origins for all our revolutionary symbols. The tree of liberty is the phallic symbol of the Egyptian cult of Osiris—carried thence to Greece and Rome. That red Phrygian bonnet of liberty which debuted tonight shouts clearly the head of the phallus."

He was getting drunker by the minute.

"And you know what? The least blessed, most hidden fact that needy mortals have ever hidden from themselves is the primitive one of cannibalism: *I* can devour *thee*. And the only way the state can really form free citizens—besides overcoming royal and religious tyranny—is to allow the natural lusts of man free play. Long live incest!"

He clinked his glass against Guillotin's on the table.

"Long live rape and sodomy, pederasty and murder!"

He clinked again.

"Yes. And therefore murder is not the job of an official, passionless executioner. Murder needs passion! Murder may be a horror, but it is never criminal. The state must tolerate it, not punish it. Passion. Vengeance. That's what makes us free. Let us rely on the vengeance of family and friends of the victim. Their passion. Their vengeance. It is only for want of the creative spirit that we do not go far enough in suffering."

"Sounds to me like a war of all against all," the doctor remarked.

"Perhaps. But preferable to the war of the *state* against all. The storming of the Bastille I called for was nothing but the drunkenness of slaves, carnivorous rabble in a whirligig of rags, precursors of storm and destruction. And the Revolution will no doubt become a staging ground for demagogues. But what is this other than the great script of Nature? I will take great delight in communing with her in the paroxysms of her implacable will."

"What do you think those drunken slaves might feel?"

"Ah, the slaves, 'the people,' as some generously call them, or 'the rabble.' We've got twenty-five million of 'the masses'—some artificially conceived unity, monstrous but dim. But far more dangerous, my friend, is the rabble of language and thought rising up among us—here and in the Assembly and at the Court—glibness which is the devil's *materia prima* from which all falsehoods, imbecilities, and abominations embody themselves, from which no true thing can come. Beware of your mouth, my dear doctor, lest your victims be thought of as your patients. Let the government be one of terror or of joy. In this Paris there are twenty-three theaters nightly; some count as many as sixty places of dancing. . . ."

The fat man shuffled his feet under the table as if to dance the carmagnole.

"I am the Revolution. . . ." he murmured.

And then the Revolution fell asleep, its head slumping down onto the tablecloth.

24.

ON THE METHOD OF
DECAPITATION

Russia had abolished the death penalty in 1754, Tuscany in 1786, Austria in 1787. But although abolition had excited much talk in French intellectual circles, no action had been taken. Robespierre's speech against capital punishment, while admired for its "philosophical sensitivity," was dismissed by both the right-wing *Journal of Louis XVI* and Marat's rabble-rousing *L'Ami du peuple*.

This, from the *Journal*:

> *The democrat, Robespierre, spoke at length against the death penalty, which he considers unworthy of a free people. His discourse is the merest philosophy, supported by some historical examples, but is without political sense and has still less the profundity that characterizes the able legislator.*

And here is Marat:

The Assembly rightly decreed, although to no avail, that the death penalty should be reserved for the gravest crimes: on this question M. Robespierre set out an opinion which does great honor to his sensitivity, but is attended by drawbacks too serious to be adopted. Society's right to inflict the death penalty derives from the same source as the right of every individual to inflict death, that is, the need to defend one's own life. Now, if each penalty is to be commensurate with the crime, the punishment for murder and poisoning must be capital, and a fortiori, *that for conspiracy and arson.*

Evidently, the time was not ripe for abolition.

The articles of Guillotin's bill that had passed the National Assembly back on January 21, 1790, had excluded considerations of rank in assigning punishment, abolished confiscation of goods, and allowed the condemned's family to take possession of the body. Because of bureaucratic delays and more pressing issues, further debate on the death penalty had been postponed to more than a year later, when, on May 30, 1791, the Assembly decided to continue it. On the 3rd of June, as noted, it determined that all persons sentenced to death would be decapitated. "All persons" . . . this stipulation meant a huge increase in the demand for such doings.

It took another four months for a committee to be formed to investigate application of the law, and that committee then consulted the civil servant responsible for its enforcement, Charles-Henri Sanson, the executioner of Paris, whose professional opinion was considered essential. His response, yet five months later, is worth quoting at length.

> *For the execution to arrive at the result prescribed by the law, the executioner must, with no impediment on the part of the condemned man, be very skillful, and the condemned man very steadfast; otherwise it will be impossible to carry out an execution by sword without dangerous scenes resulting.*
>
> *The sword is not fit to perform a second execution after the first. The blade is liable to chip, and must absolutely be reground and sharpened again. Were there several executions to perform at one time, it would be necessary to have a sufficient number of swords, all of them ready prepared. It should also be noted that swords have often been broken during executions of this kind. The Paris executioner has only two, which were given to him by the former Parlement de Paris. They cost 6 livres each.*
>
> *A further consideration is that, when there are several condemned men to execute at once, the terror of the execution, caused by the vast quantities of*

blood, will bring terror and faintness to the hearts of even the most intrepid of those to be executed. This faintness will prove an invincible obstacle in the way of execution, as the persons will be unable to hold themselves still. If the attempt is made to proceed despite this, the execution will become a struggle or a massacre. Yet it seems that the National Assembly only decided on this method of execution in order to avoid the long-drawn-out methods previously in use.

To judge by executions of another kind—which do not require anything like the same degree of precision—the condemned have been known to be taken ill at the sight of their executed accomplices, and, at least, to feel unsteady or fearful: All this is an argument against an execution in which the head is decapitated by sword. How indeed should a person tolerate the sight of the bloodiest form of execution without feeling faint? With the other forms of execution, it was easy to hide this faintness from the public, because they could be carried out without the condemned man having to remain steadfast and fearless; but, with this form, if the condemned man flinches, the execution will fail. How can one deal with a man who cannot or will not hold himself up?

With regard to these humane considerations, I am bound to issue a warning as to the accidents that will occur if this execution is to be performed with the

ALLONS, ENFANTS DE LA PATRIE

sword. It would, I think, be too late to remedy these accidents if they were known only from bitter experience. It is therefore indispensable, if the humane views of the National Assembly are to be fulfilled, to find some means by which the condemned man can be secured so that the issue of the execution cannot be in doubt, and in this way to avoid delay and uncertainty.

This would fulfill the intentions of the legislators and ensure that no breach of public order occurred.

Monsieur de Paris knew whereof he spoke. Not only was he often incompetent in hanging people, but his recollection of the Lally-Tollendal decapitation trauma, and his father's humiliating rescue, made his hand shake even as he penned his response.

Here was the paradox: The application of a universal, egalitarian penalty—at least in Sanson's hands—might very well lead to horrific and most unequal consequences. Given his history, his arguments were persuasive, and the Assembly's *procureur général syndic* Roederer asked Delegate Dr. Guillotin to "soften a punishment of which the law had not intended to make a cruel ordeal." After the "coolness on the back of the neck" ridicule of 1789, the good doctor was leery of prescribing any further, at least unsupported, and he and Roederer asked the advice of Dr. Antoine Louis, permanent secretary of the Academy of Surgery.

Louis responded quickly with his "Requested Advice on the Method of Decapitation," again a document worth pondering—especially for its language.

> *The Legislative Committee has been kind enough to consult me about two letters written to the National Assembly concerning article 3 of the first title of the Penal Code, which stipulates that all those condemned to death shall have their heads cut off. On the basis of these letters, the minister of Justice and the director of the département of Paris, subsequent to the representations that have been made to them, are of the view that it is necessary to determine immediately and precisely how to proceed with the application of the law. They fear that if, by a defect of the means employed, or through inexperience, or through clumsiness, the execution became horrible for the condemned man and for the spectators, the people might have occasion to be unjust and cruel toward the executioner, a thing it is important to prevent.*
>
> *In my opinion, these representations are correct and their fears justified. Experience and reason both show that the method previously used to cut off the head of a criminal expose him to a death much worse than the simple privation of life with is the formal requirement of the law, and which, in order to be achieved, requires that the execution be the instanta-*

neous effect of a single blow. Examples show how difficult it is to attain this.

It should be remembered at this stage what occurred during the execution of Lally. He was kneeling and blindfolded. The executioner struck him on the back of the neck. The blow did not separate the head from the body, nor could it have done so. Nothing now prevented the body from falling. It toppled forward, and the head was finally separated from the body by four or five saber blows. This hacking, if we may use the term, was witnessed with horror.

In Germany, the executioners are more experienced owing to the frequency with which this form of dispatch is used; it is the only form of execution for persons of the female sex, whatever their status. Yet a perfect execution is rare, despite the precaution, taken in certain places, of fastening the seated victim to an armchair.

In Denmark, there are two positions and two instruments used for decapitation. What one might call the honorific execution is performed with the saber. The criminal is blindfolded and kneeling; his hands are free. If the execution is to be ignominious, the patient's hands are tied and he lies prone beneath the axe.

It is well known that cutting instruments have little or no effect if the stroke is perpendicular. When examined under the microscope, they are seen to be saw-blades of greater or lesser thickness, which can operate only by sliding across the body they are intended to cut. It would be impossible to decapitate with a single blow from an axe or cutter whose blade was straight; but with a convex blade, as on the old-style battleaxe, the blow is perpendicular in effect only at the center section of the circle; but the instrument, as it penetrates further into the parts it divides, acts obliquely on each side and attains the goal with certainty.

If we consider the structure of the neck, the center of which is the spinal column, we note that it is composed of several bones which overlap at their junctures, so that there is no joint to be found. It is not therefore possible to guarantee immediate and complete separation if this task is to be confided to an agent whose dexterity may be affected by moral and physical causes. If the procedure is to be infallible, it must needs be carried out by invariable mechanical means, whose force and effects we can also establish. This is the course adopted in England. The criminal's body is laid prone between two uprights surmounted by a crosspiece from which the convex axe is made to fall onto the neck by means of a trigger. The back of the device must be sufficiently strong and heavy to act efficiently in the manner of a drop-hammer driving piles. It is well known that the force increases with the height from which it falls.

A machine of this kind is easy to construct and is infallibly effective; decapitation would instantly ensue, in keeping with the spirit and demands of the new law. It would be easy to test it on corpses, and even on a live sheep. We will see whether it is necessary to fix the patient's head by a crescent which would grip the neck at the base of the skull. The extensions of the crescent could be fixed by cotters under the scaffold. This piece of apparatus, if it proved necessary, would not cause the least sensation and would scarcely be noticeable.

Consulted at Paris, the 7th of March, 1792.

Dr. Antoine Louis, dean of an enlightened medicine allied with technology, thoughtful of his "patients."

And then a decree that would entitle the otherwise nameless Nicolas Jacques Pelletier to go down in history:

20 March 1792. Decree of emergency. The National Assembly, considering that the uncertainty as to the method of execution of article 3 of the first title of the Penal Code suspends the punishment of several criminals who have been sentenced to death; that it is necessary that these uncertainties be speedily resolved, as they may otherwise give rise to seditious movements;

that humanity requires that the death penalty be as painless as possible in its application, degrees and emergency.

    Definitive decree. The National Assembly, having decreed an emergency, decrees that article 3 of the first title of the Penal Code shall be applied in the manner specified and the method adopted in the consultative document signed by the Permanent Secretary of the Academy of Surgery, which is to be annexed to this decree. The Assembly consequently authorizes the executive to make whatever expense is necessary to implement this method of execution and to ensure that it is uniform throughout the country.

And so, first in line for execution, Pelletier had to wait, and wait, for the means of his death to be constructed.

25.

CONJECTURES CONCERNING
RECEPTION

Five paths converging at a place, and that place is the scaffold. Five roads to this engorging center, and five ways of the five men upon them.

None of the five read or spoke Norwegian. None of them was alive when *"Guten og Fanden"* was published in a folktale collection in the 1840s. Their mothers or nurses did not tell them about "The Boy and the Devil." It went like this:

Once upon a time there was a clever boy named Per, who was gathering chestnuts along the road and found a beauty—with a worm-hole in it. Curious as ever, he thought he'd take it home to find the worm and see what it might look like. So he put it in his pocket. And on the way, he met the devil.

Curious as ever, Per asked, "Is it true you can make yourself as small as you want, and even go through the eye of a needle?"

"*Of course,*" said the devil. "*I can do anything,*" which, of course, he can.

"*Could you even creep into . . .*"—Per pulled the chestnut from his pocket—"*this nut? Right through this tiny hole?*"

"*Nothing easier,*" said the devil, and whoosh, he did it. A little voice from inside said, "*See?*"

Curious as ever, and also smart, Per said, "*Neat trick,*" and clamped his toothpick into the hole: the boy had captured the devil. Interesting.

He brought the nut to his friend, Henrik the Smith, and, curious as ever, said, "*I've got the devil trapped in this nut. What shall we do with him?*"

"*'Let's smash him to bits,*" said Henrik, his hammer already in hand.

"*'OK,*" said Per. Smashing—they both liked that.

So Henrik the Smith laid the nut on the anvil and gave it a good, nut-sized whack—but it didn't break. He hit it harder—still nothing. Bigger hammer, bigger blow. Still nothing.

"*'My goodness,*" said the smith, "*I never saw anything like that.*"

The goal of killing the devil was entirely forgotten. This had become a contest of mighty Henrik versus the hardened world. He grabbed the biggest sledgehammer from the wall and gave the nut a blow that would kill an elephant. It shattered the chestnut in a thousand pieces, and he, and Per, and the worm, and the whole smithy were destroyed in the explosion. Only the sledgehammer was left. And the chortling devil.

Five is the number of the men.

- There was Nicolas Jacques Pelletier, first patient; profession, brigand; role: Body. What might have been his childhood thoughts about the story? Or his thoughts right now?

- There was Dr. Joseph-Ignace Guillotin, professor at the Faculté de Medicine, Parisian delegate to the National Assembly; role: Head. Would he have thought this through better?

- There was Charles-Henri Sanson, the public executioner of Paris; role: Arms and Hands. Perhaps a sharper tool would have done it.

- There was the *curé* Pierre-René Grenier, spiritual adviser and companion of the patient's last days; role: Heart. *Kyrie eleison*, he might have said. *Christie eleison. Kyrie eleison.*

- And finally, the builder of the machine, the "painless device," one Tobias Schmidt, German piano-maker, minor *philosophe*, ironist *avant le lettre*; role: Legs and Feet. What might he have thought? *L'homme est condamné à être libre?*

Five men; five pieces of the puzzle. The pentagram requires them all. It takes a whole man to make a guillotine. It takes a whole man to be laid upon a plank or stretched out on a wheel or gurney. And even a whole man is an uncertain tenant in a world where unreason incomprehensibly governs.

26.

TEMPO DI MENUETTO

W hy are you crying?" Schmidt asked.
Guillotin had put down his violin.

"Why are *you* crying?" he asked his pianist.

"I'm not crying. That's sweat," Schmidt said, wiping away a tear.

I'll tell you why they were crying. They were crying because in the E minor violin sonata there is a moment too beautiful to play—the trio in E major, haunting, unbearably poignant and lovely.

Guillotin had gulped at the key change, started to tear up at the first rising sixth of the theme, and by the repeat of the first phrase had to lower his instrument.

Schmidt was crying because—like the C minor moment in the *Ah, vous dirais-je* variations he had heard Mozart play—this moment, too, seemed to open a trapdoor revealing all those lurking dark forces, then shut it quickly again—but in reverse and inside out. Here it was a trapdoor not into darkness but into a universe of light, of the possible, of all that could be but isn't.

They were crying because they understood this: That such a world is hidden from us, unattainable, glimpsed only in Mozart's cruel caress. A dark E minor minuet: the dance *par excellence* of the aristocracy. Grace, beauty, decorum. Delicate but controlled and controlling. And then the intolerable knife thrust of the exquisite trio—revealing the old order for all its implications, its unsuspected possibilities of disaster.

"Is that what we're crying about?" Guillotin demanded. "An *exposé* of the old order? I thought we *knew* that. I thought we were trying a *new* order."

"That's what I, at least, am crying about," the piano-maker said. "It's not the ghastly court and the canting nobility I'm mourning, it's the stability and structure, the placidity and contentment, the state of grace they would pretend. I'm crying because I understand the loss. I fear it; I fear such transience, fear mortality—in this context of highest beauty. I'm crying because we will now have to face the great trembling—at hand—and inescapable."

Guillotin dried his eyes and wiped the rosin off his strings, and, taking this cue, Schmidt closed the piano, an instrument he had built for the music room of the Tuileries palace.

And speaking of trembling, did you know I got the commission to build Dr. Louis's decapitation machine, your machine?"

"Louis's machine, please. I don't want any more to do with it."

"Louis's machine, then."

"I didn't know you had bid on it."

"I didn't want to mention it until I knew. Some poor gentleman is waiting patiently for his fate. There was an emergency decree."

"I know. It was passed in the Assembly."

"Roederer gave the commission to Guidon, who thought he could make a fortune off it. You should have seen his bid—almost 6,000 livres. Top-quality oak, even for the scaffold, a twelve-step staircase, copper grooving on the machine, 1,200 livres for labor because he says no one would willingly want to work on such a project, and another 1,200 livres for a small-scale demonstration model, so as to avoid untoward events and demonstrate its practicability. When I heard about it I submitted a quick bid—960 livres. Roederer accepted the same day."

"It's terrible that prisoner has to be waiting two months to be executed. Every moment must be another death to him. Will it take you long?"

"I've already gathered most of the materials. Another week, maybe."

"It's not just the victim, we have to be concerned about . . ."

"Patient. Louis calls him 'the patient.'"

". . . it's detrimental to the law, it's detrimental to public safety . . ."

"I understand that the patient is huge. Big as an ox. Big, thick neck."

"I try not to think about it," the doctor said.

"Here, let me sketch my plan for you."

And on the back of the last page of the Mozart *Sonata for Violin and Pianoforte in E minor*, Schmidt penciled a drawing of his work in progress.

"How long must this board be to accommodate him?" Guillotin asked.

"Six feet at least—with the head sticking over. And thick. Maybe oak. You wouldn't want it breaking under him."

"And this hole—for his neck, to hold his neck?"

Schmidt indicated a huge mass circled by his strangely delicate hands.

"Eight inches, I'd say. We have to do this right. Someday we may be two of its patients."

The carpenter made notes on his piano part.

"It is poor form to deface one's music with workaday details," said a voice from the still open doorway.

It was the king, King Yes, the amateur locksmith, soon to be citizen king Capet, soon to be . . . no more—tooling around the palace, as was his wont, amiably checking in to see what his piano-maker and the violinist doctor might be talking about now that their music had stopped.

The story is perhaps apocryphal, but this is how it goes:

Louis XVI looked at Schmidt's sketch, with its rough depiction of Dr. Louis's convex blade, which "acts obliquely on each side" to achieve its goal efficiently.

"My friends, I see what you are aiming for with this shape. But wouldn't it be far more efficient to avoid the initial perpendicularity? Why not make the blade triangular, and have it arrive point first, for continuous slicing?"

Why not, indeed? It was the perfect solution— and obvious in hindsight. Schmidt and Guillotin properly applauded, and the king left the room, quite satisfied with his ingenious self. In less than a year, he would be able to test his design in a most personal way.

Alone again with Schmidt, Guillotin asked why he had taken on such an offensive job, humanitarian though it might be.

"Why? Do you know how many pianos I've sold since the Bastille came down? Two. One being this one. Two pianos in almost three years. Mozart—rest his soul—may have been possessed by angels, but our bourgeoisie now seems to be not very interested in them. And you know what? If this machine is a success," he slapped the paper, "I'm going to put in a bid for the other thirty-four—so our thirty-four provincial executioners will have nothing to complain about. As you said, this is humanitarian work."

"With such an easy means," said Guillotin, forlorn, "we can now behead in batches."

"*Ja.* Against a good cat, a good rat, as we Germans say. Liberty, equality, fraternity—and death. A natural quaternion, don't you think? Rich as a string quartet. For those whose liberty tramples on yours, death. For inferiors who want to be your equal, death. For those who assert presumptuous brotherhood, death. The tyranny of the small, the jealous, the incapable may very well be worse than the tyranny of the great."

"Not so loud, not so loud. The palace may have ears."

The two of them listened for listeners. After a pause, Guillotine continued, "The tyranny of the small, yes, as always. But the machine will belong to the state."

"And who will the state belong to, Doctor?" From *piano*, Schmidt began a slow crescendo. "Revolution will put the people in the place of the king, with the same absolute rule. And the people are simple, simple like violence, ruthless violence, radically simple, a simple, unifying law for society. Violence is like the law of gravity. They will love the machine, Doctor. The machine, that simple mechanism, a machine that might bear the legend 'Humanity, Equality, Rationality'—a veritable icon of civilization. We may even see the king beheaded," Schmidt whispered, *subito piano*—"if we still have our heads to see with. In a year or so children will be given toy machines. They can practice beheading sparrows."

"The danger," said Guillotin, putting his violin back into its case, "is not that a particular class is unfit to govern. *Every* class is unfit to govern. But liberty, equality, and fraternity are the only roads to peace and harmony."

Schmidt laughed sardonically. "The giant footprints of liberty may look awfully much like graves," he said. "The people will ask for bread, and we'll toss them severed heads. When they thirst, we'll offer them the blood from the scaffold."

"I'm with Robespierre: Why reinvent the world and leave the scaffold standing?"

"Too late, my friend," the piano-maker said. "Your humanitarian machine is far more persuasive than you are or ever will be. Society must avenge itself, and punish."

Guillotin spun around from his packing up. "What do you want, the wheel? The stake, skinning, burying, and boiling alive? No more administrative murder! No more executions! I never have and I never will attend one!"

Now it was Schmidt playing conductor, bringing down the volume.

"Sorry," Guillotin said. "I didn't mean to raise my voice at you."

"Does that mean you won't attend your poor child's social debut?"

"I don't need to. It will work. And it's not my child. It's Louis's."

"Ah, just watch, Doctor. This daughter will be your claim to fame whether you disown her or not. And on grand occasions the state will show off your bones and your worms."

"I'd prefer more privacy," the doctor said.

Schmidt returned to the piano and began again to play. "Ah, yes, a private death. May we all go like our E major trio, like stars falling, breathing ourselves out, kissing ourselves with our own lips, like rays of light falling into clear water."

But he played the minuet and not the trio. E minor.

"You're inscrutable," Guillotin said.

"No. Just teasing. To answer your question, I will be building machines until people start buying pianos again, which may be never, and serving our new nation, and charging a fifth as much as my competitors. My 960 francs will even provide a leather bag in which to dispose of the heads."

It was an unsettling conversation for both.

27.

IN THE CELL

The Conciergerie was the most fearsome of all the Paris prisons, a milieu pervaded by death. When the river was high, it reached the level of the prison floor: Everything was wet, water streamed down every wall, and most prisoners slept on damp pallets of vermin-infested straw.

When first entering, visitors were oppressed by the darkness, the suffocating aura, and something vaguely nauseating in the gloom, some kind of smell peculiar to such places. Iron bars, it seems, have power over light and air.

Everywhere were gothic vaults, lowered round arches, and pillars crowned with capitals—all of which can still be seen today.

As he had no money, Pelletier was spared the 18 francs a month for his accommodation—one of three condemned cells. His, number 17, was a surprisingly large room with a low, arched ceiling and stones missing from the moist floor. The room had a rusted cast-iron stove, but no wood was supplied after February. There was a large oak armchair, upholstered in leather, but torn, with the horsehair poking though, and a folding bed stinking of mold. A gendarme and a warder, relieved every three hours, guarded the murderer day and night, standing continually so as not to fall asleep. They worked their shifts in the hallway, just outside the thick wooden door. When Pelletier looked out his three-inch peephole, he often met with a staring eye.

High above the prisoner's head, a filthy barred window looked out on the quay. But the brightest sun ray cast only gray patterns through its leaded panes, which, as the day passed, elongated on the flagstone floor. Outside, not ten feet away, citizens went about their business: Vendors sold their wares, women shopped and gossiped, children played, carriages clattered by in the din of the city, and boats blew their whistles in the air, the sky, the sun, and freedom. In their homes people hugged. But for Pelletier, it was his prison which hugged him, supported him, caressed him. Carved in the wall over his bed were two hearts pierced by a single arrow and entwined by the words "Till death do us part."

He was dressed in sailcloth trousers and a twill jacket, clothing far better than that in which he had been arrested. He was fed regularly, twice a day, and though it be with sticky prison bread the color of dung and smelling as nasty, with weak soups and spoiled gruels, still it was more than he'd had when he was free. And so Pelletier was not unhappy.

He spent much of the day sitting on his bed, his elbows resting on his knees, his chin in his huge hands. He could sit that way for hours. His thoughts had no distinctness, and except for some occasional flashes, they were not about his current situation or the train of events that had brought it about. The cracks and chinks in the wall, the patterns and faces they made, the bars on the window, the shadows playing upon the floor—these were the things that occupied his mind, and although lurking behind such thoughts was a vague sense of guilt, perhaps a dread of death, he felt no more than a shadowy consciousness of it, a shapeless phantom pervading everything but having little real existence. Though he was ashamed to be afraid, sometimes he thought, "Maybe they're doing all this to frighten me. . . ." But it was impossible to hold his mind on any one point, and especially on the fate that awaited him.

He loved the spiders that spun their great webs in the vaults and arches. He would watch them, too, as well as the cracks. But his best friends were the rats. He sang to them as they ate the food he offered, songs his mother had once sung to him. They were his family now, and he the *paterfamilias*.

Sometimes he thought of his daughter. He thought of her especially when the doll-maker came to sketch him. Proud he was of being modeled, his collar open, his neck strangely long and bare. "May I have one doll for my daughter?" he asked, forgetting how old she was and that it might have been she that had turned him in. "Just the doll, not the machine that goes with it."

When he did try to think about things, he got all bollixed up. "That doesn't follow, that doesn't follow," he was forced to say. "We poor people have thick heads." He covered his eyes, and uncovered them again. Peekaboo. It *didn't* really follow, what he saw. He covered his ears and unstopped them—the same. Why don't things follow? His blanket was rough. That followed. The clock bonged, and the numbers got bigger but then got small again. He tried to put together some kind of consistent story, and this was the sequence that emerged:

Children died, but the meanest people lived on. Rich people got richer and simple people poorer, and there were many poor people and not many rich ones, and the rich ones made the rules, and the poor ones lived and died, father and son, mother and child, husband and wife, over and over, wretched and sad, homeless, and with no one to help them. And jail doors sucked them in, and gallows swung over them, and they had little chance for life, and the world rolled on. And that followed.

"So I am here by following God's world."

But that didn't really follow.

So he would try to lose consciousness without success, and little by little he felt the poisonous air filling his lungs and bringing with it a stronger, clearer consciousness of woe. And then a creeping, bone-clutching chill arose from the stone floor, and a fierce longing for freedom seized him, ordinary physical freedom, not any kind of abstraction like *liberté*.

"They are going to do something terrible to me," he thought during visits from respectable, gray-haired men with repulsive faces, and fear would rush through him like a windy roar, shameful, futile fear, and his huge body would tremble.

"Anything the matter?" they would ask, and he would say, truthfully, "No."

Father Pierre-René Grenier, seven years younger than his charge, had been sent by the Paris section to counsel Pelletier and ease his final days. In the past criminals had been executed within a day of sentencing, but this poor giant now had to wait until a machine was built which would satisfy Dr. Guillotin's new and benevolent law. The section knew that each minute must be a torture, so they tasked Grenier, at 1 livre a day, to be at the condemned man's side for the duration.

The young priest had taken the oath and was now "constitutional," allowed to serve his country and his God. And this was what he wanted—to continue comforting the afflicted, and to again be permitted to do so. The Assembly had banned ecclesiastical dress, but under his brown frock coat he wore his clerical bands.

On the day of his first visit, there was a scene that fortified him for the rest. Not knowing exactly when "the new young priest" would arrive, the prison had sent its official chaplain to call on Pelletier. Father Dupré, not realizing that the young man was a priest, asked him to leave the cell while he spoke to the prisoner. Grenier, hoping for instruction, watched and listened through the peephole.

Pelletier was sitting on the bed. The old Father pulled up the armchair and sat down.

"My son," he said. "My son, do you believe in God?"

The prisoner answered slowly: "We are created in God's image," he said, as if from the catechism. "Sand, dust, and dung."

The old priest was confused, but continued, "Do you believe in the holy Catholic, apostolic, and Roman church?"

"Yes. I do. Actually, I should laugh at the whole

business. You have to break things open to see what's inside of them."

"You seem to lack conviction," said the priest.

At which point Grenier knocked on the cell door. The old priest, happy for an excuse to end this madness, bade him enter.

"Father, I am the priest just allotted to Citizen Pelletier. Father Pierre-René Grenier. May I take over this interview, as the citizen and I had best get to know one another?"

More welcome words were never spoken, and the old priest bowed his way out of the room as quickly as possible. And a good thing, too, as Grenier felt the strongest urge to throttle him. He stood quietly in front of his charge, who was still sitting on the bed, looking up at him, waiting. But the storm of his anger had yet to pass.

"He makes a living from consoling," he raged to himself, "from confessing the condemned. It's nothing but a job to him! He leads men to their deaths with musty old formulas. His white hair no longer stands on end. If it ever did!"

He looked into Pelletier's upraised eyes. The prisoner's face seemed embittered, drawn. But his eyes. Grenier would never have thought eyes could be so pure.

This man is about to die, he thought, and I must bring him comfort. I will be with him when they tie his hands; I will be in the cart with him and hold the crucifix between him and the executioner; I will be jolted with him over the cobblestones on his trip to La Grève, be with him in the horrible, bloodthirsty crowd; I will touch his shoulder at the foot of the scaffold, and stay with him until his body is here and his head there.

"Am I a monster?" the prisoner asked him.

An odd beginning.

"There are no monsters," the priest said.

"But I'm bad. That's why I'm here. I know it. Am I a sinner? We poor people . . ." And there he left it.

"It is easier to die than to live," said the young priest.

"I don't want to die."

"Death is just a short illness from which we recover." He sat down on the horsehair chair pulled up near the bed. "A matter of a few minutes. You're a strong man. You'll get through it."

"I don't want to die," the prisoner murmured.

"Suffering is why we were put into the world, to love and to do good, to give up our lives for others. That's why we are Christians. Our God was dragged through the streets. . . ."

"Goodness—I haven't got much of that. Poor people, we don't have much goodness. That's how it has to be. Now, if I were a gentleman with a hat and a watch, then I would want to be good. Do you think that if they punish me, I can be good?"

"*They* have nothing to do with it. All the punishment in the world could not expiate a single sin. Jesus will take care of that, my son. You must only embrace Him."

Grenier felt himself falling into priest-talk. Why couldn't he say what he meant in his own words, words this parishioner might understand? Why couldn't he speak more simply, speak the universal language of the people, the language of sighs and tears?

"I had a dog once," the prisoner said. "*He* was good. He loved everyone and did his work, and he never complained. He did tricks, too, and all the people would stand around and clap, and he would wag his tail, and sometimes he'd get so happy he'd piss all over." Pelletier smiled. "Animals, they say, are in a state of nature. But us poor people, we ain't in a state of nature, Father. We even sweat in our sleep, us poor people. It doesn't follow."

"You are one with Christ. Christ is suffering in you."

This the priest believed, and couldn't have said more simply.

"They say Christ's mother is the great Mother Earth, and every tear we weep is a great joy for Her. And if I can fill the earth with tears a foot deep, everything will be joy, and there will be nothing left of my tears."

This time it was the young priest, the Jesuit, who was confused. Who was "they"? Where had he heard this about the earth and the tears?

"Human tears," he said, "human tears and human suffering are not real. Even human death is not real.

Christ is the one who wept and died. Our tears are just a shadow of His. Yes, perhaps tears do nourish the earth, and we ourselves, after our deaths. Jesus said, 'Except a corn of wheat fall to the ground and die, it abideth alone; but if it die, it bringeth forth much fruit.'"

The prisoner nodded. "But I don't know what that means," he said.

"In our tears, in our deaths, God gives us union with Himself."

Pelletier stared at him with moist, pure eyes. If man is made in God's image, Grenier thought, perhaps this is the image of God.

"In an hour, I'll have sixty minutes less to live. What if I don't want to die?"

To this the priest had no real answer.

Over the weeks they often talked past one another, but still they talked. For Grenier, the visits were far more than a duty, and for Pelletier, they were an unfamiliar kind of pleasure.

What was clear, too, over the weeks was that Grenier was seriously ill. A squeezing pain often engulfed his chest and traveled to his belly and back and then down his arm. During these attacks he felt breathless and weak, and he broke out in cold sweats. Afterward he was nauseated, restless, and frightened. Death was on *his* mind as well.

The pain would rise up and settle down again, but without ever really going away. He could no longer remember a time without it and had lost hope of ever getting better. He breathed as best he could, but he felt as if he were inhaling night.

For ten days Grenier had not prayed, not been able to, and finally it seemed to him that he no longer deserved it. God had withdrawn into some dark space, darker than the prison, perhaps beyond it. He was empty of God, but although he could share that with his charge, he said nothing.

When Pelletier went into his litany of being a sinner, of being bad, of having committed crimes, Grenier advised him that crimes, no matter how terrible, could not reveal the nature of evil. Evil could not be embodied in the likeness of man, not essential evil—that yearning for emptiness and void. The earth is quite young, he told him. Even after these centuries, evil was only at its beginning.

These points may have been too subtle for the prisoner to understand, but they were too burning in Grenier to not be stated.

Pelletier's reply, as the chimes struck the hour, was "Will the clock never stop?"

Then one day the prisoner stopped talking. The priest had the impression that something was on his mind, something he couldn't or wouldn't express.

His attention seemed elsewhere while Grenier spoke, but of what he was thinking the priest could only guess. It didn't seem to be the execution he was meditating on—he did not respond to such inquiry—but some infinite object too deep to share, some enemy faced and braved too long, and now triumphant.

28.

A Conversation Concerning Consciousness

Now though you'd have said that head was dead
(For its owner dead was he),
It stood on its neck, with a smile well bred,
And bowed three times to me!
It was none of your impudent off-hand nods,
But humble as could be;
For it clearly knew
The deference due
To a Man of pedigree!

            —W. S. Gilbert

"Well," said Sanson, "the blood flows at the speed of the severed carotids, quite quickly, then it coagulates in a big mess. All the muscles contract and vibrate. It's quite impressive; sometimes the mouth goes into a terrible pout."

"Sounds alive to me," Schmidt observed.

"No, not at all. If it's cleanly done—I've seen it

half-a-dozen times—the eyes are fixed and the pupils dilated. They aren't cloudy and opalescent like a true corpse's, but it's clear they are staring at nothing."

"Nothing, perhaps, but the great void," Schmidt said. "*You* might stare that way if it suddenly appeared before your eyes."

"The transparency is life-like, but the fixity is clearly dead. That look can last minutes, even hours, in some clients, and even I am left with a sense of vivisection, and then premature burial. But I assure you, the package is dead."

"Clients?" Guillotin inquired, appalled. "The package?"

"We call them that. What do you want us to call them, our patients?"

"But surely death is not immediate, instantaneous," Schmidt continued. "Every vital element survives decapitation. It's obvious: The heart beats, the nerves fire, the blood courses still. . . . Surely consciousness must survive long enough to perceive the fall onto the scaffold, or into a basket. Would it see another head in there right in front of it? Would the eyes stare at each other in recognition?"

"Schmidt, your notion of survival is . . . bizarre. Its premises fly in the face of what we have discovered about the nervous reflex. It's purely a metaphysical idea, a figment of the romantic imagination. Facial expression in the decapitated is not an indication of existing feeling; it's a mechanical reaction to traumatic stimulation and anoxia."

Thus the good doctor, who, though abjuring all further connection with Dr. Louis's beheading machine, was still convinced of its efficiency, painlessness, and relative humanity.

"The man, for instance, who receives a sword in the solar plexus, and whose face as a result is seized by convulsion, looks as if he laughing, though surely there is little to laugh about. His is a purely mechanical convulsion and, although his brain is perfectly intact, he surely dies unaware of what is going on."

"But we don't *know* that," Schmidt responded. "We don't know what he is feeling or thinking. We don't know that his sense of self is immediately destroyed at the moment of his so-called death. I suspect the dying may be able to see and hear long after they can no longer move and look quite dead to us."

"There are anecdotes," Sanson said, "and I underline that they are only anecdotes, as I have never seen it myself. But they are anecdotes firmly embedded in our business, anecdotes of decapitated heads actually speaking."

"Ridiculous," Guillotin said. "Where is the air coming from without the lungs?"

Sanson put forth an armpit-fart as a semiconvincing answer.

"The severed head of Mary Stuart is supposed

to have spoken. Her lips moved up and down a quarter of an hour after her head was cut off."

"What did she say, assuming she said anything?" Guillotin asked, incredulous.

"She was supposed to be whispering to God. *In manas tuas*, that sort of thing. Of course it's true that it took three chops to do her in, so she may have said something before the last."

"In Strasbourg," Schmidt said, "they used to tell of a young nobleman who was decapitated for a crime, and as soon as he was executed the surgeons—this had been arranged with him in advance—the surgeons stopped the flow of blood with styptics, and others placed his head back on his neck with all possible precision and dexterity, lining up the vertebrae, muscle on muscle, artery to artery, wrapped it all up with bandages mechanically held in place, and then gave him a good dose of smelling salts. His head, they said, seemed to come around. There was perceptible movement in his face, and his eyelids twitched."

"And?" both Guillotin and Sanson asked.

"And he was taken to a nearby house, where, after having given some very slight signs of life, he died again."

"Really!" Guillotin said scornfully.

"Interesting," muttered Sanson.

"No one is saying you can undo a decapitation," Schmidt said. "Only that life may continue to some

degree afterward. The idea that life might survive decapitation is not self-evidently false. My suspicion is
that a decapitated man retains some impression of his
own existence for as long as the brain retains vital heat.
The head is thick and round—it loses heat slowly. So
in a separated head feeling, personality, and sense of
self might remain for some time, and it might very
well feel the afterpain that affects the neck. Our impression as observers is not necessarily the same as the
subjective impression of the victim."

"But gentlemen," the doctor observed, "may I
tread upon the obvious? The brain loses heat immediately upon being separated from the body. It can't
feel the aftersensations that affect the neck; sensation, personality, and self are no longer present in
this organ."

"Look," Schmidt objected, "obviously something
is broken with the head cut off. But the brain is just
another internal organ. The sense of life lies in the
body as a whole."

The executioner was feeling left out: "What do
we know about what unites the head and the torso?
Guillotin, you might be able to prove to me that the
movements can't be voluntary and disprove all the facts
I have related, even the one concerning Mary Stuart.
But it does strike me now that you cannot prove that
thought does not survive, or that sensation is extinguished. You can't prove that the single blow that strikes

off the head immediately—poof!—shatters the mysterious unity in which head and body are bound."

"And what could be more horrible," Schmidt added, "than the impression of one's own execution followed by the knowledge of having been executed? The victim aware of that which is *par excellence* unknowable— his own death? The vocal cords being no longer connected to the lungs does, of course, prevent him from communicating this astonishing experience, or the head might speak the unspeakable sentence: 'I am dead.'"

The discussion was most unpleasant for Dr. Guillotin, who had promised the Assembly "nothing but a slight sensation of coolness at the back of the neck." And why should Schmidt, if he suspected incomplete death, be building its dreadful instrument? Only because he couldn't sell enough pianos? Only because Mozart was dead?

The fourth person in the room had been silent, observing, quietly sipping his wine.

"Tell me, Sanson, will your new victims ejaculate?" the marquis asked. "You don't know? What a pity if not. I should miss that most of all, and so will he."

The playwright and the executioner guffawed.

29.
THE MACHINE

It was fourteen feet high, its beams and posts painted blood-red—a nice touch, that. It would be called "End of the Soup," "Old Growler," "Sky Mother," "the Last Mouthful." It would be called by the feminine form of someone's name, as if it were his daughter, someone who had repudiated it. Assemblymen called it "the Timbers of Justice."

The victim, once attached to the plank, his head in the fatal window, would become a part of it, a cog in the machine of egalitarian justice. His blood would be shed not by the unsteady hand of his fellow man but by this lifeless, insensible, infallible instrument, a doctor's idea become oak and iron.

The materials now gathered, over the course of a week Tobias Schmidt and two hired workers constructed the frame. Two four-sided posts were grooved and chiseled as guides for the falling blade. When the seventy-pound holder and fifteen-pound blade came back from the blacksmith, they were fitted loosely between the posts and the posts joined by an upper crossbar with a hole for the rope. A lower crossbar was angle-braced to its stand for stability. Rope guides were placed.

On the back side of the device, the executioner's side, another crossbar was attached to hold the lunette—two wooden pieces, each with a half-circular hole to contain the client's, the patient's, the package's neck. The diameter was that of Pelletier's. A smaller one for women could be substituted as needed. When fitted together, the pieces formed a lovely "little moon" whose upper half could be lifted on a hinge to permit a head to enter.

That was it. Simple. A weighted blade and its frame. Though it required two strong men to carry it, it could be loaded onto a heavy cart and transported wherever it was needed, along with its separate bench, long and strong enough to hold a giant—or an ox— and fitted with thick leather straps.

Before dawn on Tuesday, April 15, 1792, a sound of clattering wheels was heard on southern streets two miles from the center of Paris. It was a four-wheeled wagon, drawn by two horses, carrying a long object covered with heavy black cloth and tightly bound with chains. Four guardsmen with bare swords on horseback rode silently in front of the wagon, and four behind. Bringing up the rear was a smaller wagon with several sheep. If going to market, they were being taken in the wrong direction. They advanced slowly, gray and black in the pale early morning.

The procession was heading for the suburb of Bicêtre, just outside the city gate, home to the great hospital for venereal disease, its hospice for the needy poor, and its *maison de correction*, locked wards for hardened criminals, some awaiting execution.

When seen from a distance, Louis XIII's building looks quite imposing. Set on the brow of a hill, from afar it retained something of its former splendor and the look of a royal residence. But now, three Louises later, the palace had in fact become a hovel. Its dilapidated eaves were shameful and its walls diseased. Not a window was glazed but only fitted with crisscrossed iron bars through which, here and there, pressed the harrowed face of a patient or a prisoner.

Already waiting in a small inner courtyard were Charles-Henri Sanson and his two assistants, Tobias Schmidt, and the doctors Antoine Louis and Joseph-Ignace Guillotin, the latter most reluctantly.

Early-morning eyes gawked from behind bars as the first sheep's head was placed in the lunette, its neck the size of Pelletier's. The upper half moon was locked in place. One of the assistants let loose the rope from its tie-off so Sanson could better observe.

Disaster: The heavy blade jerked stickily into motion, jolted downward between the grooves, and sliced into the animal without killing it. All mental ears were stopped against its terrifying cry. Sanson was dismayed. He had the blade wound back up and released again. It bit into the neck again but did not sever it. The victim howled. Once again the blade was raised and dropped, but the third stroke only caused a stream of blood to spurt from the sheep's neck, without the head falling. Five times the blade rose and fell; five times it cut into the sheep, which cried five times for mercy. It remained standing on the platform, an appalling, terrifying sight. Sanson straddled it and hacked away with a butcher knife at what remained of its neck. Twenty pounds of lead shot were added to the blade-carrier, and three more sheep were neatly dispatched thereby. The march of science.

After nightfall Schmidt took the machine back to his workshop in the Cour du Commerce, Rue St.-André-des-Arts, just opposite the printing shop in number 8 where Marat's paper was printed. He lined the grooves with brass for a smoother drop and bolted more weight to the blade assembly.

Two days later, on April 17, assisted by his son and his two brothers, Sanson repeated his experiments on the improved machine, this time with three human cadavers from a military morgue, three well-built men who had died in short illnesses that had not caused them to grow thin. Among the spectators were the two doctors concerned, along with Michel Cullerier, the chief surgeon of Bicêtre; Philippe Pinel, the resident alienist; several physician members of the National Assembly; and delegates from the Council of Hospitals of Paris. Strapped to the bench, the three corpses, good soldiers all, were successfully beheaded without protesting, to the applause of most of the onlookers.

IV. Le Jour de Gloire
Est Arrivé

CUM MORTUIS IN LINGUA MORTUA:
CAPITAL PUNISHMENT

> *My object, all sublime,*
> *I shall achieve in time,*
> *To let the punishment fit the crime,*
> *The punishment fit the crime.*
> —W. S. GILBERT, *The Mikado*

"An eye for an eye," says Exodus 21, "a tooth for a tooth." But not exactly.

Exodus 21:23: If any harm follows, then you shall give life for life, [24]eye for eye, tooth for tooth, hand for hand, foot for foot, [25]burn for burn, wound for wound, stripe for stripe.

Exodus 21:26: When a slave-owner strikes the eye of a male or female slave, destroying it, the owner shall let the slave go, a free person, to compensate for the eye.

Exodus 21:27: "If the owner knocks out a tooth

of a male or female slave, the slave shall be let go, a free person, to compensate for the tooth.

The principle of retributive justice. Transformed in the current climate in the United States, and quoting some recent execution counterdemonstrators, it translates as "Fry 'em all!" ("Inject 'em all," I suppose, would be more to the point but would lose its valued kinship to burning at the stake.)

An Eye for an eye. Notice, however, the *biblical* elaboration of the eye-for-eye rule of thumb with respect to owners and slaves. When men have no liberty, equality, or fraternity, they shall be granted them. That is a major adjunct to the retributive principle which "Fry 'em all" scarcely recognizes.

And why not?

Perhaps it's because the "Fry 'em all" crowd is modeling a pentagonal regime involved in continual war, whose leaders celebrate the massive use of violence. What do we do to our "nice young men," to our "brave men and women in harm's way, defending our values"? See "The Other War: Iraq Vets Bear Witness."[1]

---

[1] See quotations from U.S. soldiers in Iraq are taken from Chris Hedges and Laila Al-Arian, "The Other War: Iraq Vets Bear Witness," *The Nation*, July 30, 2007.

The soldiers' own photos from Iraq are most eloquent. One corpse is a tragedy; a million are a statistic.

What goes on, what is normalized in the dynamic of state-supported violence and murder? Some young Israeli soldiers shed light on the question: "The truth is that I love this mess—I enjoy it. It is like being on drugs. If I didn't enter Rafah, to put down some rebellion—at least once a week—I'd go berserk."

From another soldier: "What is great is that you don't have to follow any law or rule. You feel that YOU ARE THE LAW; you decide. Once you go into the Occupied Territories YOU ARE GOD."[2]

Truth, they say, is the first casualty of war. Many are credited with this assertion, Aeschylus among them. And while current war-making behavior so amply demonstrates its truth, a sister corollary also arises: Truth is the first *result* of war. For in the responses of these soldiers about the ever-present atrocities of war, an appalling truth is nakedly revealed: that in a milieu of sanctioned violence, "fresh-faced Americans" and "nice Jewish boys" can—as easily as crowds at a scaffold—be transformed into monsters. When they are given the freedom and encouraged to kill, men and

---

[2] These quotations from Israeli soldiers in the occupied territories of Palestine are from Dalia Karpel, *"Hamedovevet"* (The one who makes people talk), *Hebrew Weekend Supplement*, September 21, 2007.

women in uniform do so with abandon. "Waste 'em all!" "Fry 'em all!" "Nuke 'em all!"

Under such conditions, and the mental world that trails them, *liberté* becomes absolute freedom, absolute freedom from human values, a mockery of justice suppressive of freedom itself.

Of *égalité* and *fraternité* there is none. "A lot of guys really supported that whole concept that, you know, if they don't speak English and they have darker skin, they're not as human as us, so we can do what we want." "Oh, they'll understand when the gun is in their face."

With that kind of *liberté*, and no sense of *egalité* or *fraternité*, it is easy to imagine these soldiers coming home to support capital punishment.

For Dr. Guillotin and his colleagues in the National Assembly, and for 90 percent of the French population, *liberté*, *égalité*, and *fraternité* were dominant themes, long dreamt of and yearned for. France was on the verge of doing away with the divine right of kings and the absolute and unchallengeable power that went with it. How was it, then, that at this hinge moment of world history the new nation could not reject capital punishment as the key oppressive practice of the old regime? How did the scaffold and its new machine become transformed into *the* symbol of freedom?

At the beginning of the Revolution, none other than Robespierre denounced the death penalty. Saint-Just, too, at the same time as Robespierre, spoke vociferously against capital punishment. That pure, ascetic, fanatical soul demanded only that murderers be dressed in lifelong black, embodying a form of justice that did not attempt "to find the culprit guilty, but to find him weak." He dreamt, early on, of "a republic of forgiveness" which would recognize that "though the fruits of crime are bitter, its roots are nevertheless tender."

"It is a frightful thing," Saint-Just wrote, "to torment the people"—a perfect moment for abolition. Yet a year later, both he and Robespierre were calling for head after head. What happened, and how might those technical, social, political, and intellectual vectors still be arrowing among us in the here and now?

First there was the machine. Not that the gallows, bullet, sword, club, and fire had not served the purposes of the state—but the machine was clean, quick, and efficient, and while the mob may have found it dramatically disappointing, it reduced the ethical and emotional stress of the executioner, his employers, and his public. Today's executions, medicalized, hidden behind thick walls, restrictive of reporting, are, as a whole, even less publicly stressful. Most often victims are executed with neither public knowledge nor protest.

The tempo of executions rose markedly when conservative European powers declared war on the Revolution. The scaffold demanded French unity, purifying the land of malpractices and malpractitioners working against the Rousseauvian general will. While the external struggle could be carried on by the army, the domestic one had to be pursued by the revolutionary committees and their beheading machine. Capital punishment was the support of virtue. Us-versus-them, irrational jingoism and racism. Of this we know quite a bit today. Good guys (us) versus bad guys (them). What, then, is not permitted?

Of course it was projected by many that M. Sanson must sooner or later remove the head of the king. Abolish capital punishment? Not just yet. Louis had to die. Not Louis Capet but the Louis appointed by divine right. As Danton said so honestly, "We do not want to condemn the king. We want to kill him." That Louis Capet happened to be Louis XVI was simply unfortunate for him.

Regime change of the first order: In killing the king, the reign of Christianity over the earth would also be slain. The execution of Louis XVI initiates contemporary, secular history, the disincarnation of God. Thou shalt not kill? Turn the other cheek? Abolish the death penalty? The pressure was reduced from God-inspired ethics. It is even lower in our world today, when gang-ethics history is written only in terms of force.

America is the only Western nation still clinging to the death penalty. At present, ninety countries have abolished capital punishment entirely; eleven have eliminated it for all except under the most special circumstances; and thirty-two others have not executed anyone for ten years or more.

So what's going on with America?

The United States is the most triumphalist of the nations. National pride exists everywhere in the world, but "Num-ber ONE, num-ber ONE!" is not so common a slogan. The triumph of a murderer or torturer is made problematical by one thing: guilt. Some may feel guiltless, some are "serving their country," some are "only following orders." But in most killers, individual or state, guilt lurks and demands to be dealt with.

The most common way is via projection: It is not I who am guilty but they. They are bad, they are evil, they are less than human. They must be punished or annihilated.

The grandest of guilt necessitates the grandest of punishments.

Is there any chance of death penalty abolition in the American Republic of Virtue? Short of giving up hope, one must grab tight onto Gramsci's tragic banner, PESSIMISM OF THE INTELLECT, OPTIMISM OF THE WILL, with the other hand, perhaps, raising Klee's flag of "merrily dancing tears."

30.

COMMENCEMENT

The 25th of April, 1792. A fairer day is rarely seen. The air was mild, the city flooded with sunshine and shadow. The sparrows sang in the chestnut branches, and the sky was as clear as if it had been freshly washed that morning. It was the kind of day that opens the soul to nature, to hope, to living, to breathing, to renewal. Left Bank and Right, the spires of churches and the great cathedral could be seen rising up into the blue and showing off their every gem of tracery and fretwork, every niche and loophole.

After breakfast on this singular day, Nicolas Jacques Pelletier was visited by two armed guards and the director general of the Conciergerie and informed that his appointment at La Grève was for 3 that afternoon. Perhaps they had thought it was kindness to keep from him all week the machine's progress, testing, and revision.

Six decades later Dostoevsky would write of the

mental anguish of the condemned man as he awaits his fate with "the certain knowledge that in an hour, in ten minutes, in half a minute, now, this moment your soul will fly out of your body, and that you will be a human being no longer." Dickens's elaborate, torturing countdown for Sidney Carton's execution is perhaps the ultimate portrayal of the cruelty of the ticking clock. So perhaps it was, in fact, kindness to keep such thoughts from this prisoner, this special prisoner.

But not likely. Pelletier was in a mental state quite other than Carton's—or Dostoevsky's at the firing squad, the condition of a soul shifted outside its normal dynamics.

Father Grenier was with him at his haircut after lunch, the so-called toilet of the condemned, and from that time on. Pelletier felt the cold steel against the back of his neck and heard the squeaking of the scissors. His still brown locks fell onto his great shoulders, and the barber gently brushed them off. One of the guards took off Pelletier's jacket, and the other took hold of his hands, pulled them behind his back, and knotted his wrists together. When the barber cut the collar off his shirt, the scissors brushed against his neck, and he pulled away.

"I'm sorry, sir," the barber said. "Did I hurt you?"

The first guard bent down and tied the prisoner's feet together loosely enough that he could take small steps and then tied that rope to the one binding Pelletier's hands. The second guard threw the jacket around his shoulders and knotted the sleeves together under his chin. They must have forgotten the red shirt.

What was he thinking of as he submitted silently to this gentle, ominous treatment? He was thinking how nice it would be if God would send a bird to perch in his high window and sing to him. He was thinking of his little girl, still six in his mind. How would he explain to her that the men who would kill him didn't hate him, that most of them probably felt sorry for him but had to kill him in some kind of big ceremony?

Who would love his little girl when he was dead?

A surprise visitor, even to the staff in the cell, was Dr. Jean-Pierre Bourgogne, chief surgeon of the prison, who arrived breathlessly just as the prisoner was to be shrived. Father Grenier made room for him to intervene.

The doctor faced the shorn and bound prisoner and looked hopefully into his eyes.

"M. Pelletier, listen carefully to me. You know you will be the first patient to experience the new device. Others may—will certainly—follow you, and it would be of general benefit to society to have certain questions about it answered—from your point of view."

The prisoner looked at the doctor, looked through him, paying little attention to what the young physician was saying.

"You may know that there is a debate raging, both in the medical profession and among intellectuals and philosophers, concerning whether some gleam of real memory, thought, or sensibility survives in the brain of a man after . . ."

Here he made a neck-slicing gesture.

"Are you listening? Here's what I have to ask you. This is a very important experiment, and you could go down in history as a major contributor to human understanding. I would like to gently pick up your head afterward and, enunciating very clearly, ask you to reply by winking three times with your right eye while keeping the other one open. Got that? Right eye wink, left eye open. If at that moment you can, with this triple wink, tell me you have heard and understood, and *prove* it by thus altering, with an act of surviving will and memory, your palpebral muscle—mastering the horror, the great swell of other impressions that your existence may be undergoing. This deed will be enough to illuminate science and revolutionize our beliefs. Perhaps even cause us to do away with capital punishment. And be assured that I shall make the facts known in such a way that in the future, you shall be remembered as a great and courageous hero rather than as a criminal. May I have your permission?"

Pelletier continued to stare through him.

"Is he drugged?" the doctor asked.

"No," the young priest answered.

"Do you think he agrees to go ahead with the experiment?"

"I didn't hear him give permission."

"I'll take it up with the director general," said the surgeon, and he left.

"My son," Grenier said, "Nicolas, are you prepared?"

The *curé* had come to love this man far more than he loved himself. His heart was pounding, his chest was aching, and his left arm hurt so that he had to hold up the crucifix and make the sign of the cross one-handed. Nevertheless, on the storm tide of his feelings, it would do. *Ça ira, oui, ça ira.*

"Are you prepared?"

Nicolas focused his eyes on those of his friend. More than that he would or could not do or say. As the guards and barber watched, Grenier administered the last rites of the Catholic Church. He gave the prisoner absolution, conditional on contrition, as he would to a sick man, unable to confess. Laying aside his crucifix, he anointed Pelletier with oil and touched the consecrated host against his lips. The condemned opened his mouth, took the wafer on his tongue, and began to suck. Finally Father Grenier pronounced the viaticum, the provision for the journey.

"We commend to you, O Lord! the soul of this your servant Nicolas, and beseech you, O Jesus Christ, Redeemer of the world, that, as in your love for him, you became man, so now you would grant to admit him into the number of the blessed.

"May all the saints and elect of God, who, on earth, suffered for the sake of Christ, intercede for him; so that, when freed from the prison of his body, he may be admitted into the kingdom of heaven— through the merits of our Lord Jesus Christ, who lives and reigns with the Father and the Holy Spirit, world without end. Amen.

"May the blessing of God Almighty the Father, and the Son, and the Holy Ghost descend upon you and remain with you always. Amen."

Instead of dying alone, Nicolas, he hoped, would die with Christ, who would lead him to eternal life.

"It's just a few minutes that have to be lived through," he said. "Courage." And then he signaled to the guards that they might proceed. They took the prisoner by the armpits and assisted his walking, though his steps were small and wobbly. In the hallway outside his door, a prisoner yelled out from a neighboring cell, "Lucky bastard. So long, friend." At the courtyard doorway the turnkey said, "Monsieur, you may be on your way. Your carriage is at the door."

The tumbrel was waiting in the courtyard, an ordinary cart, newly painted red, drawn by a rawboned nag. Its driver was wearing a blue gardener's smock embroidered in red. Pelletier climbed in, his leg ropes barely permitting him to make his way up the stepladder set against the cart at a steep angle. "A brave fella," the doorman mumbled. The two guards climbed in after him, followed by Grenier. Armed horsemen framed the wagon, fore and aft, left and right. "Seven of them, all for me," the prisoner thought.

Out through the Conciergerie gate, and a turn toward the Pont-au-Change bridge, the iron-shod wheels rattling over the cobbles or knocking against the wagon as they jolted from rut to rut. The procession moved at a walking pace through the fragrance of the Quai aux Fleurs, and the girls stopped making bouquets to stand and take in the procession.

A little way along from the square tower which stands on the corner of the Palais de Justice were alehouses whose balconies were packed with the people— mostly women—delighted to have such a good view. The landlords would do a good business this day. Every vantage point was mobbed by spectators.

Running ahead of the wagon and stopping with it at crowded intersections and squares was the public crier, along with a drummer, probably his son. The huge man took his announcement from a bag around his neck and, after a drum roll, said in a voice as loud as Mirabeau's, "The Commune of the Paris Sections . . ."

A cheer went up from the crowd.

"By virtue of the orders given, and the power granted by the National Assembly, and in accordance with Article 17 of the Decree of Emergency of the

20th of March which has ordered a new and more humane form of capital punishment for crimes resulting in death . . ."

"What was that decree?" a peasant asked his neighbor.

"Something about an emergency."

"What is capital punishment?" asked another.

"I don't know," his neighbor answered.

Others must have had similar questions, as the murmuring markedly increased.

"Attention," the crier called out. "Listen!"

The boy beat the drum to stop the noise.

"The individual designated by the name Nicolas Jacques Pelletier . . ."

"He looks like a big, dumb ox," a storekeeper was heard to say, considering the big-shouldered man in the cart.

"The individual designated by the name Nicolas Jacques Pelletier will be put to death this afternoon at 3 P.M. in the Place de Grève."

Yelling, booing, hissing, and many epithets were heard, directed at Nicolas, perhaps at the crier, perhaps at . . . any and everything. Nicolas had heard his name, and he was proud he was now famous. He, Nicolas Pelletier, the dumb one.

"Let it be further noted," the crier continued, "that, under pain of death . . ."

The crowd quieted down to hear.

". . . under pain of death, it is forbidden to assist the prisoner named. Anyone who tries to help him escape will be court-martialed and executed forthwith."

A drum roll indicated the end of his announcement; he and the boy handed out sheets printed with the announcement and ran on ahead to the bridge.

"What did he say?" an old man asked.

"Under pain of death, you are not to help the prisoner."

"What prisoner?" the old one asked.

Nicolas watched the good people of Paris trying to stay ahead of his cart. At each step it rolled, the crowd dispersed behind, and many ran forward the better to attend his journey. On the bridge the tumbrel could only inch along, so dense were his followers. Grenier saw him gazing at Notre Dame, and this was his cue, he thought, to hold up the crucifix for Nicolas to kiss. But the prisoner began to shiver and seemed not to see it. Gendarmes in front, gendarmes behind, crowds, crowds, and more crowds, and a sea of heads ahead on the Place de Grève.

Pelletier could no longer see or hear. All those heads jammed at the windows, all those people in doorways, the children and young men perched on the lampposts. All those cruel and bloodthirsty spectators. *This crowd, they think they know me, but I don't know any of them.* Pelletier's eyes fell to watching the shop signs go by. And Notre Dame again, from the other side of the river, its windows blazing in the sun. Crowds of people up there on the towers, trying to get a good view.

Shops rolling slowly past him, their signs, and a street cobbled with filthy faces laughing, yelling, and stomping in the mud. Suddenly the row of shops gave out on the corner of the Place, and the square was revealed, shaking with noise from ground to rafters. The bridges chimed in, and the riverbank, too. The Hôtel de Ville loomed ahead, with its steeply sloping roof, its pinnacles and big white clock, its columns running along every floor, its thousand windows watching. It stood there level with La Grève, grimy with age, gendarmes at every door, faces at every window.

With the appearance of the cart, the crowd grew louder and more excited. A row of police horses opened the way, and a detachment of soldiers was drawn up in battle order to clear the path.

The cart jerked to a halt, and its four inhabitants were nearly thrown to the floor. Grenier caught Pelletier and tried to steady him. The prisoner's pants were wet with urine. A stepladder was brought up to the back of the cart, and the guards helped the shackled prisoner down. Once on the ground, he took a step, turned, and froze. Between two lamps on the embankment, he saw a nightmare object, unnamable, a steel triangle glinting at the top of two uprights. *But everything has the right to live,* Pelletier thought, *everything, this little fly here, buzzing at my face, that bird. Why not me?*

The answer? Jeers and insults from the crowd of *sans-culottes, tricoteuses,* shopkeepers, and aristocrats there to witness his spectacular, original end. Laughing they were, hissing, sniggering, yelling, hooting, whistling, singing—together it made in Pelletier's mind an unending, incomprehensible noise, like the great wind outdoors, the great rain, the great ocean. The sight they were waiting to see was calculated to bring out the lowest of the population and the highest, both for sport, not justice, devoid of generous impulse and already turning hateful. For some it was a festival, a day of license. "Kill the rich!" one yelled. A few were there to witness the benefits conferred by a new, enlightened regime, egalitarian, dedicated to the reform of capital punishment. But even among *them,* as among all the others, there lurked the fear of death mixed with a strange desiring.

Death, fascinating and enticing. They had gathered to see how the victim would accomplish his grand, last act. At the heart of the ritual was the singular privilege to explore the mystery of what it was to lose one's life.

Father Grenier was confounded. The last hours had left him with a profound spiritual and physical listlessness, fatigued, anxious, breathing quickly and shallowly to minimize the pain. The killing machine he had imagined turned out to be unexpectedly slender, like a reedy young girl, decked out in red, surveying her potential conquests. Lust again, he thought, young lust, and his soul shivered. Surveying the mounted soldiers ringing the scaffold, he focused on their horses, calmly standing under them, breathing softly, taking in the warm spring air, their ears occasionally twitching. The only genuine ones among us, he thought, the only innocents.

At the bottom of the scaffold Sanson was waiting to escort his charge up the stairs. He was dressed "à la Sanson" in his three-cornered hat, his celebrated dark-green riding coat and dapper striped trousers. Near him, in complementary colors, the red cart to remove the body and, hitched to its yoke, a new leather bag.

Elsewhere, Paris in all her beauty and immensity, bathed in the merry sunshine, oblivious to the happenings at La Grève. April hope filled the air; for all the poverty and political crises, citizens felt themselves optimistic, expectant, young men felt happier, women more beautiful.

Elsewhere in Paris news was spreading that the monarchs of Austria and Prussia had just declared war on revolutionary France. The previous night, in Schmidt's border town of Strasbourg, Claude-Joseph Rouget de Lisle, a young engineer, had written a song to inspire the people's army to resist the anticipated Hapsburg attack. *"Allons, enfants de la Patrie,"* he wrote, *"Le jour de gloire est arrivé!"* Its sanguinary lines were sung with special zest by the newly arrived group of volunteers from Marseilles, good seamen all.

And now, all over Paris, the many clocks and many bells tolled 3.

Here at the Place de Grève, in the square before the immense Hôtel de Ville, the new machine stood in rectilinear purity and stretched its two red arms into the sky, as if inviting angels, a hell-colored light glinting off its blade.

When Sanson walked over to the group at the tumbrel, Father Grenier addressed him with a speech he had brazenly prepared.

"Monsieur Executioner, I know it takes courage to carry out your work. You and I walk toward the same end, but by different roads. Yours represents human justice, and mine the mercy of God."

Sanson nodded, pleased by the equivalence. He had always felt himself a kind of pontiff, with the scaffold for his altar. This is my blood. This is my body.

The priest continued, "May I ask a favor in God's name?"

Sanson nodded again.

"Please do not give the signal to strap him down until this poor man pronounces the words 'May God commit my soul to His keeping.' Will that be permissible?"

Before he could agree, a large, long-haired dog broke free from his master in the crowd, came bounding up, barking, and leapt round the priestly conference wagging its whole body, wild with glee at who knew what. And then, before anyone could stop it, the dog jumped up on the prisoner, trying and trying to lick his face. One of Sanson's assistants rushed to help, but it danced and frolicked out of his grasp, taking everything and everyone as part of the game. Pelletier, held tightly by two guards, looked on indifferently, as though this were yet another formality to be endured. It was a minute or so before the embarrassed owner managed to catch the dog, leash him, and drag him away, still straining and whimpering.

"I may not hear him if he speaks too softly," Sanson said to the priest, "so I'll just wait for a signal from you."

He nodded to his assistants, who, holding the condemned man by each arm, led him slowly to the stairs, guiding him carefully around a puddle in the path. They held him carefully, in a caressing grip, as though needing to make sure he was still there, supporting him and at the same time pushing him forward. He hardly noticed and did not resist.

One of them thought, This man is about to die. Yet right now he is alive—like me. Everything in his body is chugging along—his stomach is churning on his last meal, making a last load of shit, his heart is beating, his hair is growing, without any of them knowing what's about to happen. It's very strange.

The other wondered if the blade would cut through such a neck.

They helped him clumsily up ten steps. Ten. That many. His dreadful journey was over.

Guillotin was in his study, not a mile away, pouring over his papers, trying fearfully hard to not think or feel.

Schmidt hid anonymously in the crowd, intent upon the consequences of his craftsmanship, mechanical, social, and political.

Sanson was the last to appear on the scaffold. At his appearance the unruly crowd hushed quickly into the solemnity of habitual deference, awed by the majesty of authority, its nobility vindicated despite itself. There they stood on the scaffold above the crowd: the priest, the execution team, and the patient. The client. The package. The condemned. In the silence, birds twittered above the soldiers' bayonettes.

There was an old French tradition whereby an execution might be aborted if a woman shouted out a proposal of marriage to the prisoner before his death. You may remember such a moment in *The Hunchback of Notre Dame*. Even now, when such behavior was understood as merely quaint, one would occasionally hear women calling out above the crowd, if only in jest, to save the life of a prospective victim. But not today. The death machine had no ears to hear—no eyes to acknowledge. So much of the excitement concerned the machine itself. Procurer General Roederer had written to Lafayette, Commander of the National Guard,

"Measures must be taken to prevent the machine from being damaged. I therefore consider it necessary for you to order the gendarmes who will be present during the execution to remain after it has taken place in sufficient number in the square and its exits to facilitate the removal of machine and scaffold."

Protect the machine, not the executioner. The victim and executioner were relegated to the background, the headsman now a simple functionary, an "agent of public works." Who said the people were cannibals?

Grenier turned to his charge, the pain building in his chest and arm. With his good dexter hand he gripped Nicolas's huge left shoulder. With his sinister one he held the crucifix up before the condemned man's eyes.

"Nicolas—will you say after me, 'May God commit my soul to His keeping'?"

Nothing. Behind the prisoner's eyes he could see nothing. He could see nothing because behind those eyes something very dark was fermenting. Why should I love God? Pelletier thought, that Pelletier whose stomach was making shit and whose nails were growing. God loves only the rich. For death, at least, we are all the same.

Standing silently at the edge of the abyss, he felt time and space swell up like a great wave within him, and all of a sudden he understood the whole. All of a sudden it all followed—what he should have known—that born as he had been, and raised as he had been raised, he had no right to any hope for mercy.

And he closed his eyes as if in prayer, and in his thoughts he called down the wrath of God on the rotting earth. He cursed it, the earth and all its victims, now and in the past and in the future. And to that curse, he thought, Amen.

Grenier looked at those closed, praying eyes, and thought he understood the answer to his question. Nicolas didn't have to say it. He could just think it.

"Courage," the priest said, and signaled to Sanson that his charge had said the saving words.

The team went into well-rehearsed action. Sanson took Pelletier by the left arm, his senior assistant by the right, and another by the legs; in a flash the patient was lying prone upon the bench. In a series of smooth motions, they strapped him down, slid the bench up so his head was across the lunette, and lowered the top of the lunette around his neck. Sanson walked around to the side of the machine and released the rope suspending the blade. Smoothly it fell, with a hollow roar ending in a thud.

And still the sun shone, and flowers bloomed, and pitiless Nature showed herself gorgeous in the face of abomination. In the midst of barbarous murder and the shameful grotesqueries of human law, the

crowd was chastised by the sight of holiness, the re-
proach of sweetness, the serenity of the firmament, the
dazzling beauty of eternal spring.

All came off without a hitch. Those up front
may have gasped, but most, behind crowds and soldiers
and horses, saw very little. Sanson should have held up
the head. Next time.

Disappointed, the people wanted their gallows back.

> Give me back my wooden gibbet,
> Give me back my gallows . . .

became a popular song.

*There are three things that belong to God and
not to man: the irrevocable, the irreparable, the
indissoluble. Woe unto man if he introduces
them into his code of laws.*

—VICTOR HUGO

CONFITEOR

Confiteor—I acknowledge, I confess. And I can't think of the word without hearing Bach's great fugue over its hugely marching steps, with the plainsong chant weaving through it, woof to its warp.

Those three elements—the continuo, the fugue and the chant—serve well to structure my *Confiteor* for *The Good Doctor Guillotin.*

The continuo is, of course, the march of history—that of late-eighteenth-century France and—clearly implied—that of our own time. The French went through oligarchic waste to mass poverty, revolution, and a terroristic war on terror. Their history dethroned the rich, disbursed the power, and articulated the rights of man. Our own course has gone far to reverse that. Clinging to that pendulum, I write.

The fugue is the busyness and themes of the writing: my use and abuse of truth and fiction. A few examples will suffice. *Confiteor* a few shenanigans with respect to people, place, and time:

- Robespierre made his great anti-death-penalty speech *after* Pelletier was executed. But I wanted to get that astounding fact in there, before the end of the book, into Guillotin's considerations. So I lied.

- The good doctor was not at Mirabeau's deathbed as described—but he could have been, a famous doctor, a colleague in the Assembly. However, I made it up.

- As I did concerning the *Così* performance in Paris: I needed Guillotin to see it, and think about it, and I wanted to play with its themes. The real border would have been hard to cross, but it was easy enough on the page.

- Schmidt was a Parisian piano-maker all right, but he was not piano-maker to the king. He would not likely have been playing chamber music with Guillotin at the Tuileries palace. But that was a good place and a good time to bring him together with Guillotin over Mozart, and the two of them with the king to redesign of the blade of the machine. So I simply appointed him, sold one of his pianos to the court, and with it gained him entry to the palace.

There are some other stretchings. The fact is, we know very little about the five characters of the book.

- Of Pelletier there is recorded only his name, crime, and sentence. We also know he was the first patient.

- Of Schmidt we know only that he was a German piano-maker come to Paris, and that he was awarded the contract to build the first machine, and subsequent ones.

- Of Guillotin we know a bit more, but mostly concerning his many activities as a politically involved medical professional. We know where he was born, what he studied, whom he married, what commissions he was on, what bills he introduced. But he was a decorous, reticent man who left few personal communications—at least few that I could find.

- Of Sanson we know quite a lot. He was a figure of fascination in revolutionary Paris, a self-promoting and self-doubting man, a rich contradiction of prissy moralist and bloody swine. Many wrote about him and his work.

- Of Grenier—well, I just made him up. I thought there would likely be a clergyman present to help Pelletier through his extraordinary end, and I found the struggle around religion to be one of the most fascinating dimensions of revolutionary history.

Confiteor.

Confiteor, too, to frank literary theft. I make music with a Pelletier, Vin Pelletier, a professor of French and a bass in my chorus. Vin is a big guy, and that being the way things start *chez moi*, I imagined Nico to be big. And that brought to mind Steinbeck's Lennie, and then, many will recognize, Büchner's Woyzeck—a poor man overwhelmed by the structures of his time, victimized in the military, a guinea pig for scientific experimentation, and finally totally confused, engulfed in violence. I gave Pelletier some Woyzeck lines, took him through Woyzeck's despair, and added to that some of Büchner's wildness from his short story "Lenz." And so our "patient," our "package" comes with some grand literary history—Woyzeck, Lenz—the unforgettable products of Enlightenment oppression on the human soul—valuable baggage to import, I think, for those who may recognize and claim it.

Confiteor again, this time the crucial contributions of an editor, a reader, two consultants, and a wife.

Fred Ramey, as usual, has picked up his editorial baton and run alongside, poking me with it to encourage my first noncomic novel and keeping me on track. Another musical colleague, friend, and professor of German literature, Dennis Mahoney, did a careful reading and provided many valuable corrections and suggestions. I wish there were room for the essay on Büchner we contemplated. Again, as so often, I want to thank my daughterly medical consultant, Mario Trabulsy, MD. Even in fictional histories, characters have to die in real ways, of real conditions. My Bread & Puppet colleague, Genevieve Yeuillaz, was helpful on geographical details and regional names in her native land. Finally, there is, as ever, sitting upstairs or in the chair to my right, my dear wife, Donna, she-who-knows-all, including whether I should "cut this or not."

The third element of the *Confiteor* is the *cantus firmus*, the simple chant which infuses all that flows around it. I am a member of Vermonters Against the Death Penalty. I ponder why it is that unlike other Western industrial nations, we seem unable to rid ourselves of this domestic barbarity. Much evidence demonstrates that death-penalty states show no higher, and sometimes lower, murder rates than those without—so where is its preventive aspect?

Many death row inmates, freed after further investigation, demonstrate the fallibility of the system, its vulnerability to mistakes which, once made, can never be reversed. Racial disparities make things even worse. Plus the torturous wait times and unneeded expense. There is nothing to be rationally said in its defense.

But *ir*rationally? Ay, there's the rub. There is the demand for "closure" on the part of ever more vocal victims' families, covered ever more fawningly by the media. In spite of the fact that there is no medical or psychological evidence for such "closure," whereas the murder of another human being simply increases the number of victims and the turbulence created around them, still families argue for "closure." They cry real tears in front of juries inescapably moved. And the death penalty marches on.

Revenge—another dimension. Imprisonment in secure lockups would surely minimize public danger, but that goal seems parenthetical to some. Even lethal injection seems too kind to the "Fry 'em all" crowd. "I want to see them suffer."

Confiteor. I thought I'd use this subject matter, this research, to better understand the issues here— cultural, political, psychological—to explore the technological imperative, the function of fear, the epidemic paranoia that invests state killing.

Confiteor. In remissionem peccatorum.

Burlington, Vermont 2009

Bibliography

Arasse, Daniel. *The Guillotine and the Terror.*

Arendt, Hannah. *On Violence.*

Ariès, Phillipe. *The Hour of Our Death.*

Becker, Earnest. *Escape from Evil.*

Billington, James. *Fire in the Minds of Men.*

Bloch, Ernst. *The Principle of Hope.*

Brockliss, Laurence, and Collin Jones. *The Medical World of Early Modern France.*

Büchner, Georg. *Lenz.*

Büchner, Georg. *Woyzeck.*

Buranelli, Vincent. *The Wizard from Vienna: Franz Anton Mesmer.*

Burton, Anthony. *Revolutionary Violence.*

Camus, Albert. *The Rebel.*

Camus, Albert. *Resistance, Rebellion and Death.*

Canetti, Elias. *Crowds and Power.*

Cantor, Jay. *The Space Between: Literature and Politics.*

Carlyle, Thomas. *The French Revolution.*

Conner, Clifford D. *Jean Paul Marat: Scientist and Revolutionary.*

Darnton, Robert. *The Great Cat Massacre.*

Daumal, René. *A Night of Serious Drinking.*

Farge, Arlette. *Fragile Lives.*

France, Anatole. *Les Dieux ont Soif.*

Garrioch, David. *The Making of Revolutionary Paris.*

Hildesheimer, Wolfgang. *Mozart.*

Hsia, R. Po-Chia. *Trent 1475:* Stories of a Ritual Murder Trial.

Hufton, Olwen H. *The Poor of Eighteenth Century France, 1750–1789.*

Hugo, Victor. *The Hunchback of Notre Dame.*

Hugo, Victor. *The Last Days of a Condemned Man.*

Hugo, Victor. *Les Misérables.*

Hugo, Victor. *Ninety Three.*

Janssens, Jacques. *Camille Desmoulins, le premier républicain de France.*

Jones, Peter, ed. *The French Revolution in Social and Political Perspective.*

Kafker, Frank, and James Laux, eds. *The French Revolution:*
   Conflicting Interpretations

Lever, Maurice. *Sade, a Biography.*

Levy, Barbara. *Legacy of Death: The Remarkable Saga of the Sanson Family,*
   Who Served as Executioners of France for Seven Generations..

Linguet, Simon Nicholas Henri. *Memoires of the Bastille.*

Luttrell, Barbara. *Mirabeau.*

MacNulty, W. Kirk. *Freemasonry: Symbols, Secrets, Significance.*

Nabokov, Vladimir. *Invitation to a Beheading.*

Reynolds, Beatrice Kay, ed. *Spokesmen of the French Revolution.*

Rudé, George, ed. *Robiespierre.*

Sade, Marquis de. *Drame Complète.*

Sade, Marquis de. *Letters from Prison.*

Sarat, Austin. *When the State Kills.*

Schama, Simon. *Citizens.*

Scurr, Ruth. *Fatal Purity: Robiespierre and the French Revolution.*

Solomon, Maynard. *Mozart: A Life.*

Soubiran, André. *Ce Bon Docteur Gillotin, et sa Simple Méchanique.*

Spender, Stephen. *The Year of the Young Rebels.*

Thompson, J. M. *The French Revolution.*